PRAISE FOR FIONA VALPY

'Love, love, loved it . . . Brilliant story, I was completely immersed in it, so moving and touching too. The research needed must have been hard to do but it brought the war . . . to life.'
—Lesley Pearse, author of *You'll Never See Me Again*

'A novel that will whisk you to another time and place . . . a tender tale of hope, resilience, and new beginnings.'
—Imogen Clark, bestselling author of *Postcards From a Stranger*

'Fiona Valpy has an exquisite talent for creating characters so rounded and delightful that they almost feel like family, and this makes what happens to them feel very personal.'
—Louise Douglas, bestselling author of *The House by the Sea*

'A wonderfully immersive novel set against a vivid and beautifully described . . . setting. I loved it!'
—Victoria Connelly, bestselling author of *The Rose Girls*

'A moreish story of love, war, loss, and finding love again, set against an atmospheric . . . backdrop.'
—Gill Paul, author of *The Second Marriage*

The Sky Beneath Us

OTHER TITLES BY FIONA VALPY:

The Cypress Maze

The Storyteller of Casablanca

The Skylark's Secret

The Dressmaker's Gift

The Beekeeper's Promise

Sea of Memories

Light Through the Vines (previously published as *The French for Love*)

The Recipe for Hope (previously published as *The French for Christmas*)

The Season of Dreams (previously published as *The French for Always*)

The Sky Beneath Us

Fiona Valpy

LAKE UNION

PUBLISHING

Text copyright © 2024 by Fiona Valpy

Published by Lake Union Publishing, Seattle

www.apub.com

Amazon, the Amazon logo, and Lake Union Publishing are trademarks of Amazon.com, Inc., or its affiliates.

ISBN-13: 9781662516863
eISBN: 9781662516856

Cover design by Emma Rogers
Cover images © Gary Qian / Getty Images; © photonova © Dewin ID
© Prutti Singkittaya © Christopher Moswitzer © lakkana savaksuriyawong
© Asep ginanjar © Galina Bolshakova 69 © Niraelanor / Shutterstock

Printed in the United States of America

For Tashi Lama, Dipa Rai
and the Sherpa people of Phortse.

We're all just walking each other home.

Ram Dass

PART ONE

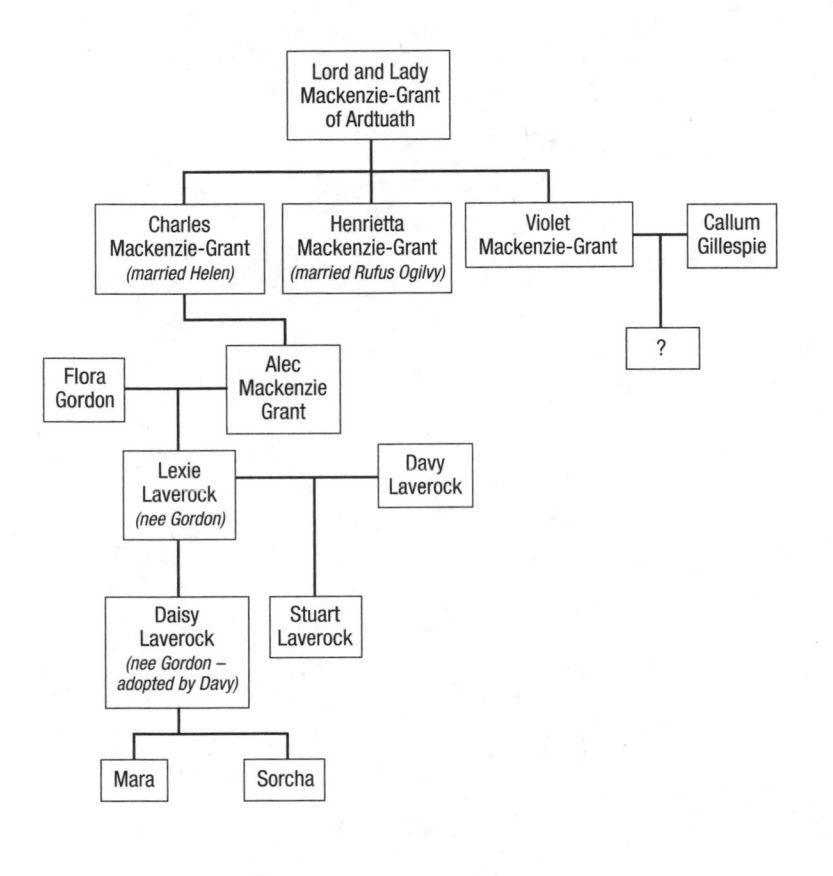

Daisy – March 2020

I crash through the door of the ladies' loo, startling a woman in a burqa who's washing her hands very, very thoroughly, carefully following the instructions on the laminated notices posted above the basins. Her eyes watch me, warily, from the mirror. I dive into one of the cubicles, where I flip the lock and collapse on to the seat with my head in my hands.

The scent of the perfume that I sprayed on my wrists just a few minutes ago in the duty-free shop engulfs me, sickening me. How could I have done something so frivolous? I'd put the sample bottle back on the counter to rummage in my bag for my phone, answering the call from Mum. I thought she'd be telling me her flight had just landed, that she'd be meeting me in the transit lounge in a few minutes. But instead of joyful excitement, her voice was tight with anxiety as she told me she hadn't been allowed on the plane, just before the battery in my phone went dead.

I know that from this moment on, whenever I catch a whiff of this scent I'll remember these queasy, panicked moments, locked in the toilets in the transit area of a shiny Middle Eastern airport, feeling utterly alone.

I shed a few tears of self-pity, then tear off a length of loo paper and blow my nose loudly. Taking a deep breath, I unlock the door and emerge to wash my hands over and over again at one of the basins. Never mind the warning signs about the spreading of the virus, I'm just trying to erase every last drop of the perfume. I catch sight of the reflection of a forty-something-year-old woman in the mirror, and for a second I think how frazzled she looks, her skin stark and pale, lit by the unforgiving overhead lights, before realising she's me. It's something that's been happening all too often lately. I hardly recognise myself these days.

I splash a little water on my face and scrape my hair back into a ponytail, composing myself. My body clock tells me it's some ungodly hour of the morning, whatever time it may be here, and there are dark circles under my eyes. I've already been travelling for more than six hours and have the same again ahead of me to endure.

You could go back, my image in the mirror tells me. Then deep frown lines crease its brow. *But of course, that would mean giving up on the trip of your lifetime. You won't get your money back, because the insurance won't cover Wimping Out. It's far too late to cancel now – you're already halfway there.*

I stare back at myself blankly, knowing turning round and going home is not an option. I've maxed out my credit cards paying for this trip, so I'm not even sure I could afford the cost of a last-minute ticket back the way I've come.

'You'll just have to go on alone then, won't you,' the woman in the mirror tells me. She glares at me, angry and afraid. I square my shoulders, pick up my backpack and, without a backward glance at my frightened reflection, go out into the terminal to find the departure gate for my onward flight to Nepal.

When I finally reach Kathmandu and my hotel, feeling more than a little disorientated after the long flights and the terrifying chaos of the traffic on the taxi ride into the city from the airport, I fling down my bags on one of the beds – the one that should have been Mum's – and try to work out what time it is in Scotland. Nepal has its own time zone, a rather strange five hours and forty-five minutes ahead of the UK, so it must be about seven in the morning there. Mum's an early riser, so I reckon I can call her. It takes a while for my phone to charge enough, and to work out how to connect to the Wi-Fi, and then my call cuts out the first few times I ring her mobile. But at last it rings through, and relief floods through me as I hear her voice.

'Daisy? Where are you? Are you in Kathmandu?' she says at the same time as I say, 'Mum! How are you feeling? Are you at home?' My eyes fill with tears at the sound of her voice, so familiar but so far away.

'Don't worry about me,' she replies. 'I'm sure I'll be fine. So much fuss over this dratted virus. I thought it was just a wee bit of a cold, but then they were checking everyone's temperature at the airport and they pulled me aside. Told me I wasn't allowed on the plane. Davy hadn't even got out of the car park, so he came back and scooped me up, once I'd managed to retrieve my luggage, and we're back home at Ardtuath now.' She coughs – a tight, harsh-sounding hacking noise – and then continues. 'Anyway, don't you mind about me. You're the one we're all worried about, on your own out there. How is it?'

I look around the hotel bedroom with its embroidered wall hangings and gleaming en-suite bathroom. We'd decided to book ourselves a little bit of relative luxury for our first few days in Kathmandu, before setting off on the more challenging part of the trip. 'It's lovely, Mum. But it would be a whole lot better if you were here too.'

She sighs, then stifles another cough. 'I'm sorry. I was so look-ing forward to it, after all these years of planning! But you can do this, Daisy. And you'll have the guide with you for the trek, so you won't be on your own. Don't worry about us, we're honestly fine. I'm sure all the fuss about this coronavirus thing is a storm in a teacup. Stick to the plans we made. And send me lots of photos so I can imagine I'm there with you. It's going to be a fantastic trek. Remember, you're walking in Violet's footsteps, and if she could do it in the 1930s then you can do it now. Do it for us both.'

'I know, Mum. It's going to be great. I'll keep you posted . . .' Then I realise the connection has dropped and I'm talking to thin air, my words of reassurance hanging there in the emptiness. I try to call again, but without success. After a few minutes I give up and plug my phone in to charge again before busying myself with unpacking my rucksack. It doesn't take long to put my leggings and tops into the wardrobe that sits against one wall of the room, its carved panelling smelling faintly of dusty spices.

I feel drained and my brain seems to think it's the middle of the night, despite the glare of the sun and the bustle of the city outside my window. I lie on the bed, stretching out my legs and back, which ache after all those cramped hours on the plane, but I'm too wired to sleep. So I reach for the zip-lock bag containing the notebooks and letters that have brought me here. Their familiarity gives me a little reassurance as memories of my childhood come flooding in.

◆   ◆   ◆

I found Violet's letters and journals many years ago at the bottom of an old cedarwood chest in the library at Ardtuath House. I must have been about twelve years old, I suppose. I loved spending hours playing among the leather-bound books and the botanic prints that lined the walls. We lived in a cottage on the estate in the north-west Highlands of Scotland, but spent much of our time in the big house, which my mum, Lexie, had inherited from the better-off side of the family. Sadly, though, that inheritance didn't include enough money to cover the maintenance of the house with its leaking roofs and draughty windows. To make it pay, she and my stepdad, Davy, run it as a music school, covering everything from classical to contemporary but with a particular focus on keeping alive the traditional music of the Highlands. So I grew up on the side of a wild sea loch surrounded by hills, to the accompaniment of an ever-present soundtrack of fiddle music and flute scales, as well as the occasional distant wail of a lone piper who'd been sent out into the grounds to spare everyone else's ears from the worst squawks and squeals of bagpipe practice.

There was quite a gang of us local kids in the village and we ran wild much of the time, taking for granted a freedom where we could poke in the rock pools along the shore and make dens in the pine woods on the estate to our hearts' content, largely untroubled by any interference from our parents.

I suppose we'd all taken that childhood wilderness for granted when we were wee. And then I missed it like mad when I went away.

As well as growing up surrounded by hills and sea, the famous gardens at Inverewe were just a few miles away across the loch, and as children we visited them often when Davy drove the boat across to pick up tourists from the pier there and take them out on trips. While we waited for the visitors to wend their way through the gardens to the departure point, I would often clamber ashore and play hide-and-seek among the rhododendrons and tree ferns. Those gardens are a magical place, full of surprisingly exotic plants that thrive in the mild dampness of the Gulf Stream, which kisses those far north-western shores. I suppose that's where my fascination with Violet's story began, making fairy teacups from fallen rhododendron flowers and gathering the cones from the pine-needle carpet covering the peat-sprung ground. Finding that my great-great-aunt had also been a keen plantswoman only served to inspire me further, and I credit that inspiration with kindling my ambition to become a gardener myself.

Violet's journals captured my imagination and I'd pore over them for hours, seeing her story unfold in my mind's eye. Until, that is, they came to an abrupt end. At various times Mum and I have tried to find out what happened to her, but all our efforts have come to nothing. She just seemed to disappear. Life's journey took her to a remote village in the Himalaya, where she apparently vanished into thin air, leaving us with many questions, as well as the desire to make the trip of a lifetime some day and come to Nepal to try to find out more.

The day I found Violet's papers, I was supposed to be minding my wee brother, Stu, in the library at the big house while Mum and Davy were busy teaching. Stu was in a crotchety mood, it having rained solidly for the past week, leaving us stuck inside for much of the time. I'd peeked into the cedarwood chest before and seen that it apparently contained nothing more interesting than a pile of old blankets; and that day it struck me we could put them to good use in making a den, which would keep Stu busy for a while. So I raised the heavy lid and hauled them out. At the bottom, hidden beneath the layers of dry, dusty wool, were two large, flat cardboard boxes marked with the name of an Edinburgh dressmaker, which Mum later told me would have probably once contained ballgowns or pieces of fine tailoring. When I looked inside them, I found a small treasure trove.

Stu's pestering was insistent, though, so I had to set my newly discovered cache aside while we built the den and played a game of pirates in it until he was worn out. We wrapped ourselves in the blankets and I read him a story for a while, until his eyelids drooped and he fell asleep, lulled by the distant sound of a single fiddle playing 'The Skye Boat Song'.

Then I reached for the first of the boxes and discovered it contained the story of a whole intriguing life. That life belonged to my great-great-aunt, Violet Mackenzie-Grant, and she lived it far beyond the austere walls of Ardtuath House and the persistent Scottish rain, beneath breathtaking mountain peaks and a soaring Himalayan sky. Intriguingly, there was also a tiny leather shoe stitched from soft calfskin, just the one, missing its partner.

In the second box, there were other items – watercolour paintings of exotic botanical specimens, some folded pieces of card enclosing tissue-paper-thin pressed flowers, and dozens of little brown envelopes of seeds. But it was her letters to her sister and her journals that drew me in.

It's taken me more than thirty years, but I'm finally here to walk in Violet's footsteps. She left a trail to follow, not of breadcrumbs but of paintings and seeds and dried botanical specimens. I'm here to piece it together, to try to fit the pieces of this jigsaw in place and make sense of her life. And to try to find out what happened to her in the end, once the letters and the journals stopped.

But the beginning of Violet's story – once Mum and I had pored over the contents of the boxes and sorted the muddle of letters and notebooks into some sort of order – was a lot closer to home.

Violet

Sunday, 28th August, 1927

Dearest Hetty,
Tomorrow is the day when at long last I can call myself a student of the Edinburgh School of Gardening for Women! And I admit to feeling more than a little trepidation this morning as I sit writing this to you. How I wish you were here to distract me with the latest news from home, to make me laugh at myself for these last-minute qualms, when we both know how much I've wanted this and been looking forward to making a start.

After all the years of pleading with Ma and Pa to allow me to apply to the school, my stomach is now a-churn with equal measures of excitement and worry at the prospect of actually beginning the two-year course. *The hard physical work every day doesn't alarm me, but will I be up to the evening classes in bookkeeping and agricultural chemistry?* Two years is a long time to study when there's no assurance of a career at the end of it. I hope all those hours spent working for Mrs Hanbury will stand me in good stead. Without her encouragement and her trust in letting me loose on her beloved gardens at Inverewe, I wouldn't be here. I don't want to let her down, nor do I want to prove our parents right when – like so many others – they've made it so very clear they heartily disapprove of my ambitions and think horticulture an entirely unsuitable occupation for a young lady. 'If you really must turn yourself into an unkempt harridan with dirt engrained beneath her fingernails, then I suppose I can't stop you' were Ma's parting words to me when she bade me goodbye at the station. She may be right. But at least I'll be a happy unkempt harridan!

Fortunately, I have a sister-in-arms as a room-mate. Her name is Marjorie Howard and she too starts at the gardening school tomorrow. The other lodgers at The Laurels are what I'm sure our parents would consider suitable young ladies, pursuing careers of a secretarial nature in the city's law firms and financial institutions. I sense they rather look down their well-powdered noses at the strange pair of cuckoos who've invaded the nest, ruffling feathers with our ambition to ruin our complexions, out in all weathers wielding trowels and grubbing about *in the mud. We are watched over by our landlady, the formidable Mrs MacDougall, who runs her establishment with an iron fist. 'There will be no gentlemen callers and I expect my lodgers to make their beds every morning and not outstay their welcome in the bathroom' were her words of greeting when I arrived yesterday. There's no danger on either of those fronts, as far as I'm concerned: I've already overheard the other girls complaining of the lack of young men in Edinburgh, as in all other corners of this land where the Great War has taken such a toll, as you and I are only too well aware; and the bathroom is even draughtier and less welcoming than those at home at Ardtuath, where at least one could run a hot bath when needed. Here at The Laurels guesthouse, we are ordered to make do with a bath containing only an inch of lukewarm water on our allocated evening of the week (mine is a Thursday, so I will have to jolly well make sure I don't get too dirty on Fridays, when all that will be available to me is a cold washcloth at the basin in the chilly room Marjorie and I share).*

We are at the very top of the house and Marjorie, who is a good few inches taller than I am, has already given herself a good crack on the head standing up too quickly where the ceiling slopes beneath the eaves as she was unpacking. We have a chest of drawers each and a shared cupboard in which to hang our gardening smocks and skirts. The sink in one corner at least saves us the ordeal of tramping down a steep flight of stairs to wash our faces and brush our teeth before turning in. From the dormer window of this hilltop perch, when the smoggy haze allows it, I can see all the way across to where the castle stands proudly on its rocky crag, with Arthur's Seat crouching like a lion beyond it, reminding me of our hills back at home. If I crane my head as far to the right as is humanly possible and peer over the thick laurel hedge that surrounds the property (no doubt another deterrent to any potential gentlemen callers), I can just make out the gates of the gardening school. So we are very conveniently placed, unlike the secretaries, who have to catch the tram into town to reach their own places of work.

When I first stuck my head out of the window, I heard the strangest noises — a sort of jabbering, high-pitched babble of voices, reminiscent of a madhouse. Marjorie laughed at my expression of astonishment and explained that it was only the sound of the monkeys in the ape house at the zoo, which is just a few hundred yards away. I suppose I'll get used to it, although last night I fell asleep imagining I was in some tropical jungle rather than suburban Edinburgh. It made my feet itch with an instant longing to travel and see such exotic places in real life!

Yesterday, Marjorie and I ventured into the city and strolled through Princes Street Gardens, admiring the floral clock and the neat squares of bedding plants. The design is certainly a far cry from the more natural approach we take at Inverewe and Ardtuath, and far too regulated for my taste, but I suppose it's appropriate for a city centre park. The bright colours of begonias and pansies certainly cheer up the grime of the surrounding buildings: Auld Reekie is aptly nicknamed. After our walk, we decided to treat our-selves to tea at Jenners and splashed out on a shared currant bun as well. Luxury indeed!

I shall finish now, dear Hetty, and walk down the hill to the postbox so this will catch the mail tomorrow. I'll write with more news soon. In the meantime, I'll enjoy picturing this letter chugging its way to you across the country on the mail train and then meandering in Colin McTavish's post van from Achnasheen to Aultbea and Ardtuath.

Pass on best love to Ma and Pa for me, and I hope Charles's headaches have abated a bit. And I'm sending lots more love to you, of course.

Your sister,

Violet.

Daisy – March 2020

I wake with a start, my mouth dry and sticky with the remnants of a troubled sleep, and reach for the bottle of water next to my bed. Violet's letter lies beside it and I refold it and return it carefully to the plastic bag containing the rest of her letters and notebooks.

Outside my hotel window, an altercation breaks out in the street with a blaring of car horns and a storm of shouting. I open the curtains and squint in the glare of bright sunlight. Despite my body clock telling me it still feels like the middle of the night, it's already late morning and Kathmandu is a hubbub of noise and commotion. I check my watch. Having tossed and turned for much of the night, I've now overslept and missed the hotel breakfast. Everything is different here, even time. It's not just the hours and minutes that are strangely offset from the rest of the world. Nepal is a country with six seasons, not the four I've been so used to, and has its own calendar, the Nepali *patro*, in which the number of days in the months vary annually. And simply by landing here, I've been catapulted forward almost fifty-seven years. Things I'd always assumed were certain and dependable have been turned upside down, calculated instead by reference to holy festivals, the location of a sacred mountaintop and the arrival and departure of monsoon rains. I suppose, now I think about it, these things are just about as arbitrary as lines of latitude and the phases of the moon, and probably a good deal more relevant to the people who live here.

I climb into the shower and let the blast of tepid water wash away some of the bleariness of my jetlag and the muddle of my thoughts, trying to bring myself back down to earth.

Once I'm dressed, I check my phone, hoping for a message from one or other of my twin daughters, Sorcha and Mara. Instead, there's a reassuring text from Elspeth: *Lexie's doing okay. Don't worry, and don't change your plans. I'll keep everything running here.*

She's my mum's best friend and has been since childhood. She's always helped run the music school and has been like a surrogate mother to me.

And there's another message, a light-hearted one from Elspeth's son, Jack. I guess she's told him what's happened. I've known Jack just about my whole life and he's as much of a brother to me as Stu is. When we were kids, Jack was always the ringleader on our expeditions. He thought he could boss me around, being almost two years older, and some of the time I let him because he often came up with the best ideas for building rafts out of flotsam and jetsam or going down to the pier at Aultbea to catch crabs on our handlines.

After I left school our paths parted, although somehow we've always kept in touch, through all of life's ups and downs. And there have certainly been a few downs, over the years, for both of us. Though my own preoccupations pale into insignificance against what Jack and Elspeth went through.

His dad ran a fishing boat out of Gairloch and the sea seemed to run in Jack's veins. He was on his dad's boat the day of the accident. I don't think he's ever stopped blaming himself, even though it wasn't his fault his father's foot got caught in the bight rope while they were shooting creels, dragging him overboard and pulling him under. And although Jack was quick to cut the engine, by the time he managed to pull his dad from the water, it was too late. Jack couldn't bring himself to work the creels after that, even though Davy tried to help him.

It was about that time that I began to see Jack in a new light. Instead of a sometimes annoying older brother figure, I suddenly saw him in his own right, as the devastated young man he'd become. He was so changed by his dad's accident, and the grief that engulfed him and his mum.

He got roaring drunk at my wedding, and soon afterwards he left Aultbea for good. I think it broke Elspeth's heart to see him go, but she said she couldn't bear seeing him so sad and so lost and she'd rather he went away to find his happiness if it wasn't to be found at home.

Jack took off to explore the oceans and picked up work along the way skippering fancy yachts in the Caribbean for millionaires. He still sends me texts and WhatsApp messages from time to time – photos of white sand beaches to make me jealous and jokes to make me smile.

This latest message, sent to cheer me up a bit I guess, looks as if it's been taken in some exotic port. It's a photo of a man with a quiff of suspiciously black hair and long sideburns, wearing a satin shirt undone almost to the navel. *ELVIS LIVES* is the caption. Followed by *I intend communicating only in anagrams from now on. SAFE TRAVELS = FARTS, LEAVES*. I text back a laughing face emoji, then set my phone aside and pick up the itinerary that Mum and I spent so many hours putting together, researching places to visit during our first three days in Nepal.

We'd planned to spend the time acclimatising in Kathmandu before catching the plane to Lukla to meet our guide and begin our trek into the mountains. Sightseeing on my own isn't nearly such a tempting prospect though. I decide to head straight for the Garden of Dreams, where I hope to soothe my frayed nerves and find something to eat. When we read the name, Mum and I both immediately agreed we had to go and see it, even before we'd found out anything more about this magical-sounding place in the middle of the city. I put the first of Violet's journals into my backpack to take with me. If I have to do this alone then at least I can take the spirit of my great-great-aunt along with me for moral support.

◆　◆　◆

The garden isn't far from my hotel, but it takes me more than half an hour to get there. There are several roads to cross and the cease-less stream of tooting mopeds and taxis terrifies me. I watch for a while to see how the locals navigate their way across and realise it's a case of taking your life in your hands, stepping out in front of the oncoming traffic with your heart in your mouth, praying that they'll either stop or swerve just enough to avoid you. I wait for a small group to gather on the kerb before taking my lead from them. Miraculously, no one is run over and the veering, hooting scooters manage to avoid one another by a hair's breadth.

I trot along the uneven pavements, picking my way between the potholes and rubble. More than once, as I struggle to read the map, I trip over paving stones and tree roots, staggering, almost losing my footing. I'm attempting to look confident and purpose-ful, as the guidebook tells me I should, in order to avoid attracting the unwanted attention of hawkers and hustlers, but I know I am easy prey. I carry on walking, doing my best to shake off the small procession of street vendors that trails in my wake. I'm thoroughly relieved when I turn in at the gate that marks the entrance to the garden. Barked at by the guard, the retinue melts away in search of other prey, and I pay for my ticket at the kiosk.

Immediately, it's like stepping into a parallel universe. The Garden of Dreams is an oasis of calm, the clamour and bustle of the city streets muffled beyond its high stone walls. I sink gratefully on to a bench, giving myself a few moments to allow the pounding of my heart to subside, regathering my tattered nerves.

The first thing I then notice is the birdsong. I suppose it's everywhere in the city, but it's only when the din of the traffic fades that it can be heard. The bass cooing of pigeons is overlain with the treble notes of other birds, high and pure as a flute or soft as an oboe's liquid tones. It reminds me of walking along the hall-way at Ardtuath House, hearing the sounds of instruments being practised behind closed doors. I sit for a while, closing my eyes to absorb the sounds.

When I open my eyes again, I become aware of the play of sunlight over my face and a sweet scent drifting on the air, entic-ing me deeper into the gardens. I gather up my bag containing Violet's papers and begin to walk. The space is filled with colour and perfume from the plants that grow here – cascades of jasmine, a tapestry of roses, the teardrop flowers of angel's trumpets, and a clump of headily fragranced white orchids hiding in the shade of a fig tree. As I wander along the paths, I imagine I feel the presence of Violet beside me. The exotic birds and trees remind me of the descriptions I've read in her journals and the flowers seem familiar to me from the botanic watercolours she painted, crowding the walls of the library in the big house. I pull out my phone and snap some photos to send home to Mum, my spirits lifting a little as I do so.

The focal point of the garden is a pavilion, its domed cupola supported by elegant cream columns. According to the leaflet I was given with my ticket, this is where the café ought to be. But I find the doors locked and a hand-scrawled notice saying it's closed until further notice due to the virus. I spot a white marble plaque set into the wall and step closer to read the writing on it. It bears four stanzas translated from the *Rubaiyat of Omar Khayyam*, but they're made difficult to read by a cobweb of cracks radiating from the third of the verses. I peer at it more closely.

> *Ah, love! Could thou and I with fate conspire*
> *To grasp this sorry scheme of things entire,*
> *Would not we shatter it to bits — and then*
> *Re-mould it nearer to the heart's desire!*

And then I read the engraving on a smaller metal plate set beneath it:

> *The crack in the marble plaque, now disguised as a creeping vine, is said to have been the only damage to the garden caused by the Great Earthquake of 1934.*

Instead of replacing the broken slab of marble, someone has instead turned the damage into a part of the design by etching leaves and flowers along the cracks. I sit on a bench beneath it, turning every now and then to reread the words and absorb their broken beauty. It's as if Violet has reached out to me and taken my hand to guide me here. If I needed a sign of encouragement to continue on this journey, then surely here it is. The message is loud and clear . . . life falls apart; and maybe some things can't be mended, but perhaps they can be reshaped into something even more beautiful. In the sighing of the breeze and the calling of the birds, I imagine I hear her voice too. *Keep going*, she says. *Keep putting one foot in front of the other, just as I did. You've taken the first steps — now see where the path takes you.*

I pull her journal from my bag and settle down in the jasmine-scented shade to read.

Violet's Journal

My first week as a student of the Edinburgh School of Gardening for Women has passed in a blur and it's a relief to be able to sit down for a few minutes at last and write up my impressions. So much for my resolution to keep this journal on a daily basis! It's been all I can do at the end of every day to drag myself upstairs to my room and collapse into bed. Marjorie is the same. We scarcely exchange a word before falling into the deepest of sleeps, and then my dreams are filled with Miss Morison's lectures on the care of glasshouses and the best ways to propagate herbaceous perennials.

Even though today is Sunday, I've come to the Royal Botanic Garden to explore the glasshouses, which are on a far grander scale and filled with infinitely more exotic specimens than those at the gardening school. I'm writing this sitting on a bench in a corner of the Tropical Palm House, beneath the fronds of a tall Bermuda palmetto. Outside, beyond the white ironwork and towering panes of glass, a biting autumn wind is tousling the heads of the trees, turning the maples scarlet and making the sweet-chestnut leaves tumble. But in here the air is more pleasantly balmy than the warmest of summer days back home on the shores of Loch Ewe (and with the added bonus of being without the swarms of midges).

A young man was sitting on this bench. I nodded to him as I sat down and he took off his cap and wrung it in his hands, betraying his discomfort at my presence. His hair was the reddish brown of a conker and there was grime beneath his fingernails, although the skin surrounding them was clean. His hands had the chapped appearance of having been well scrubbed with soap and water – a condition with which I am rapidly becoming all too familiar myself.

I took out my sketchbook and began to draw the palmetto with its clusters of ripening berries. When I paused to remove my coat – the heat of the glasshouse beginning to make my skin prickle – from the corner of my eye I caught the young man looking at my efforts. I turned to face him and held out the sketch. He blushed as pink as a beetroot. I couldn't help noticing the warmth in his hazel eyes when he finally plucked up the courage to meet my amused gaze.

'You have an interest in plants?' he asked. He couldn't disguise the surprise in his voice.

I suspect I couldn't keep the pride out of my own voice as I replied, 'I'm a student at the School of Gardening for Women.'

Instantly, his demeanour changed and the air around us seemed to cool a few degrees along with his expression, despite the muggy warmth of the glasshouse. I supposed he must be one of those people who disapprove of young ladies dirtying their hands, or perhaps he agreed with those who say we take jobs from young men who need them and would be better off staying in the kitchen where we belong.

'You draw well enough,' he said. I couldn't place his accent precisely, although his words had the brusque edges of the Scottish east coast about them.

'It's most kind of you to say so,' I said. I nodded towards the palmetto. 'That particular specimen is the oldest one here. It was moved to this location from the old botanic garden on Leith Walk nearly a hundred years ago.'

I'd gleaned this fact from one of Miss Morison's lectures in the preceding week, but rather than receiving it with polite interest, the young man abruptly got to his feet. He settled his cap back on his head and bid me a gruff 'Goodbye', before disappearing into the undergrowth of the tropical forest surrounding us. I heard the door bang shut behind him as he left and caught a glimpse of him hurrying along the path, pulling the edges of his jacket together and stooping slightly against the buffeting of the wind.

I shook my head at his incivility and finished my sketch, then settled down to writing up this journal. The first week of the course has passed in a blur of new names and faces, and my mind is full to bursting with Latin botanical nomenclature as well as the challenges posed by lectures in bookkeeping and chemistry. We have to attend evening classes in those subjects at the College of Agriculture, requiring a lengthy tram ride into George Square at the end of an already long day's toil.

Miss Morison insists upon her students learning all aspects of horticulture and takes a most pragmatic approach. She has told us of her own career, which began when she became one of the first practitioner gardeners at these very same botanic gardens at the turn of the century. It was the prejudice she encountered here that prompted her and her colleague, Miss Barker (sadly no longer with us), to start the Edinburgh School of Gardening for Women. 'It is up to you to prove our male counterparts wrong in their assertions that you lassies are welcome to come and play in the garden, but the "tall and braw laddies" – as they like to call themselves – will pity your struggles with the spade,' she told us on our first day. 'We are no fair-weather gardeners at this school, and we have no use for dilettantes and dabblers here. You will dig and plough and plant and hoe, just as the men do, even though you do so in skirts. We have already proven ourselves their equals, joining our suffragist sisters on the march to winning the vote so very recently. It is up to you to do justice to the women who have gone before you, to prove yourselves worthy of their efforts and to keep opening new doors for those who come after you.'

Next week we begin the practical classes too at Corstorphine. I look forward to the introduction to ploughing – having already made the acquaintance of the School of Gardening's resident plough horse, a stocky grey named Bessie – as well as getting to grips with the market garden, where the season's fruit and vegetables are ready for harvesting.

Manuring is on the syllabus as well, though I reserve judgement on just how exciting that particular topic will be.

Daisy – March 2020

Kathmandu has always conjured up images of a mysteriously remote and exotic city, but nothing I've read has prepared me for the noisy, crazy, colourful chaos that engulfs me each time I step out of the doors of my hotel. The air is filled with dust and traffic fumes, and the stench of raw sewage makes me gag as I cross a bridge over a murky stream. Madly haphazard loops of electric wiring run above every pavement, and I wonder how often people are accidentally electrocuted. I snap a photo and send it off to Jack, adding the tagline *Just one of the hazards on the streets of Kathmandu. Probably a faster and less painful way to go than being run over by a hundred scooters though.* There's no reply, but then it's still the middle of the night in Bermuda, which was the last place he texted me from. He'd said he was fed up with sailing yachts for other people and was looking for a more modest boat of his own to buy.

The sense of overwhelm I feel as I attempt to navigate my way through the city streets is compounded by the drip-feed of news of the pandemic. Here in Nepal a few people are wearing paper masks, but most seem to be carrying on their lives as normal. News flashes come through sporadically, when the Wi-Fi is working in the hotel. The prime minister has said all non-essential travel should be cancelled, so I feel guilty about being here. But it's too late now, and maybe flying back would just help spread the virus more. Some people are saying it will take twelve weeks to turn the tide of the virus. Nearly three months . . . that would be a long time to be stuck out here. But surely things will get better before then? Most people seem to think it'll only be a couple of weeks at most.

I woke this morning to find a message from Davy, saying Mum's doing okay. She's still in bed, sleeping for much of the time, but her temperature's coming down and her breathing is getting a little easier. *Don't worry, I'm looking after her for you*, he'd typed, and I had a sudden yearning to feel his strong arms around me, looking after me as well. He may be my stepfather, but he's all the dad I've ever needed.

Do you think I should come back? I asked him, forgetting it must still be the middle of the night there and he'd sent the message hours before.

But even so, after a few minutes his reply flashed back: *No, do your trip. She loved the pictures of the Garden of Dreams. It's helping her to know you're carrying on. We love you.*

I'd felt a lot happier knowing Mum seemed to be on the mend and had managed to eat a hearty breakfast earlier that day.

I'm supposed to be meeting a guide this afternoon from the company we'd booked the trek through, ready to confirm all the arrangements for my departure tomorrow. The last email I received from them was a week ago, so I've been assuming the plans haven't changed. I check the address of the office again. This is definitely the place, but when I try the door, it seems to be locked. I peer in, but the lights are off and there's no one inside. Then I notice a piece of paper stuck to the inside of the window. Scrawled on it is a brief message: *Closed due to Covid-19. Please call for refund.*

I feel the panic rising in my chest. Now what? But I can't lose it completely, here in the middle of a busy Kathmandu street, so I make myself take a few deep breaths (trying not to choke on the mixture of dust and petrol fumes), and walk back to find a café where I can sit and try to gather my thoughts.

Miraculously, the café has Wi-Fi as well as excellent coffee, and I manage to connect. After a moment's hesitation – and calculating that it's mid-morning in Scotland – I call Davy's number, needing to hear his voice. I attempt a video call and catch a glimpse of his face before it cuts out again. He looks thinner, grey with exhaustion, and suddenly both my parents seem old and vulnerable. He rings back immediately – without the video – and the voice call connects.

'It's so good to hear from you, love. I'm here with your mum,' he says. 'Hang on a sec, I'll put you on speaker . . .'

She chimes in, 'How are you getting on, Daisy? All set to start the trek tomorrow?'

I swallow hard, as the emotion wells up at the sound of their voices, at once so familiar and so distant.

'There's been another glitch.' I explain about the sign in the trekking company's window. 'So I'm thinking maybe it would be best to try and arrange a flight home . . .'

There's a silence at the other end, followed by the sound of coughing. I hear a brief, muffled conversation and then Mum's voice comes through loud and clear.

'Daisy Laverock, don't you dare give up yet. This trip is your chance to find what you've lost . . .' She draws a wheezing breath. 'You're not just searching for Violet, you're searching for the Daisy you used to be. That's why I was so keen for you to go. In fact, I only agreed to come along because I knew you wouldn't do the trip otherwise.' There's a pause while she coughs again. 'At least try to find out a bit more about where Violet went. And while you're at it, try and find out what's happened to the fearless, audacious girl you once were, so full of dreams.'

Tears are running down my face now. Suddenly, I can see how right she is. I've lost my own sense of self and have come looking for Violet by way of a distraction, to avoid admitting that fact. But now I'm stranded here alone I'll be forced to come face to face with myself. And perhaps that's what I fear the most.

The thousands of miles between us are filled with a silence loaded with pain and fear and love. For a moment I think the connection's dropped again, but then I hear Mum's voice, gentler and softer this time. 'We love you, Daisy. Do this for me, please. And I'll be with you in spirit, every step of the way.' Her breath seems to catch, and I can't speak either.

'You okay, love?' It's Davy's voice this time, and he steadies me. I imagine him holding Mum's hand and the pair of them reaching out together across the distance that separates us to hold me and support me as they always have done.

I swallow hard. 'I'll be fine. I'll see what I can do. You're right. After all, it's taken half my life to get here and who knows when there'll be a chance to come back again. I'll keep you posted,' I promise. 'And I'll send some photos from the mountains.'

I don't know where to go or what to do to try to find another guide. But I realise I haven't eaten since breakfast, so I decide to go out into the city again and look for a restaurant. I wander aimlessly, letting my feet lead the way. I find I've joined a river of people walking along a wide avenue and allow myself to be carried along, letting go of any last shreds of purpose.

It feels like I'm surfing, carried along on a wave, and a memory flashes into my head of Jack teaching me and Stu to surf on a white sand beach many, many years ago. 'There's no point trying to fight it,' he told us. 'The sea is way stronger than you'll ever be. Let it take you where it wants to. Just try to stay balanced, feel the play of the water and go with it, not against it.' I remember the grace and power in his body as he showed us how.

When the wave of people breaks, spilling out into a wide square, I find myself standing in front of a vast temple. A pair of piercing, brilliant-blue painted eyes stare down at me from the golden spire that sits on top of its white dome. I recognise it immediately from the pictures in my guidebook. It's the Boudhanath Stupa. One of the most sacred sites for Buddhists in Nepal. Skeins of prayer flags flutter in the evening breeze, scores of pigeons wheeling between them on air heavy with the smell of incense. I think there must be some sort of ceremony going on, judging by the stream of people still arriving in the square.

A whirlpool of humanity swirls around the stupa, everyone moving in the same clockwise direction, so I step into the stream and am swept along in the flow. Some people walk in silence, reaching to spin the prayer wheels set into the stupa walls, while others recite mantras as they walk. There are monks in earthen-coloured robes, pilgrims wearing traditional clothes striped in brightly coloured silk, and tourists, like me, in my ordinary dress. The all-seeing eyes painted on the four sides of the stupa's golden tower scrutinise the walkers below.

At the top of the square there's a brightly painted temple with a vast prayer wheel in the entranceway and a huge bronze bell hanging in a golden frame in front of it. People pause here to light butter lamps, which burn brightly, the flames dancing in the evening breeze. Incense smokes in bronze cauldrons and more pigeons swoop through the haze, coming in to land in a section cordoned off by ropes where bowls of seed are provided for them. Back home we'd consider them pests, but here in Nepal they are sacred – as are all living things. I perch on the temple steps for a while, watching the scene unfold.

A pilgrim wearing a garland of marigold flowers stops to talk to a red-robed monk sitting next to me and I pluck up the courage to ask them if this is a special ceremony. The monk replies in perfect English, with a hint of a German accent, that it's just a normal evening. 'In fact,' he says, 'it's quieter than usual. People are staying away because of the virus, and many who live in Kathmandu are leaving the city to return to their families in the countryside, where it's safer.' He asks me where I'm from. 'Ah, Scotland is a great place.' His face crinkles in a smile. 'You will be missing your mountains, I suppose. But we have some here in Nepal too, you know.'

I nod. 'I was supposed to be going there, but my plans seem to have fallen apart. So I'm not sure what I'm going to do now . . .'

Instead of sympathising, he smiles again. 'That's good,' he says. 'Because it's only when we stop clinging on to the plans we've made that we step on to the middle way – the way of the unknown. We call this the sacred path of the warrior.' He must notice the uncertainty in my expression because he reaches into a pocket beneath his robes and brings out a length of fine red string. 'Here,' he says. 'You tie it around your wrist. This is called a *sungdi*. It will bring you strength, love and luck. It will also give you spiritual protection. And I think you may be in need of a little of that on the journey ahead. Remember, you are never alone.'

I look down at the thin red bracelet I've tied and then begin to thank him, but he's already rejoined the tidal swirl of the crowd, his terracotta-coloured robes disappearing into the throng as it surges on its way.

I ponder his words. I don't entirely understand their meaning, but somehow the simple moment of connection – and the gift of a length of red string – has made me feel less alone. And that makes me a little braver. I complete my own circuit of the stupa, but don't want to tear myself away from the square just yet. The sun is setting, bathing the sky in a glorious pink light, and the breeze has dropped now so that the thousands of prayer flags flutter more gently, then become still. I climb the stairs to a restaurant's roof terrace and take a seat at a table overlooking the stupa. There's only one other occupied table in the whole place, two men who are tucking into heaped plates of rice and lentils, scarcely glancing in my direction. The waiter takes my order and brings me a cup of mint tea, which I sip as I take photos of the golden tower against the glow of the evening sky. I feel more at peace than I have done since I arrived in Kathmandu. Perhaps the monk was right – letting go of my carefully laid plans might be liberating after all if I can just accept there's nothing much I can do about it. And now I have my red string *sungdi* to protect me, bringing me strength and love and luck – things that have been missing from my life for many years now. I touch it with my fingertips and smile.

I eat with more appetite than I've had in the past few days. The two men at the table in the corner have finished their meal now and seem to be having some sort of argument. I can't understand a word of what they're saying, but the older of the two raises his voice while the younger one shakes his head vehemently and leans back in his chair, his body language exuding a stubborn refusal of whatever his companion is urging.

I'm concentrating more on my supper than on their conversation, when suddenly I hear a word that makes me prick up my ears. Phortse. The name of the village in the mountains that is familiar to me from Violet's journals. At first I think I must have misheard, or be misinterpreting some other word, but the older man says it again and the younger one repeats it, shaking his head again, speaking more forcefully too now. Then he catches me looking across at them and smiles ruefully.

'I am sorry,' he says, his English fluent but heavily accented, the consonants soft. 'My father and I are disturbing your meal with our argument.'

'Not at all.' I take another sip of tea, and then, emboldened by the *sungdi* tied round my wrist, I say, 'I didn't mean to eavesdrop, but are you talking about the village of Phortse? A Sherpa village in the Khumbu?'

The older man turns to look at me. 'You know Phortse?' he asks, surprised.

'I was supposed to be going there,' I say. 'But everything has changed and now I don't have a guide.'

'Why do you want to go there?' the younger man asks. 'Surely you'd rather go to Everest Base Camp, like all the other tourists? Even I don't want to go to Phortse, and I live there! That's what my father and I are speaking about. He wants me to come home with him and I want to stay in Kathmandu.'

His father turns to him, exasperated, and says in his broken English, for my benefit, 'Stop to keep arguing, Sonam. Now is not good time to stay in the city. Can't you see what's happening in the world? There will be no work for us here. Everyone leaving. We must go home and help your mother. Is going to be hungry times ahead otherwise, for all.'

His son slumps in his chair and reaches for the bottle of water that sits between them, pouring more into his glass.

The older man looks across at me again. 'But why *do* you want go to Phortse?'

'I'm following in the footsteps of a long-lost relation. I had a great-great-aunt who lived there nearly a hundred years ago. I've always wanted to see where she went. My mother was supposed to be here with me, but the virus stopped that . . . and now I'm here on my own and everything has changed and the guide I'd booked has cancelled . . .' I stop, aware that my explanation must sound increasingly garbled to them. I touch the red string bracelet again for courage and take a deep breath. 'So if there's any chance you're going to Phortse, please can I come with you?'

He looks at me appraisingly. 'What your name?'

'I'm Daisy Laverock. Daisy – like a flower.'

'And this relation you follow? They have name?'

'It's Violet Mackenzie-Grant. Also like a flower.'

He repeats it, almost as if it's a surname: 'Violet Like-A-Flower?' The man's expression doesn't change but he nods, then stands and comes across to my table, placing the palms of his hands together in front of his heart in the traditional Buddhist greeting. 'We are Sherpa. My name is Tashi, this my son, Sonam. Our work cancelled now because all the climbers and tourists are not coming, so we will take you to Phortse.' He says something to his son in their own language and, with some reluctance, Sonam seems to give in, because he slowly gets to his feet too and comes to stand beside his father.

I scramble to my feet as well, excitement rising in my chest. 'That would be wonderful! I'm so grateful. You have no idea what this means to me. How much would you charge?'

'Is not an easy journey,' Tashi warns, ignoring my question. 'We will fly to Lukla and then it take four days trekking to reach Phortse. Do you know this?'

I nod. 'Don't worry, I've been preparing for months. And I already have a ticket booked for the flight to Lukla.' I have it in the plastic folder in my bag. I pull it out to show him. It's unlike the plane tickets we're used to at home as it doesn't actually specify a time and date, it's just a note stating that we have paid for seats on a Yeti Airlines plane flying from Kathmandu to Lukla – a tiny airstrip on the side of a mountain, which has a reputation for being the world's most dangerous airport. I scribble down my phone number and the name of my hotel on the back of the sheet of paper and hand it over.

He reads it carefully, then folds it and puts it in his pocket. 'OK, Mrs Daisy. Then is agreed,' he says. 'We have few things to

35

sort out here, but we will be at your hotel in two days' time. No worry now, you travelling with Sherpas – number one best mountain guides in the world. I give you my word.'

'*Namaste*,' I say, placing my palms together in front of my heart as they have done. And then I watch them leave, wondering whether I'll ever see them again and only realising, when it's too late, that I don't know how much it's going to cost. I've also handed over my air tickets to a pair of complete strangers and I don't have any way of contacting them. But I head back to the hotel with my spirits a little higher than they have been in days. Something in Tashi's face makes me believe in his promise to guide me into the Khumbu. I'll worry about the money later.

With a surge of excitement, I send an email to Mum, Davy, Stu and my girls to let them know the good news. I just may be able to follow all the way in Violet's footsteps after all.

I lie down on my bed, twisting the thin red bracelet around my wrist. The fluttering of the prayer flags and the flickering flames of the butter lamps beside the stupa seem to enfold me still as I reach for Violet's journal and begin to read, reminding myself again of the origins of her story and the path she eventually trod: the path of the warrior.

Violet's Journal

FRIDAY, 9TH SEPTEMBER, 1927

Miss Carmichael, our botany instructor, announced this morning that we would be studying at the Royal Botanic Garden at Inverleith today – our first official visit there as her class of gardening women. In her stentorian tones, she instructed us to bear in mind AT ALL TIMES that we were ambassadors for the school and would be judged accordingly by the gardeners and keepers we were about to encounter. 'There will be no chattering,' she said, fixing a couple of the more talkative girls with a particularly stern look. 'You are there to learn, remember, and some of the staff still don't take kindly to our presence. Miss Morison has used her influence to create a partnership of sorts with the Botanics and we are privileged to be allowed behind the scenes in the Glasshouses and the Library. Do not let her down.'

We obeyed as best we could, although as we walked through the tall iron gates there were a few excited outbursts, quickly silenced by another look from our teacher. We walked in silence, two by two, along the path. My visit to the Tropical Palm House at the weekend had been as a member of the public, but now my heart beat a little faster as we entered the main building as gardening women. I was eager to see behind the scenes, coming one step closer to the famous names of horticulture, plant hunters like Forrest and Sherriff whose specimens are housed here.

Following a welcome from the Regius Keeper himself – even the redoubtable Miss Carmichael seemed overawed by his presence – we were allowed into the Library. Never have I seen such a collection! We wandered in silence amongst the shelves of books and portfolios of botanical drawings. My fingers itched with a longing for my paint-box and pencils. And then we were shown the drawers of specimens. The collection seems to take up acres, and the librarian drew forth folder after folder containing pressed leaves, flowers and seeds, each one neatly labelled with its scientific name and the descriptions of where and when it had been found. We will have access to all of this in our future visits, so I shall have ample opportunities to bring my sketchbook along and make my own drawings. A blue poppy from the Himalaya caught my eye in particular. How I long to capture that extraordinary colour on paper and send it home for Ma and Pa to see.

We emerged at last into the open air of the gardens again. It was a glorious autumn day, far warmer than it had been last Sunday, although the wind still blustered through the trees, sending more flurries of leaves tumbling, so Miss Carmichael allowed us to take our packed lunches to a secluded corner of the arboretum she knew of, away from public view.

We turned the corner and disturbed a group of men who had already claimed the picnic spot. One of them got to his feet as we approached and greeted Miss Carmichael.

'Good afternoon, George,' she said. 'This is my new class of gardening women, here on their first visit.' She turned to us. 'Ladies, these are some of the gardeners who work hard to keep the Botanics in such a good state all the year round.'

The man nodded, muttering a greeting to us.

'I apologise for intruding,' Miss Carmichael continued. 'We'll take ourselves elsewhere and leave you to finish your lunch in peace.'

'Och, it's no intrusion at all,' George replied. 'There's space enough for us all and the shelter this corner provides keeps the wind off. Please, make yourselves at home.'

We settled ourselves at a little distance from the men and took out the pieces we'd brought with us from our lodgings. I discovered I was suddenly ravenous after our morning's excitements, and the egg sandwiches Mrs MacDougall had prepared for Marjorie and me became the sole object of my concentration. It was only when Marjorie nudged me and hissed in my ear that one of the gardeners seemed to be glaring at me that I looked up.

A young man sat with his back against the trunk of a red oak, a penknife and short stick in his hands. He'd been whittling at it when we arrived, his head bowed over his work. But now he had abandoned his task, distracted no doubt by the interruption. As Marjorie had observed, he appeared to be staring straight at me with a look of disdain in his clear hazel eyes and I recognised the young man I'd encountered in the Palm House on Sunday.

Mortification flooded through my veins as I recalled how I'd told him about the palmetto. No wonder he'd been annoyed. It must have sounded so condescending, and to one who knew the plants there far better than I.

Determined not to be cowed by his hostility, I smiled in recognition and raised the hand holding the remains of my egg sandwich by way of salutation.

'Violet Mackenzie-Grant!' snapped Miss Carmichael, having witnessed my gesture and, I suppose, interpreted it as a brazen flirtation.

A few of the gardeners laughed out loud and I saw one of the girls nudge her neighbour and whisper something behind her hand.

Chastened, I dropped my eyes to my lap and felt my cheeks burn with embarrassment. But when I slid a furtive glance towards the young man again a few moments later, I saw he was smiling at me. It could have been simple amusement at my public admonishment, but I thought there was more warmth in his eyes so perhaps there was some sympathy there too.

Marjorie cut an apple in two and passed me one of the halves.

'Thank you,' I whispered, my gratitude not just for the apple but for the gesture of friendly solidarity.

The lads got to their feet and went back to their tasks in the gardens, leaving us to finish our lunch. I didn't dare raise my eyes as they left, not wishing to draw more of Miss Carmichael's disapprobation down upon myself. But one of them walked close by where Marjorie and I were sitting and something fell at my feet as he passed. Making sure no one was looking (apart from Marjorie, who witnessed the whole incident with much amusement), I reached out and picked up a piece of wood that had been whittled into the form of a palm frond, a perfect miniature facsimile of those of the palmetto.

I tucked it into the pocket of my smock. And now it sits on the bedside table in my room at The Laurels as I write this.

He appears to be a really rather extraordinary young man, that lad with the hazel eyes.

WEDNESDAY, 12TH OCTOBER, 1927

At lunchtime today I was called in to Miss Morison's study. We'd been working in the market garden that morning, harvesting the last of the spring-planted onions and the first of the neeps, so I kept my hands behind my back as I stood before her desk, to hide my dirt-engrained fingernails. Despite my best efforts with the scrubbing brush and carbolic soap, the rich black soil of the vegetable beds persists in clinging stubbornly to the roughened skin. Mother has sent me a jar of Hinds hand cream, with a note urging me to use it often and to wear a pair of kid gloves at night-time, in a last-ditch attempt to prevent my descent into harridan-ism. It may be effective for women who 'do housework, play golf, and run a car or a typewriter', as the advertisements claim, but I'm afraid it doesn't make much of a dent on the after-effects of ploughing, digging and turning compost heaps.

Miss Morison has a stern outward demeanour but beneath it lies a deep vein of kindness. I was a little nervous as I stood before her, wondering which of my mistakes I was to be dressed down for. There'd been that incident with the insecticide for the Brussels sprouts the other day (although Marjorie agreed with me afterwards that the instructions for its dilution had been less than clear), and last week I'd bent the ploughshare on a stone when attempting to create one of the new market garden beds. But she smiled at me so warmly that I felt the tightness across my shoulders release a little as I shifted my feet on the oriental rug that is the one concession to comfort in her study, lined with its horticultural tomes.

'How are you enjoying your time with us, Violet?'

My heart sank a little again, nerves a-flutter in case this was her opening gambit in telling me I wasn't cut out for the course.

'Very much indeed, Miss Morison,' I assured her. 'The work is hard, and I know I have a lot to learn, but I love it here.'

'Good,' she replied. 'Your tutors tell me you are doing well.' She glanced down at a note on her desk. 'We have received a request from the Regius Keeper at the Botanics. It's somewhat unusual, but he has mentioned you by name. It appears your proficiency at illustration has not gone unremarked. They have recently received a large number of specimens from George Forrest's latest expedition to Tibet and there is much to be done to catalogue and illustrate them. Ordinarily, we would assign such an opportunity to one of our second-year students, but I'm afraid to say none of them has your proficiency with pencils and paint. I am prepared to let you undertake this work – and it is an excellent opportunity – but only on the condition that you make up the elements of the course here in your own time. Is that something you'd be prepared to do?'

I think I stood in flabbergasted silence for several moments, my mouth opening and closing like a landed trout, before I was able to burst out my excitement and gratitude. 'To be one of the first people in the country to see those exotic specimens, to be able to study them and be one of those responsible for presenting them to the world . . . ! I'd love to, Miss Morison. And I'll be sure to make up the course work too. Oh, thank you, thank you for this opportunity.'

She smiled again, but then quickly readjusted her expression into one of sternness. 'Very well, Violet. But you must remember that you are representing the Edinburgh School of Gardening for Women and I expect you to behave with decorum at all times. You will be under the scrutiny of some of the most knowledgeable and influential men in British botanical circles. I hope I can trust you to make a good impression.'

I was so excited I could scarcely concentrate on this afternoon's lectures on the propagation of herbaceous perennials. I think I shall scarcely sleep a wink tonight. I am to present myself at the Library of the Royal Botanic Garden tomorrow morning.

SUNDAY, 16TH OCTOBER, 1927

Conscious of keeping my word to Miss Morison, I have forced myself to copy up Marjorie's notes on pest control for brassicas before allowing time for writing up my journal today. What a week it has been!

As instructed, I made my way through the gates of the botanic gardens and up the path to the Caledonian Hall, which houses the Herbarium. I had to keep pinching myself to be sure it wasn't a dream, that I really had been selected to help illustrate the latest findings from one of the world's most renowned plant hunters. Despite its grand name, the hall more resembles a pretty cottage built from honey-coloured stone, its gables decorated with carved wooden filigree. I paused before the door, adjusting the leather satchel containing my art materials across the front of my coat like a protective shield, to give me confidence before knocking. The man behind the desk fixed me with a most suspicious glare when I gave him my name and said I was expected. He is clearly the type of custodian who believes it his duty to preserve the collections in his care from the prying eyes of anyone who might be termed a member of the general public. Reluctantly, he told me to take a seat and wait whilst he spoke to someone on the telephone. Whatever was said, it seemed to convince him that I really was to be allowed into the inner sanctum, because he raised his eyebrows, replaced the receiver without further comment, and told me someone would be with me shortly, before returning to the pages of the vast leather-bound ledger before him.

The silence, broken only by the loud ticking of the clock on the wall behind the man's desk, merely served to increase my jitters. I reminded myself of the confidence placed in me by Miss Morison and the other lecturers at the School of Gardening, as well as the encouragement given to me by Mrs Hanbury in the gardens at Inverewe, and clutched my bag a little more firmly on my lap to stop myself from quaking. I told myself I deserved my place here amongst the men. And I would need a steady hand if I was to draw and paint George Forrest's specimens.

After what seemed an eternity – although a glance at the clock told me I'd been waiting less than ten minutes – a door off to the

43

side of the entryway opened and another man appeared. The door-keeper stood up from his chair. 'Good morning, Dr Kay,' he said with some diffidence. 'This is Miss Mackenzie-Grant, the young lady who is apparently a botanic artist.' He glanced at me disparagingly, as if he very much doubted this to be true.

The man fixed me with an appraising look as I scrambled to my feet. 'I'm pleased to meet you, Miss Mackenzie-Grant. We have heard good things about your skill with pencil and paintbrush. I am Francis Kay, the principal curator.' He shook my hand with a reassuringly firm grip. 'We are grateful to Miss Morison for sparing you to help us. Please, follow me.'

I trotted through the doorway after him, leaving the custodian to his ledgers, and entered another world entirely. I blinked as we stepped into the central hall, its walls and ceiling painted with whitewash that reflected the autumn light streaming in through tall windows. At one end, the room was lined with shelves and panelled cupboards housing the collections that had already been catalogued. Cluttered workbenches filled the central floor space and around them were piles of wooden crates, many stamped with foreign characters and covered with paper labels, recording the long and sometimes tortuous journeys they must have made to end up here in Edinburgh. Dr Kay led me to a workbench near one of the windows. As we approached, a young man who had been hunched over a desiccated-looking branch straightened up and grinned at me. I think I must have gaped at him like an idiot in return. He set aside the scalpel he'd been holding and held out his hand to shake mine.

The curator introduced us. 'Miss Mackenzie-Grant, I believe you have already encountered Callum Gillespie. He speaks highly of your artistic skills, and it was on his recommendation that I approached Miss Morison to see if we could avail ourselves of your services.'

Regaining my composure, I replied, with what I hoped sounded like calm professionalism, 'Our paths have crossed on occasion whilst at work in the gardens. It is a great honour that my drawings might be considered of a standard to help catalogue the new arrivals here.' I cast a look around the room, meeting the glances of other men who had paused in their work, disturbed by the arrival of a female interloper.

Dr Kay nodded. 'Very good. Well, I'll leave you in the capable hands of Mr Gillespie. He can make some space and show you the specimens we've set aside for drawing.'

I thanked him and then set my satchel on a stool alongside the workbench, unbuttoning my coat and removing it ready to roll up my sleeves and set to work.

'You can hang that on one of those hooks over there.' Callum pointed towards the door and then began stacking several of the thick card folders that were scattered over the worktop one on top of the other, clearing one end of the bench.

Perched on my stool, I listened carefully as he showed me how each specimen was processed. 'These crates are a bit like a lucky dip. You never quite know what you're going to pull out next. And you never know what state the plants might be in, either. Some are useless, mouldy and rotted by seawater, and have travelled all this way only to end up as compost. Others are so perfectly preserved they almost still show signs of life. But most are like this rhododendron here' – he picked up the dry branch he'd been working on – 'and whilst we have enough to go on to catalogue them and preserve them in the Herbarium, sometimes a bit of artistic interpretation helps bring them back to life. That's where you come in.'

He passed me a pile of folders. 'These will get you started. They're well annotated, so it should be fairly easy for you to get the colours right. See, here, someone's written this lily is "*the colours of the sunrise*". Other specimens will need a bit more detective work as the notes are a bit sketchy. You'll need to look up similar species in the books we have to get more accurate clues as to what the flowers look like in the wild.'

I opened the first folder, revealing a pressed rhododendron bloom. The sheet of paper on which it had been stuck carried the official stamp of the Botanic Garden as well as a number of neat, handwritten notes detailing the location and date of collection and the name of the collector: G. Forrest.

Callum must have seen the awe in my expression when I read the name because he moved a little closer to look over my shoulder. 'Pretty impressive, isn't it?' he said, his hazel eyes alight with enthusiasm. I've noticed they seem to shift from brown to green to golden, depending on the light and his mood. 'To think, George Forrest himself clambered up some rocky slope somewhere on a Himalayan mountainside and picked this. See here, the altitude is recorded too. Twelve thousand feet. Just imagine being part of an expedition that takes you to such places, finding plants like this one that haven't been seen in the world beyond those mountains!'

I found myself smiling back at him, swept up in his passion as he described some of the other specimens he'd been working on from that same expedition. The whitewashed walls of the hall seemed to melt away, replaced by the landscape he described. Soaring mountain peaks, covered in snow and far higher than anything we have in Scotland, appeared against a dizzyingly blue sky. I felt a little breathless, imagining the effort of trekking in the thin, cold air and the wildness of the places where banks of these miraculous coral-coloured flowers blanketed the inhospitable terrain.

'These are my favourites, I think. We've just received them from Colonel Fairburn's latest expedition to Tibet.' He pushed another stack of folders my way and I opened the cardboard cover to find a beautiful pressed blue flower on a slender stem. '*Meconopsis* – the Himalayan blue poppy. Aren't they extraordinary?'

'Extraordinary,' I echoed. 'Lilies the colours of the sunrise. And poppies the colour of sky.'

I'd seen flowers like this one before, because Mrs Hanbury has begun cultivating them at Inverewe. They seem to thrive in the damp but temperate climate there, moderated even in winter by the Atlantic's Gulf Stream current. In May, their sky-blue petals glow against the woodland backdrop, nodding on tall stems as they stir in the ocean breeze. When I told him that, he said, 'I'd love to see the garden at Inverewe one day. I hear it's full of wonders that cannot be grown in other parts of Scotland.'

'Well, maybe one day I can show you round,' I replied. There was a moment's silence and in it I realised something had shifted between us. His gaze, which had seemed awkward and confrontational on our previous encounters, suddenly felt like the sun coming out from behind a cloud on a spring day. He must have felt it too – perhaps my own eyes were shining with the same light – because he blushed and turned away, busying himself with setting the piles of folders back in place.

'Right, well,' I said, as businesslike as anything, 'I'll get on with it then.' I set out my drawing things, opening the tin box holding my brushes. I took out the little carving of the palmetto frond that he'd dropped at my feet those weeks before. 'I never had a chance to thank you for this, by the way.' The wooden leaf nestled in my hand, and I curled my work-roughened fingers around it.

His cheeks flushed a deeper red and he seemed stuck for words.

'I think I owe you an apology too,' I went on quietly, not wishing the others around us to overhear. 'That day we first met, in the Palm House. I didn't realise you were a gardener. I must have seemed awfully condescending, lecturing you on the provenance of the plants you tend. I was sorry I drove you away.'

'Aye, well, perhaps I should have introduced myself properly. It's a warm spot to sit on a Sunday when the east wind's blowing.

The room in my digs catches the draught full on and the Palm House makes a good refuge. But there's no harm in sharing it with others.'

I felt all the worse, realising it was probably one of the few places he could go to get warm on his day off that didn't involve having to find the cost of a cup of tea.

'Perhaps another time you could show me round,' I said, opening my sketch book and picking up my pencil. 'I'm sure there'll be plenty more cold and damp Sundays ahead of us in the winter months.'

He didn't reply, and we set to work in companionable silence on the specimens before us. As I mixed my watercolours, attempting to make exactly the right shade of cherry red to bring my sketch of *Rhododendron barbatum* to life, I heard him whistling faintly under his breath. And I couldn't be sure, but I think the tune just might have been a song I'd once heard about a bonny lass and the man who loved her.

Daisy – March 2020

I have two more days in Kathmandu to prepare for trekking in the mountains. Top of my list of priorities is to lay my hands on some pills to help with altitude sickness and a supply of loo rolls. Apparently, the former are readily available but the latter are scarce in the more remote parts of Nepal and I'm worried about the possibility of them being suddenly and catastrophically needed. We'll be staying a day or two in Namche Bazaar, to acclimatise to the change in altitude. My guidebook warns that everything is available there but at greatly inflated prices. Every single item has to be carried up to the hill town – one of the main waystations on the trek to Everest Base Camp – on the backs of porters and mules.

Ironically, when I return to the hotel in the evening with my booty, a BBC news update on my phone describes a severe shortage of toilet paper in the UK as a result of panic buying, so I take a photo of the two rolls I've managed to buy in Kathmandu and send it to Jack with a message saying, *Eat your heart out!*

He must be within reach of shore somewhere because a text pings back almost straight away: *Did you know that an anagram of HEART is HATER? Bog paper situation not yet critical here. But good to know I can call on you in case of dire emergency.*

Where are you? I ask.

Bought a boat in Bermuda. She's a beauty. Called Skylark. The name reminded me of you, Laverocks, it being the Scots word for a lark and all, so I knew she had to be mine the minute I saw her. Now anchored off Grenada. Turned away at every port. Attempting to reprovision and then going to make for the Azores. Might as well do lockdown crossing the Atlantic.

On your own??

What could possibly go wrong? He adds a laughing face emoji.

Take care, I text back.

Is that the pot calling the kettle black? comes the reply. *Are you in the mountains?*

Heading that way.

Watch out for yetis.

And you watch out for sea monsters.

I wait, hoping for another reply, but his connection must have dropped or perhaps he's busy with the boat because there's radio silence.

I stuff the loo rolls into my pack and then swallow the first of my altitude pills with a gulp of water before turning off the light. But sleep is elusive, and I toss and turn, worrying about the trip ahead.

I try not to think too much about the description in my guidebook of Lukla airport and its frightening reputation. From the photos I've seen, it seems to be a single runway tucked into a narrow meadow high in the mountains, which ends abruptly just before a wall of merciless-looking rocky peaks. I imagine it will be busy at this time of year, the beginning of the Everest trekking season, packed with climbers far more experienced than I who will be making the eight-day trek to the foot of the world's highest mountain. I'll be leaving the path about halfway up, climbing into a quieter valley where the village of Phortse clings to a vertiginous slope. The name gives me a tingle of anticipation. Phortse: the Sherpa village where Violet Mackenzie-Grant once lived, now home to Tashi, his wife and his son, Sonam.

I'm champing at the bit to get going, and at the same time worried that my plans may be cancelled once more – or perhaps Tashi and Sonam won't turn up. If that happens, I decide, then I'll definitely head home. The thought that I might never see them again brings with it a confusing surge of disappointment and relief. I realise a part of me is hoping the latest plan will unravel too and I can abandon this crazy journey once and for all. I could be back in London by the end of next week. Nobody can say I haven't tried. I can return with my head held high, my red string bracelet round my wrist, and my photos of Kathmandu to prove to everyone, myself included, that at least I was brave enough to come this far on my own.

Another message pings on my phone and I reach for it, thinking it will be from Jack. But to my surprise, this one's from Mara. *So glad you're doing this, Mum. Inspirational!*

It's as if she's read my thoughts and realised I might be in need of encouragement. It's also the first communication I've had from her in a while. Sorcha is naturally the more communicative of my twins. I tell myself I'm glad they're both so independent and since starting their university courses (Mara's acting studies at RADA and Sorcha's degree in ecology at Imperial College), it's probably only natural they should gravitate more towards their dad. He now lives with his wife, Claire, and their five-year-old son, Max, in a large house in Wandsworth. But there's a nagging voice in my head that worries whether it's the best thing for them emotionally. The instinct to protect them from being hurt is still strong. Their dad never showed much interest in them when they were growing up, but recently they've drawn closer to him.

Before my departure on this trip, I'd tried to arrange to see both Mara and Sorcha, but Mara had cancelled at the last minute as she had to be at an important rehearsal. So Sorcha and I had dinner at a fancy restaurant in the West End. She'd talked about how cute her half-brother Max was, how cool her dad was with him, and how Claire had been busy recording a studio album but might be going on tour again, while 'the boys' stay at home and mind the fort.

I'd tried to swallow another overpriced chip, while choking down my concern and resentment. Then chided myself silently. I didn't want to be the bitter, rejected ex-wife, consumed with jealousy. But I'd sacrificed so much for him and his career, and now I felt I'd lost everything I ever cared about, so perhaps a pang of anger every now and then was justified.

My ambition to become a gardener like Violet had led me to study for a diploma in garden design and to do an apprenticeship in horticulture. I'd begun to establish my own landscape gardening business and it was gathering momentum. My big break came when I was asked to design one of the smaller gardens for the Chelsea Flower Show and it had won a gold medal, catapulting me into the gardening stratosphere. But that all changed when I met my husband – whose name I can't even bring myself to think, let alone say, so much does his betrayal still hurt.

He came to the music school at Ardtuath to record a folk singer who went on to become a global presence on the music scene. His job as a sound engineer took him all over the place, wherever the next tour went, but he insisted we had to make our home in London, saying it was easier for him, logistically, as he never knew where he'd be flying off to next. It was a big sacrifice for me. Getting married and moving to London meant starting all over again, building a client base in the city. People there wanted instant, low-maintenance designs involving much hard landscaping and plants that would behave themselves, a far cry from the exuberant wildflower meadows and wildlife-friendly habitats I loved to create.

And we could only afford a small flat in an apartment block, so I didn't even have a patch of garden of my own.

I still remember the moment I found out about the affair. And although years have gone by, the memory still makes my stomach clench with the physical pain of his betrayal. I suppose I should have suspected something before I did. It seems the wife is usually the last to know. Claire – the now-famous folk singer – and he had grown closer at the same time as he and I had drifted apart. Inevitably, I suppose, as our worlds became so very different. Mine involved fitting in my work around school runs and nagging over homework, while his involved air tickets and tour buses and stadiums packed with fans – glamour, with the added risk of a free-lancer's sporadic salary. No wonder Mara and Sorcha were drawn to him like moths to a flame, readily exchanging my boring, cramped flat for holidays in exotic places and backstage passes to gigs.

The betrayal, followed by the aftershocks of divorce and life as a single parent, made me feel completely inadequate. Sometimes I used to think I'd leave me too, if I could.

I switch on the light and prop myself up on my pillows to compose a message in reply to Mara's, trying to sound confident and not come across as too needy, too worried, too nagging . . .

Thanks, love. Enjoying my adventure! Hope all good there. What will you and Sorcha do if a lockdown happens and the universities close?

All good. Don't worry, we'll go to Dad's.

I begin to type, then backtrack hitting the delete key and in the end settle for a thumbs-up emoji. By the time I send it, Mara has gone offline, and it sits there unseen. Perhaps she saw I was typing and deliberately retreated, knowing the mention of staying at her father's would send me into a tailspin. Because of course I'm worried. I'm anxious that spending more time with their father will only set them up for hurt and rejection. He took absolutely no interest in the twins when they were younger. They'll be useful, I suppose, as childminders and entertainers. But will Claire want them in her home for weeks on end now her latest tour will have been cancelled? And how will they be able to keep up with their studies with the universities shutting down?

I shake my head, trying to snap myself out of the tailspin of rumination. I'm just jealous, I tell myself firmly. This is not the woman I want to be. And anyway, perhaps it will work out well and the girls will be safe and happy as the world descends into chaos. They're adults now. And they certainly don't need me butting into their lives from halfway around the globe.

I check my phone again in case Mara is back online, but the falsely cheery emoji remains hanging in the space between us.

As I plug in my phone to charge, I catch sight of myself in the mirror hanging on the opposite wall and once again my reflection takes me by surprise. I always used to look as determined as I felt, but both my appearance and my confidence are melting away, becoming fuzzy and indistinct. I don't like what I've lost: my self-possession; my role as a mother; my previous relationship with my girls; the ability to catch a man looking at me and to smile back at him, feeling wanted. Nor do I like what I've gained: ten pounds in weight; a layer of flesh settling like a snowdrift around my waist and thighs; and a single, disconcertingly coarse hair sprouting on my chin, which stubbornly resists all my attempts to permanently eradicate it with a pair of tweezers.

My mother also gently pointed out one evening, when I'd been weeping into my glass of wine during a heart-to-heart with her, that history has an uncanny way of repeating itself. There were certainly a few parallels with my own father, who had deserted Mum when he'd found out she was pregnant as it was far too much of an inconvenience to his own career as a composer to contemplate supporting a wife and child.

That conversation prompted me to visit a counsellor but it didn't help me much to know I'd just ended up writing the same old story all over again and passing it on to my girls.

We all do it, don't we? Unwittingly making the same old mistakes, over and over again. Except perhaps Violet. I think she's a good example of someone who defied her upbringing and wrote a new story, all of her own. When I was going through some of my darkest moments, her journals continued to inspire me.

Since there's now no chance of sleep, I pick up a letter of hers from the bundle of her papers and start to read.

◆ ◆ ◆

The Laurels

12 Corstorphine Gardens

Edinburgh

Sunday, 27th November, 1927

Dearest Hetty,
Well, I've almost completed my first term and despite Ma's predictions I have neither got myself expelled nor have I dropped out. In fact, it's been everything I dreamed of and more. My assignment to the Herbarium at the Botanic Garden has been going well and my drawings and paintings have, I think, added to the recording and cataloguing of many of the specimens. The chilblains on my fingers are worth it! Ma

will have kittens when she sees the state of my hands (the only one of her predictions that HAS come true). The heating in the Caledonian Hall consists of a temperamental monster of a boiler that only barely manages to raise the temperature of the room by a degree or two at best, so I often work wrapped in my coat, wearing a pair of fingerless gloves so as to be able to use my pencils and brushes. But as I draw and paint, I forget the cold and the damp and the grey skies beyond the soot-speckled windowpanes and am transported to lush tropical valleys filled with bright rhododendron blooms and rugged, snow-capped mountainsides, where poppies the colour of a summer sky nod amongst carpets of starry white saxifrage. Oh, how I should love to see such sights one day! Of course, women are rarely included on the plant-hunting expeditions that send these treasures back to us. But maybe, somehow, one day I will travel further than the Scottish railways can carry me.

Speaking of which, I'm so looking forward to coming home to Ardtuath for Christmas. There is much to tell you about the past three months here, and whilst I suspect the botanic and horticultural details will bore you rigid, I do have some news of a romantic kind that will interest you more. One of my colleagues at the Herbarium is a most personable young man by the name of Callum Gillespie. It has taken a few weeks, but he has finally plucked up the courage to ask me to accompany him on a walk beside the Water of Leith next Saturday. I must confess, I find his shyness rather attractive. So far, he is most comfortable talking about the plants we work on together, but I have managed to extract from him the information that his family comes from Perthshire, where his father is head gardener on an estate near Dunkeld. Ma will have even more kittens when she learns this is the sort of person I socialise with nowadays. But, after all, we are equals at work (indeed, he is a couple of years ahead of me in experience and holds down a far more responsible role than I do at the Botanic Garden). I like him very much indeed. He is a great deal more interesting than anyone we were ever introduced to at those hunt balls.

Is there anything in particular you would like me to bring from Edinburgh, dear Hetty? I look forward to treating you to such luxuries as silk stockings and scented bath salts, as well as some of those rose cream chocolates you love.

Counting down the days until I see you . . .
Your sister,
Violet xx

Daisy – March 2020

I'm all ready to leave tomorrow morning, having packed and repacked my bags several times. With time on my hands, I return to the Garden of Dreams to spend time among the jasmine and roses. I sit on the bench beneath the marble plaque and read the words of the verses again. This time, it's the first one that speaks to me most clearly:

> *One moment in annihilation's waste,*
> *One moment. Of the well of life to taste –*
> *The stars are setting, and the caravan*
> *Starts for the dawn of nothing – oh, make haste!*

Well, Mr Omar Khayyam, no one can say I'm not seizing the moment, stepping far out of my comfort zone and on to the middle way of the unknown.

A feeling of serenity descends over me as I sit gazing out across the neat lawns and the beds overflowing with colour. I get to my feet at last, and take one final walk along the path that circles the outer edge of the garden. In the far corner, I notice a gate I haven't seen before. It's as finely wrought as the others punctuating the garden walls here and there, embellished with ironwork scrolls and the heads of lions. The word 'DREAMS' is picked out in gilt along the top, just as it is on the entrance gate at the other side of the garden. But as I draw closer, my sense of serenity evaporates when I see what lies on the other side of the railings. It's a scene of total devastation. Heaps of rubble and splintered wood are piled there haphazardly, as if a whole building has collapsed. It must date from the last earthquake, five years ago. I stand before it, shocked by the juxtaposition of the wording above the gate and the annihilation beyond it. *Dreams in ruins*, I think. *How apt.* It's a sobering reminder of the forces of nature that are capable of racking this country without warning. My confidence wavers again, but I turn away and walk briskly towards the exit before anything else can shake my resolve to carry on with this misbegotten trip. If someone's trying to tell me something, I'm not listening.

On the way back to the hotel, I stop in at Himalayan Java again, now my favourite café, and have one last cinnamon bun and decent cup of coffee. I know such luxuries will be hard to come by in the mountains. Just as I'm picking the final crumbs from my plate, my phone rings. I answer it, expecting it to be Tashi Sherpa calling to confirm the pick-up time for tomorrow and the arrangements for getting to the airport in time for the first flight to Lukla. But it appears our plans have been stymied once again.

Tashi tells me there are no more flights to Lukla for tourists. Because of the developing situation with the virus, as of today internal flights in Nepal are to be used only for transporting essential supplies.

I clutch my hair in exasperation. Perhaps the universe really is trying to tell me to abandon this trip and go home. But then I think of Violet, how she never had the luxury of bailing out even when her own dreams lay in ruins. And I remember Mum's words: *This trip is your chance to find what you've lost . . . not just searching for Violet, searching for the Daisy you used to be.* I feel a new surge of determination. 'So is there anything we can do?' I ask Tashi.

'Should be no worry, Mrs Daisy. We can walk to Lukla. Five more days trekking, maybe six. But maybe too a good way for you to climb more slowly. Sonam and I meet you at hotel tomorrow, seven in morning.'

Should be no worry. But I think of the dwindling bundle of cash in my money belt. I've already had to pay for my extra days in Kathmandu. And now there'll be five more days on the trail. Or maybe six, Tashi said. But still, no worry. And then I realise he's right. Somehow, here in this extraordinary country, where everything I once thought I knew about time has evaporated and the ability to feel in command of my plans has been removed by forces far outside my control, deadlines and schedules no longer seem to matter. After all, according to the increasingly alarming news flashes, the world outside has become equally as chaotic, so perhaps I'm just as safe staying in Nepal. I've been trying to cling on to the last shreds of agency I once thought I had over my plans, but that seems laughable now. What's the point? To my surprise, I find there's a huge sense of liberation in finally letting go. Perhaps this is what the monk at the stupa meant when he talked about the middle way. I rub the length of red string tied around my wrist between my finger and thumb.

All I know for sure now is I'm going to take a leap of faith. I will walk into the mountains, on the path of the warrior, putting my trust in a pair of strangers. I'm doing it for Mum. I'm doing it for Violet. But most of all, after so many years of putting others first, I'm doing it for myself.

I pay for my coffee, stepping out of the café and back into the frenetic hustle of the city's streets.

Despite my efforts to discard anything non-essential, my backpack still feels awfully heavy when I test it out in my hotel room in the thin light of dawn the next morning. Reluctantly, I pull out a bottle of moisturiser, my deodorant and a spare fleece top, and set aside the comfortable slippers I'd imagined putting on my tired feet at the end of each day. I'll just have to wear my socks and smell. The loo rolls add to the bulk, but have to stay in, obviously. I try the backpack again. If anything, it seems to feel even heavier now. How can that be possible? It'll have to do.

I ease my feet into my hiking boots and tie the laces firmly, then manhandle both my pack and the bag I'll be leaving at the hotel downstairs to the lobby. I force myself to eat some breakfast. The altitude pills I've started taking add to the dryness of my mouth. It's an effort to swallow the toast and honey I order, and I gulp it down with cups of milky chai.

Perhaps Tashi and Sonam won't turn up though, I think, and I'll be able to book myself back into my room and spend the rest of the day arranging my flights home. The hotel is half empty and the waiter at breakfast told me they're receiving more and more cancellations because of the virus, so I know accommodation won't be a problem if I have to extend my stay by another day. But from a mirror on the dining-room wall, my reflection looks back at me, its frown lines deepening as if it disapproves of this defeatist attitude. I stand, shouldering my pack with a grunt, and push open the door without a backward glance.

Tashi and Sonam are already waiting outside the hotel when I emerge. I raise a hand in greeting, hoping my smile disguises the churning of my stomach and the final pang of regret I experience at the realisation that I've run out of excuses, and am now actually going to have to do this. Sonam takes my pack from me and swings it with ease into the back of the jeep that will take us to Shivalaya, where we'll pick up the trail into the hills. I climb into the back seat, where he joins me.

'All ready, Mrs Daisy?' Tashi asks from the front seat.

'All ready,' I reply.

I ask again what I owe him for the trip, but he dismisses my question with a wave of his hand, saying, 'Later, later.' I just hope my scant budget is going to cover it.

The driver turns the key to start the engine, with a cough and a splutter, and we jolt forward into the morning traffic.

◆ ◆ ◆

Despite the early start and a lack of traffic on the roads out of Kathmandu, we end up not doing any walking at all on the first day. At first we sail along, the wheels of the jeep humming over the tarmac until we reach the town of Jiri, where we stop for lunch, five hours later. But then the road becomes an unmade, potholed track. We make slow progress and I'm tired, hot and thirsty. Every bone in my body hurts from the jouncing and swerving (to avoid goats, cows and people, not just potholes).

'All okay, Mrs Daisy?' Tashi asks from the front seat. I nod and smile and give him a thumbs up. 'Only few more miles to Shivalaya. No worry.'

I'm longing for the car to stop, and then all of a sudden it does, in the middle of nowhere, behind a large truck that has its back wheels stuck in a deep pothole, completely blocking the track. Dense bushes line both sides of the road, hemming us in. Our driver, Tashi and Sonam jump out and go over to talk to the truck driver, so I ease my stiff legs out of the jeep too, and stand in the dust, thankful – at least – for the opportunity to stretch.

After an animated discussion and a couple of failed attempts to push the truck out of the hole, our driver comes back to the jeep and cheerfully pulls a long, machete-like knife from the boot. I go over to see if I can lend a hand. He begins to hack at the bushes and Tashi and Sonam start pulling the cut branches away. 'No, no,' they tell me, insisting I go back to the relative comfort of the jeep, showing me the vicious thorns on the stems of the brush.

Darkness is beginning to fall. I take out my phone but there's no signal. Half an hour later, the men return to the car, having cut a way through the thorn bushes and hefted several large rocks out of the way to form a new, makeshift track. 'We can go now,' says Tashi, as calmly as if we've stopped for a rest rather than a stint of road building.

'But what about the truck?' I ask.

'No worry. We will send tractor from Shivalaya in morning.'

By the time we reach the village the sky is pitch black, studded with a million stars. We drive slowly along what appears to be the main street. Only one or two houses have a light in their windows and the few teahouses appear to be shut.

'Is there anywhere for us to stay?' I ask. I want the driving to stop. I want to be able to wash my hands and face, which are covered with dust. I want to change out of my stale, sweat-stained clothes. I want to lie down on a bed and stretch out my aching body. Such luxuries as food and sleep seem extremely unlikely, but I don't even care any more.

Tashi's smile gleams from the front seat. 'My cousin has teahouse just here. We will stay there tonight, no worry.'

And we do. And there is a room with a narrow bed that seems like one of the most comfortable things I've ever lain on. Not only that, there's also a shower with a trickle of warm water, and a dish of lentil dhal and rice that's one of the most delicious things I've ever tasted. I can hardly keep my eyes open as I stumble up the stairs to my bedroom and I fall into my bed and a deep, deep sleep.

◆ ◆ ◆

I wake to the sound of rain. I'm used to Scottish rain – everything from a drizzle to a downpour – but this has a different quality to it. It sounds like the roar of the ocean in a storm, crashing on the tin roof of the teahouse and engulfing us from all sides. I pull on my clothes and hurry downstairs. Tashi and Sonam are already sitting at the table, cups of steaming tea before them, and the cousin who owns the teahouse sets another one down in front of me.

'No walking today, Mrs Daisy,' Tashi says, his smile undimmed as he shares this news. 'The rains should be stopped by now, but very late this year. So we stay here and keep dry. Leave tomorrow, no worry.'

'Do you think the rain will stop by the morning?' I ask, taking a sip of my tea. While I'm disappointed by yet another delay to stop us getting going on the trek, my aching body could certainly do with another night's rest in a comfortable bed. And Tashi's cousin's wife is an excellent cook, too. I take a spoonful from the bowl of some sort of vegetable stew that's been put in front of me for breakfast, relishing the taste of garlic and herbs.

'For sure,' says Sonam. 'Shouldn't be raining now anyway. But the climate's changing here, like everywhere else. We're at the very tail end of the winter rains now though. This won't last long.'

After we've eaten, I settle myself on a pile of cushions by the iron stove in the corner of the room. It's not cold – in fact, it's still pretty muggy – but the dampness pervades everything, and the glow of warmth from the stove helps dispel it a little. I feel strangely contented, cocooned in the teahouse with the sound of the rain, overlain by the noises of pans clattering in the kitchen and the murmur of the men as they talk quietly around the table. There's no internet here, no phone signal, nothing. So I curl my feet beneath me on the cushions and take out Violet's journal.

I reread the pages detailing her studies at the gardening school – she continues to struggle with chemistry but enjoys her time working in the Herbarium at the Botanic Garden as winter gives way to spring. She describes the first colour appearing. And as the snowdrops emerge and the early rhododendrons begin to bloom, her relationship with Callum blossoms too.

Violet's Journal

MONDAY, 9TH APRIL, 1928

Home at Ardtuath for the Easter break. It feels so very strange to be back. I hadn't realised how much the distance has grown with having been away and experiencing such a different world in the city.

Callum is here too. I persuaded him to come as I wanted to introduce him to Ma and Pa. A momentous step, and one that both of us faced with a good deal of trepidation. Correctly so, it turns out, because it's been something of a disaster. Rather than being welcomed as a guest of the house, Callum has been put in the keeper's cottage, given a bed in the attic room there, and it has been made very plain that my parents see him as nothing more than another labourer.

Ma insists on calling him 'your friend the gardener'. And when we first arrived, sitting uncomfortably in the drawing room with teacups – not the best ones, I noted – perched precariously on the wobbling side tables at our elbows, Pa asked him what wage he'd expect if he were to be employed up this way. As if it was a job interview, presumably because that could be the only possible reason for him to be here at Ardtuath House. It was mortifying. Callum is taking it all with good grace, though I can tell it wounds him.

Today we went to Inverewe, where we both felt far more at home in the gardens. Mrs Hanbury was her usual interesting and interested self and I could tell she warmed to Callum. His knowledge of Himalayan plants rapidly earned her respect as we walked amongst the rhododendrons and sweet-scented azaleas, with the bristly leaves of the blue poppies beginning to show alongside the path leading to the shore. We could almost imagine ourselves in the mountains of Nepal or Bhutan and I knew Callum was in his element.

He always seems more at ease outdoors, pursuing his passion for plants. He's not had much in the way of formal schooling, but his natural thirst for knowledge and sharp, enquiring mind have made me realise that education is of secondary importance: it's innate intelligence that really matters. I love that in him. I love a lot of other things about him as well. But most of all, I love him because he is so completely and utterly himself, unburdened by the veneer of social strictures, and that speaks straight to my heart.

After showing us the latest plantings in the walled garden, Mrs Hanbury left us to walk at leisure and told me to bring Callum back every day whilst we're here. I think she'd guessed how we would be being treated at Ardtuath.

We walked through the woodland to the point, and I showed him Cuddy Rock and the hidden bay. We sat there for a while, turning our faces to the sun, and I felt – for the first time since arriving back home – that I could breathe again. Ardtuath is stifling, with Ma and Pa's unspoken disapproval of 'my gardening friend' all too apparent, and Charles worse than ever with his headaches and moods when he condescends to call in. I do love Helen, though, she's such a kind and gentle sister-in-law, and little Alec is a delight. I don't think Charles realises how lucky he is to have them there to brighten his dark moments.

There's more news on the wedding front, too. Hetty is to marry Rufus Ogilvy. She saved the news to tell me herself, coming to my room on my first night back. I feigned delight, of course, although I'm sure she can guess my reservations. He's so much older than she is, a widower with two grown children and I doubt he will be wanting more. It seems a sad sacrifice to make. I asked Hetty if she is truly happy and her smile was just a little too bright when she replied, 'It's a good match, Vi, and he's a kindly man.' He offers her financial security and the promise of a good home, of course, but I was left feeling that what I share with Callum – our true intimacy and mutual understanding – is worth more than all of those worldly considerations.

As Callum and I sat side by side on the rocks by the shore at Inverewe, he talked about the caste system in India, which he'd read about. I realised he was relating it to his situation here, being made to feel a second-class citizen, his 'place' being made all too apparent by the treatment he's received at the hands of my parents. I worried he was trying to tell me that we cannot be together, that society conspires against us in ways too powerful to overcome. To reassure him, I pointed out that he and I are at exactly the same level in society because of our chosen profession. He laughed a little hollowly at that.

'What you mean to say, Vi, is that you have taken a step down to join me.'

'Not at all,' I retorted. 'As a woman, I'm already a second-class citizen. One could argue we were born equals. And I should much prefer a marriage on that basis to one such as Helen or Hetty have opted for.'

I flushed as pink as the wind-blown azalea flowers scattered amongst the stones at our feet, realising I had surely overstepped the mark with my reference to marriage. But Callum simply turned to face me and took hold of my other hand too. 'You would consider such a union then, would you, Miss Mackenzie-Grant? A marriage far beneath your station?'

I shook my head and laughed. 'I would only ever consider a marriage to a man I loved, heart and soul, one who loved me back in the same way. That, surely, is the only equality that matters.'

He was quiet then, and the only sounds were the hush of the waves and the sighing of the wind in the trees. Then he said, 'I want to be worthy of you, Vi. I want to be able to give you the life you deserve. And I shall work every day God gives us to be able to offer you that.'

He put his arm around my waist, and I rested my head on his shoulder. For those few blissful minutes as we sat there like that in the sunlight, cocooned for a while in a world beyond the strictures of social hierarchies, it felt as if nothing could ever tear us apart.

When I got back to the big house, having left Callum at the keeper's cottage, a delegation was waiting for me in the drawing room. My parents sat stiffly on the over-stuffed sofa facing the door and my brother Charles stood in front of the fire, shoulders squared, his hands clasped behind his back. Nervously, I smoothed down my hair and smiled, trying to ignore the atmosphere in the room, which seemed so heavy it made it hard for me to breathe. Why was Charles here, and where were Hetty and Helen?

'Is there any tea left in the pot?' I asked, with a pretence at nonchalance.

'Sit down, please, Violet,' Pa said.

'Is something the matter?' I said, perching on the edge of an armchair, although I knew full well exactly what it was.

'The matter,' said my brother, his tone caustic, 'is that gardener you've brought here. What on earth were you thinking? It's hardly appropriate for you to be running about the place with him. People will jump to conclusions.'

I lifted my chin and met his disgusted gaze with defiance. 'Let them. Who knows, perhaps those conclusions are correct?'

My mother gasped, raising a hand to her chest, and Charles's face flushed deep puce with fury.

'This is exactly what we were afraid of, Violet.' My father's voice was deliberately calm, trying to sound reasonable. 'And that's why we need to have this talk. I want to make absolutely certain that you understand our position.'

I tried to interject, but he raised his palm to stop me. 'No, let me speak.' His words were sharper now, edged with steel. 'Your mother and I have humoured you in your whimsical desire to do this gardening course in Edinburgh. Knowing how headstrong you can be, we thought it might be wise to allow you to get it out of your system. But if you are to continue, we expect you to be more discerning in the company you keep there. So when you return, you will no longer see that young man.'

'Really, Vi,' my mother added, 'Edinburgh must be full of people who'd make suitable husbands. I thought it might do you good to be in the city and meet a wider circle than is available to you here. But this . . . boy . . . is most certainly not what any of us had in mind. Please, dear, listen to your father.'

'Because if you don't,' said Charles, unable to refrain from butting in again, 'you will either come home or we will send you off to a finishing school where you'll be taught to behave properly.'

I looked from one to the other. My mother's expression was pleading and scared; my brother's was straining at the seams with his barely suppressed rage; but my father's was the worst. He simply watched me in a manner so cold and detached that I realised nothing I could say would make any difference. It was as though all pretence had fallen away in that moment and I saw myself through his eyes.

He didn't even see me as a human being, let alone an equal. I was worthless to him – the second daughter and the third child. The most I could aspire to was not to be a burden on the family. I was nothing. And all he wanted me to do was make a suitable marriage, in which I would continue to be nothing for the rest of my life. Nothing but a good and biddable daughter. Like Hetty.

I got to my feet. 'I see,' I said, as levelly as I could. 'Well, you've made the position absolutely clear.'

'I mean it, Violet,' said my father, in that same even, emotionless tone. 'We've given you more than enough leeway. This is your final chance and if you disobey me then I will take the appropriate steps.'

'You'd do well to remember who pays your allowance,' Charles added. 'We can stop that straight away if you don't do as you're told. Life won't be much fun if you've been cut off without a penny.'

My mother reached across the space between us and patted my hand. 'Go and get yourself tidied up, dear, and then come down for dinner. We'll say nothing more about this unpleasantness, as long as you see reason. We just have your best interests at heart, you know.'

I walked out and climbed the stairs to my room, moving automatically, stunned by my father's coldness. I sat down at my dressing table and picked up my hairbrush, then put it down again, unable to move. Earlier, I'd cut a sprig of cherry blossom and put it in a vase, setting it where it would be reflected in the mirror of the vanity table. A few of the petals had fallen on to the marble top, scattered between the brush set and my little Wedgwood trinket box. I was frozen with the sudden icy clarity of my situation. Until now, I'd imagined I had choices, a degree of self-determinism about where my life would lead. But now I saw it through my father's eyes. He and Charles held all the power. I was merely another one of their belongings, and rather an inconvenient one at that.

I raised my eyes to the mirror. The flowers reflected there were delicate and fleeting. And yet each one held within it the potential to form a fruit, containing a seed from which a whole new tree might grow.

So much potential.

I brushed the fallen petals lightly with my fingertips, feeling the softness of decay already upon them.

Such a waste.

And then I lifted my chin and smiled at my reflection, knowing what I would do.

Because I, for one, simply cannot bear waste.

Daisy – March 2020

Violet's words and the sound of the rain on the roof of the teahouse transport me back to the shores of Loch Ewe – the childhood home I too dreamed of leaving for a wider world and finding love and respect such as she and Callum seem to have shared. Her descriptions of Ardtuath and Inverewe stir up a tidal pull within me, a flood of longing for my childhood home. It's a familiar feeling. I remember walking along the shore with Jack just before I left for London, taking leave of the place and the people who'd given me so much.

Jack stopped at the end of the beach, where the sand meets the rocks, and stood gazing out to sea. 'You'll miss this, Daisy,' he said. 'More than you know.'

I nodded, suddenly unable to speak as un-spilled tears choked me.

He turned to look at me then, searching my face for something. He swallowed hard and then said, 'Are you sure this is right for you? Uprooting yourself and everything you've been working towards, to go and live in a city? So far from the things you love?'

I shrugged, trying to look and sound more sure of myself than I really was. 'It'll be an adventure,' I replied. 'And a good challenge for me.'

He'd been right though. I did miss it. So much, sometimes, that the loss felt like a phantom limb, still hurting after it had been amputated. But by then it was too late to go back, and I was stuck in a place I'd never really wanted to be.

I turn back to Violet's journals, as I have done so often to live vicariously, escaping from my own life into hers. I read until lunchtime and then nod off, lulled by the warmth of the stove, and when I waken, it's late in the afternoon and the rain has stopped.

Next morning, we're ready to set off again at last. I seem to have done nothing but read, eat and sleep since we got here, and I feel all the better for it.

There's an awkward moment in the teahouse as I fumble in my money belt, asking Tashi how much I owe for the two nights' food and lodging. He shakes his head. 'This is family, Mrs Daisy. I already settle up. And also, I have money for you.' To my surprise, he pulls a sizeable roll of Nepali rupees from his pocket and hands them to me. 'Refund for your air tickets to Lukla. You and your mother's.'

I'm overcome with relief. I'd written off ever seeing the money again. 'Tashi, you're a miracle-worker! How did you manage to get this?'

He shrugs. 'I know someone who works in Yeti Airlines ticket office.'

'Let me guess,' I say with a grin. 'A cousin?'

He looks a bit surprised. 'No,' he replies. 'My cousin who works there is not authorised to pay out refunds. It was my uncle who arranged it.'

I laugh and reach for my heavy backpack, but Tashi gets there first. 'You don't carry this, Mrs Daisy. We have porters. They come with us to Lukla, then my cousin there will arrange new ones to come to Phortse.'

Outside, on the porch, Sonam stands chatting with two smiling men. Tashi hands one of them my pack and he swings it on to a large, fan-shaped bamboo basket as if it weighs nothing at all. The basket is already filled almost to the brim with sacks and cardboard boxes, so he uses a piece of rope to tie my bag in position, then hoists the load on to his back, drawing a strap over his shoulders and adjusting it to take the weight around his forehead. Before I can express my mixture of horror and admiration for the heavy load he's about to lug into the mountains for four days, he and his friend set off down the road, quickly disappearing into the distance.

At a more leisurely pace, Tashi and Sonam shoulder their own packs and say their goodbyes to the owner of the teahouse. I clasp my hands together in the universal gesture of thanks to him and his wife, then follow my Sherpa friends as they set off in the direction the porters took. I feel strangely light, stepping out unhindered by my heavy pack and with only my phone and a bottle of water in my smaller rucksack. I feel my weakness, fear and uncertainty evaporate, replaced by a new sense of purpose. I'm on my way.

It's a long day's hike, but the track is well made, winding into the hills where wisps of mist hang like cobwebs in the valleys as the storm clouds lift. We walk steadily, through dense forests of pine and glossy-leaved needlewood trees that drip a patter of yesterday's rainfall on to our heads and shoulders. My waterproof jacket is completely useless, though, as I quickly grow so hot inside it that sweat drenches my clothes. I take it off and tie it round my waist, resigning myself to being soaked. We trudge upwards, our trajectory steep. At last, we emerge from the forest on to a more open stretch of track and I gasp in amazement. It's as if the entire hillside has been turned into a vast Jackson Pollock-like canvas, splashed with paint to form a tapestry of colours as rich as a Persian carpet. Scarlet rhododendrons jostle for position alongside the amethyst blooms of Pride of India trees, interspersed with splashes of bright pink camellias. The hills stretch away, row upon row, leading the eye upwards towards the far horizon where the lifting clouds have begun to reveal the higher peaks, topped with snow.

I pull out my phone, trying to capture the scene in a photo, but nothing can do justice to this view. We move forward again, walking over a carpet of rain-bruised blossom, and I snap away as we go. We pass a small house beside the path and some children come out to watch us, their dark eyes smiling as they return my wave.

By the time we reach Kenja and tonight's teahouse, every muscle in my body is screaming at me to stop walking and lie down. On this, my first day of trekking, we've climbed to an altitude of nearly three thousand metres to get over the pass at Deurali and then dropped back down by more metres than we've climbed to reach Kenja. And tomorrow we'll be climbing even higher. But my personal aches and pains seem irrelevant as we walk through villages where the terrible earthquake of 2015 still leaves its mark. Five years on, houses lie in ruins, little more than heaps of stones, and the hillsides are scarred with stretches of bare earth. This whole area was badly hit, Tashi explains. They're trying to rebuild, but it's hard getting materials in such a remote place. Even though years have passed, people are still surviving in shacks and makeshift shelters.

The air is still warm, but the humidity has gone now and the setting sun bathes the terraced rice fields in gold as we walk the final kilometres into the village. People stop and turn to watch us passing by, calling out their welcomes. We haven't seen any other trekkers since the top of the pass, which is lucky because much of Kenja lies in ruins too. Tashi tells me there were many teahouses here before the earthquake, catering for the steady stream of walkers on the trail. But only a couple are open now and we are the only guests in the one we stop at.

I wash off the sweat in a basin in the shared bathroom, and drag a brush through my hair, attempting to tame the frizz a little. Then I check my phone for any news bulletins about the pandemic, both at home and here in Nepal. It's difficult to find any clear information, but the Nepal Tourism Board has a helpful page, advising that I'm not alone: there are still thousands of foreigners stranded in Nepal. It says to register with the British Embassy in Kathmandu, via their website. One sentence in particular grabs my attention: *Conditions are most likely not going to be better in your country and the trip back is going to be long and dangerous.* It goes on to say, *Don't worry about your visa, Nepal has granted amnesty on foreign visas and it will be sorted out later.* So I send an email to the British Embassy, letting them know where I am, only slightly reassured that perhaps my decision to stay will turn out to have been the right one.

Over supper, I can hardly keep my eyes open. But as soon as I get into my sleeping bag, my legs begin a relentless twitching, as if they're still climbing the trail, and I'm wide awake again. In the end, I turn over and switch on the light, pulling Violet's journal out of its plastic wrapper and reading until – at last – my restless legs and mind quieten enough for me to sleep.

Violet's Journal

Sunday, 4th November, 1928

We were given a week off at the end of October, once the harvest in the market garden was over and next season's onion sets and overwintering cabbages had been planted. I didn't bother going home to Ardtuath. After the ultimatum delivered by my father and Charles in the spring, I no longer feel part of that world in the way I used to. I've chosen my path. If I'm to share it with Callum then I know it must lead me away from my childhood home. We will need to find our own place in the world. In the meantime, I intend keeping my plans from my parents, of course, so that I can complete my course and have a proper career to fall back on once I leave. I hate the deception. But needs must.

Callum managed to get some time off from the Herbarium too. He wanted to take the opportunity to go home to his parents in Perthshire and introduce me to them. So we boarded the train and chugged northwards, crossing the Firth of Forth and heading towards the hills.

We received a warm welcome at the gardener's cottage, having walked from the station and dropped off my overnight bag at a local hotel on the way. Mrs Gillespie had baked us a fine tea, with scones and cakes and the butteriest shortbread I've ever tasted. She and Callum's father seemed a bit ill at ease, though, and the conversation was a little stilted. I got to my feet to help out with clearing the tea things, but his mother shooed me away from the sink.

'At least let me help dry,' I begged, picking up a tea towel, keen to lend a hand and leave Callum and his father to talk by the fire.

'Och, no, a young lady such as yourself has no place in the kitchen,' she said.

'Honestly, I'm very used to fending for myself these days. Living in digs has made me a good deal more useful than I was before.' I picked up a saucer and began to dry it, and she relented with a smile.

'I suppose you'll be enjoying the gardening,' she said. 'Learning to prune roses and so forth. And Callum has told us how good you are at your painting too.'

'I love it,' I replied, reaching for a teacup. 'I think my favourite times are spent in the Herbarium, but I've enjoyed learning to plough and dig and turn compost too.'

She glanced at me in surprise. 'And what do your parents think of you doing such menial work?'

'Not much,' I admitted cheerfully. 'But I've always been happier outdoors than in, and I love learning about the plants we see coming back from far-flung places. It makes me feel I'm seeing the world even though I've not been further south than Edinburgh.'

'Well, Perth's south enough for me,' she replied. 'I've not been to the capital for years.'

'You'll need to come and visit one day. We can take tea in the North British Hotel and go shopping in Jenners.'

She shook her head, plunging her hands back into the soapy water. 'Oh no, I don't think so. We're so busy here on the estate, it's hard to get away. And Callum's dad doesn't like cities at all – says they're full of too many folk getting in the way when you try to walk down the street.' She tipped out the bowl of dishwater and turned to take the tea towel from me. 'I'll finish up here,' she said, with a firmness that brooked no debate. 'Thank you for your help, Miss . . . er, Violet.' She stumbled awkwardly over my name. 'You go back and sit by the fire for a minute. Then you'll be needing Callum to walk you back to your hotel if he's to be back here in time for his supper. You don't want to be walking along that road in the pitch dark, not when tomorrow's the eve of Samhain.'

Callum had told me how his mother – despite being raised a good Christian woman – still held the belief that the bounds between this world and the Otherworld grow thin on the night of the pagan festival of All Hallows' Eve, allowing the souls of the departed to return. She would set an extra place at the table, he said, and put out an offering of food and drink to make sure of their protection through the winter months ahead. As if to endorse her words, a sudden gust of wind rattled the branch of a rowan tree against the kitchen window, its bright orange berries shaking in a flurry of falling leaves. I remembered that it's another ancient Scottish custom to plant a rowan tree beside the home in order to keep the witches away.

When I went back through to the parlour, Callum and his father were sitting in silence and it seemed to grow heavier as I walked through the doorway. To spare them the awkwardness, I asked if we could look around the estate's walled garden. The afternoon was already growing darker so there wasn't time to see everything that day, but Callum had told me his father took a particular pride in the neatly laid-out kitchen garden, protected from the autumn winds by a high wall of red brick.

'Suit yourselves,' Mr Gillespie grunted, kneeling to put another shovelful of coal on the fire. 'But there's not much to see at this time of year. And you'll need to be getting back to your hotel, Miss Mackenzie-Grant.'

We put on our coats, and Callum was silent as we walked along the path.

'It seems my parents are not the only ones to disapprove of our relationship,' I observed.

'I'm sorry, Vi,' he said. 'It's just hard for them to get their heads around a lady of your station taking up with a lad like me. You belong in the big house, not the gardener's cottage.'

I think we were both troubled by the reminder of the hurdles we faced as little more was said until he dropped me at the hotel entrance, a mile along the road from the estate. I'd taken his hand as we walked back, but he pulled away a little when we reached the pool of light cast from the hotel's front window, as if he was afraid someone might see us and pass yet more judgement.

'Good night then,' he said, twisting his cap awkwardly in his hands. I took a step towards him, wanting to kiss him goodnight, but he shook his head and drew back. 'We can't, Vi. Not here where someone might see us. Your reputation . . .'

I smiled, but I'm sure the sadness I felt must have been reflected in my face. 'Good night, Callum,' I said softly. 'See you tomorrow.' I climbed the steps to the door of the hotel. Before I pushed it open, I turned to look back, but he'd already walked away and the darkness had swallowed him.

◆ ◆ ◆

Next morning, after a fine breakfast of Arbroath smokies in the hotel's dining room, I put on my walking boots and gathered my coat, settling myself before the fireplace in the ladies' lounge to wait for Callum to arrive. It was a fine day and the Perthshire hills were clad in red and gold where the trees were turning. We'd planned to have a tour of the estate's gardens and then to walk along the river in the afternoon. But I knew straight away something was wrong when Callum appeared. He tried to smile, but his expression wavered and his eyes were clouded with discomfiture.

Instead of walking back on the road towards the estate, he led me down to the riverbank and we wandered along the path there a little way. On a bench beneath the arching branches of a clump of larches, I sat down and took his hands in mine.

'What's wrong?' I asked.

He shook his head, reluctant to speak, but then lifted his eyes to meet mine. 'Sorry, Vi. I thought they'd be okay with this. But I've had a fight with my dad,' he said. 'He's not prepared to show you round the gardens today. Says women don't have any business taking jobs from the men and I should send you back to the city where you belong.'

I was taken aback but laughed hollowly. 'Now I know just how wretched my parents made you feel,' I said. 'So at least we're equals on that front too.'

We sat in silence for a while, watching the current sweep past. I remembered how it had felt to sit with him on the shore at Inverewe, and how easy our companionship was as we worked at our shared bench in the Herbarium. 'Callum,' I said, turning to face him. 'Let's go somewhere where it's just the two of us. Away from the judgement of others.'

He lifted his eyes to mine and I read in them a desperate mixture of love and hope and anguish. 'But Vi . . .' he began.

I put a finger to his lips. 'But nothing,' I replied. 'I know what you're going to say about my reputation and what our parents will think and say. But I don't give a fig about all that any more, if I ever did. We've given everyone a chance to be nice to us, to support us and be a part of our lives together. And if they refuse to take it then that's their choice. But Callum, I choose you. And if you are prepared to choose me then that's all I need to know. No one will miss us. My parents think I'm visiting yours and yours will think we've gone back to Edinburgh. Is there somewhere we can go, to be together, just the two of us?'

He nodded slowly. Then he leaned forward and kissed me, and I kissed him back and that was all the certainty either of us needed. 'I'll get some things,' he said, 'and I'll meet you at the hotel in two hours' time.'

◆ ◆ ◆

Instead of walking across the bridge and back to the train station, we went in the opposite direction, into the hills. Callum had a pack on his back and took my overnight bag from me, whilst I carried a basket of food he'd coaxed from his mother, claiming nothing in the big city could match her cooking. We quickly left the village behind, climbing above its cluster of white houses, and turned off on to a narrow track that led into the woods. We walked for miles, past a small loch and into more open countryside where the heather had begun to turn from purple to brown with the first frosts of autumn. It was a fine day to be out in the hills. The sun shone and the breeze was soft, gently coaxing the birch trees to let fall their leaves in a flutter of golden confetti. Our spirits lifted as we put more and more distance between ourselves and the rest of the world.

At last, as the sun was beginning to slip behind the far range of hills, we came to a little stone bothy tucked into a side valley. Beside it, a foaming burn tumbled down the hillside and high on the ridge above us a herd of deer stood watching. 'Will this do you, Miss Mackenzie-Grant?' Callum asked, holding open the door for me to step inside, his eyes far brighter than they had been in the morning.

'I do believe it's the finest hostelry Perthshire can offer,' I replied, looking around at the single room. The floor was of earth and the ceiling of red-painted tin, but there was a fireplace at one end and a wooden bench along one of the walls where we could set out our provisions.

'We'd best collect some firewood,' Callum said. 'You don't want to be outside when the ghosts of Samhain come visiting.'

I'd forgotten it was All Hallows' Eve. 'We'll make sure we set an extra place for them then,' I laughed. 'And you'd better leave them a bit of your mother's gingerbread instead of guzzling down the lot!'

As dusk fell, we gathered bracken and the driest sticks we could find in the scrubby woods that grew alongside the stream. An owl hooted and the deer melted away from the ridge above us, disappearing silently into some secret fold in the hills. We piled the firewood beside the hearth and shut the door on the approaching night. Callum began to set the sticks, but before he lit them he reached up into the chimney breast and pulled a small object from the soot-grimed stones.

'Look at this,' he said, showing me a tiny shoe that fitted easily into the palm of his hand. 'When the shepherd and his family were living here, they'd have put this wee shoe in a niche in the chimney piece to keep the fairies from stealing away their bairn. It's an old tradition.'

'How on earth did you know it was there?' I asked, gently stroking the smoke-cured leather.

'I was sleeping here one summer's night, with no need for a fire, and a crow came tumbling down the chimney. I suppose it was nesting up top, or maybe just looking for trouble, as crows often do. It dislodged the shoe. Once I'd chased the bird out the door and dusted off the soot, I realised what this was. It will have been here for a hundred years or more, I'd guess. So I popped it back. Not wanting to be stolen away by the fairies myself, you understand.' He set the little shoe on a rickety wooden shelf above the fireplace and then stooped down to light the sticks.

We soon had a good blaze going and the bothy warmed up, despite the nip of frost in the clear night air outside. Through the age-warped glass of the single window, the first Samhain stars appeared, pinpricks of light in the darkness. We spread a blanket on the floor and from the basket Callum produced some slices of cooked ham, a jar of Mrs Gillespie's homemade chutney and a neat stack of shortbread. He tucked two potatoes into the fire to bake and then handed me a bottle of ginger beer.

'What a feast!' I exclaimed, taking a long draught from the bottle before handing it back to him.

'And whilst we're waiting for the tatties to cook, I have a snack to keep us going.' He pulled a knotted handkerchief out of his pack, showing me a cache of hazelnuts. He broke the glossy brown shells on the hearth with a stone and handed me a few of the creamy kernels.

We sat there contentedly, watching the flames make leaping shadows around the walls, happy to be cocooned in a sanctuary all of our own again. This would be the nature of our future together, I realised. We'd need to find a place where we could be together without judgement from others. But if it had to be this way then I, for one, felt I could be perfectly happy.

Once the potatoes were cooked, we scooped the soft insides from their burnt skins and mashed them with a knob of butter. Our meal was quite delicious. And we remembered to set a bit of it aside to ensure we were in the good books of the night's returning souls. 'I reckon we'll be needing all the luck we can get,' said Callum, his eyes shining in the firelight. 'At least the ones who've passed over might be on our side, even if the living aren't.'

After supper, we sat on the blanket watching the fire settle and shift as the sticks burned down. Callum picked up the last two remaining hazelnuts and rolled them together between his fingers.

'Do you know the superstition about these?' he asked. I shook my head. 'It's believed that if a pair of lovers puts two hazelnuts in the fire on Samhain, it will foretell how they are to fare together. If the nuts pop and crack, it bodes ill, meaning the relationship will break. But if they burn calmly, side by side, it means the pair are well matched and are meant to stay as one.'

I reached out my hand. 'Give them to me, then.'

'Vi, no, it's only a silly superstition.' He closed his fingers around them, reluctant to release them to me.

'What are you scared of, Callum Gillespie? Do you worry they will explode and we'll have to part?'

He shook his head, then nodded it slowly. 'I suppose I do. I couldn't bear to lose you, you see.'

'Well, I'm not afraid,' I replied. I prised open his fingers and placed the two nuts side by side in the glowing embers at the edge of the fire. He drew me close to him and we sat and watched as they began to burn. I think we were both secretly holding our breath. And I knew if they popped then I would laugh the whole thing off as a silly bit of superstitious nonsense. But they burned steadily, giving off an unwavering flame until they had crumbled away to ashes.

'There.' I turned to face him. 'It's official now. We are supposed to be together. The laws of Samhain have decreed it.'

I kissed him and then my fingers went to the buttons of his shirt. As I began to undo them, he clasped my hand, stopping me from opening it further. 'Vi . . . are you sure?'

'Sometimes in the river of life, Callum, you just have to throw your heart in and dive in after it.'

He released his grip and his eyes were alight with a smile that spoke of his love for me more eloquently than any words could ever have done.

I drew a blanket around us, and we lay together in the dying glow of the firelight, with only the stars and the spirits of the dead keeping watch over us until daybreak.

Daisy – March 2020

After four more days of trekking – following the path up and up over high passes in the hills marked with piles of carved stones and strings of tattered, fluttering prayer flags, and then down and down again into the terraced farmland of the valleys – we finally see Lukla clinging to the mountainside above us. As the path skirts below the town, a propellor plane comes in, flying so low over our heads that the roar of its engines forces me to clamp my hands over my ears. I turn to watch it make the landing on the infamous airstrip above us, engines screaming as it makes a stomach-churning last-second swerve to the right at the top of the short runway to avoid the sheer wall of rock in front of it.

I can't help feeling glad I've managed to miss that particular experience. But from this point on, where our path joins the main Everest Base Camp trail, the climb into the higher mountains really begins. I tip my head back to look up at the snow-covered peaks emerging from the clouds on either side of the valley.

Tashi Sherpa seems to brighten visibly the further he gets from Kathmandu and the closer he gets to his home in the mountains. He answers my questions about the birds we see soaring above us – mostly vultures, but he spots an eagle too – with a ready smile. And he laughs and jokes with the few people we meet along the way. There've been almost no tourists in the past few days. The few we have crossed paths with have all been heading in the opposite direction, back towards Kathmandu and the possibility of a plane home. Sonam, on the other hand, becomes a little quieter and more preoccupied with each mile we cover, every step carrying us closer to Phortse.

'Three more days, Mrs Daisy, no worry,' Tashi tells me as I shrug off my backpack and sink thankfully into a chair on a terrace outside the teahouse in Phakding. It's been another long day's hike and the sun is setting, bathing the snow-capped peaks in rosy light. I gratefully accept the welcoming cup of tea the owner's daughter brings me, feeling a pang of guilt as I notice our porters' baskets propped against the wall by the door with my heavy bag still tied to the top of the load.

'We get to Namche Bazaar tomorrow. Stay two nights there so you don't get sick. Then Phortse day after that.' Tashi goes to get the keys for our rooms, while Sonam pulls out his phone and flicks a little despondently through his messages before placing it face down on the table.

'Beautiful view,' I say, gesticulating with my cup towards the last of the light as it slides up to the very top of the mountains, chased by the dark shadows of evening. 'Amazing sky.'

He shrugs, attempting to summon a little enthusiasm, and his phone buzzes with an inbound message.

'News from your friends?' I ask him, nodding to where it sits in its plastic case on the table between us.

He picks it up and glances at the screen. 'Not good news,' he says. 'But then it never is these days. This virus is affecting everyone.' He puts it back down and gazes morosely out across the valley again.

I shiver as the last of the light slips away and the chill of night immediately envelops us. In an attempt to cheer Sonam up a bit, I pull my own phone out of my pocket and scroll through until I find a photo of my girls. 'These are my daughters,' I say, holding it out for him to see. 'They're about the same age as you. Not easy times for young people everywhere.'

He takes it from me and examines the picture carefully. 'Very beautiful,' he says, smiling a little more widely. 'What are their names?'

I point. 'This one's Sorcha and that one's Mara.'

'Mara?' he asks. 'Is that a Scottish name?'

I nod. 'It means the sea, in Gaelic.'

'In Buddhism, Mara is a demon,' he says.

I laugh. 'Well, she can be a bit of a demon sometimes, I suppose. But mostly she's okay.'

'And the other one – Sorcha? What does her name mean?'

'Shining light,' I reply. 'I grew up on the shores of a wild Scottish sea loch, so you don't have to look very far to see where I got my inspiration from. Does your name have a meaning?'

'Sonam means merit, or good karma,' he replies. 'And my dad's name means good luck. It can be quite a lot to live up to. We get given our names by the monks, depending on what is auspicious at the time of our birth. Although a lot of people just get called after the days of the week, which is why you'll meet a lot of Mingmas, Lhakpas and Pembas in the Sherpa community.'

He hands me back my phone. 'What do your daughters do?'

'They're both studying at university. Although I guess that's probably about to grind to a halt if this lockdown they're talking about actually happens.'

'Same here,' he says. 'Same all over the world.'

'What was the course you wanted to do in Kathmandu?' I ask him.

'Computing. I want a good job in the city. But instead maybe I'll have to become a guide like my dad and take people up Mount Everest. My parents don't want that for me – it's a dangerous career.

It's a good way of earning money, but it comes at a cost too, because the mountain gives but she takes as well. In 2014, many Sherpas were killed in an avalanche on the Khumbu Icefall, just above Base Camp. Maybe you heard about it?'

'I read the newspaper reports. It was a terrible tragedy.'

'Terrible for the ones who died. Terrible, too, for the widows they left behind who depended on the money they should have made from guiding. And for the more than fifty orphans, and the elderly who they supported as well. This is a tough place to survive, Mrs Daisy, no matter how beautiful it is.'

He gets to his feet, stuffing his phone into the pocket of his jacket. 'We better go inside. It's getting cold now. You can check into your room and then have something to eat. Tomorrow is a hard day's climb to Namche Bazaar, and we will cross the Hillary Bridge, so you'll need to keep your strength up.'

Tucked up in my sleeping bag that night, I rub my feet together, trying to warm them. Sonam's words ring in my head. I knew this trip would be a challenge, of course, but the dangers are very real and getting closer. I feel we've reached a tipping point on the trek now we've passed Lukla. I guess I could still turn back, return to Kathmandu and try to get a flight home. But we're over halfway to Phortse now. I check my emails to see whether there's anything more from the British Embassy, but there's no reply to another message I sent yesterday asking for advice, apart from an automatic response saying the staff are working hard to handle queries, but due to the pandemic there will be unavoidable delays.

I toss and turn in my bed, once again physically exhausted but still somehow unable to sleep.

The screen on my phone lights up with a message and I reach to read it, hoping it may be from Mum. But it's a newsflash from one of the Nepali news channels I've been following. 'All domestic and international flights in and out of Nepal are now cancelled until further notice.' So that's that, then. Definitely no turning back now.

Giving up on trying to fall asleep, I turn on the light, swallow the big lump of loneliness that rises in my throat and reach for Violet's journal to help keep it at bay.

Violet's Journal

SUNDAY, 11TH NOVEMBER, 1928

It was a relief to return to Edinburgh, immersing myself back into the routine of my studies and the work in the Herbarium. Neither of the trips north with Callum, to my home and to his, had exactly been a rip-roaring success. But the night of Samhain had fully cemented our bond and I know, more than ever before, that he's the man I want to spend my life with.

He was silent on the train ride back to the city, his face turned to the window to watch the countryside pass by. I guessed what was on his mind. When we rattled across the Forth Bridge and the city came into view in the distance, I took his hand and said, 'It doesn't matter what our parents think. All that matters is that we love each other.'

He gave my fingers a squeeze, and I felt the reassuring strength in his own, but there was a sadness in his eyes when he turned towards me. 'I love you more than anything on this earth, Vi. But I can't ask you to sacrifice your position in society for me. I want to be able to support you, to give you the life you deserve. Instead, being married to me would deprive you of your friends and family and many of the choices that are your birthright.'

'So you're thinking of asking me to marry you, are you?'

He laughed and reached up with his other hand to tuck a stray lock of hair behind my ear, the tenderness of his gesture making my heart turn a sudden somersault. 'That is what you take from what I've just said? I'm telling you how impossible it is.'

'No,' I replied firmly. 'It is most certainly not impossible. Don't tell me that. All I know is how much better my life would be with you. And if you feel the same way about me then nothing should stand in our way. We'll find work, make a home together. Once I've finished my course, perhaps we can look for a position together as gardeners on an estate in the south, far away from the judgement and disapproval of your parents and mine. Or we can stay in Edinburgh. You can carry on your work in the Botanics and I'll make a living with my paintings. There is such a demand for illustrating the new specimens coming to these shores from the expeditions. We will find a way.'

His eyes still held doubt, but I saw a glimmer of hope there alongside it. 'It would be a sacrifice, Vi.'

'What, giving up the opportunity to marry some stuffy neighbour of my parents and never be allowed to get my hands into the earth again? It's not much of a sacrifice, Callum, if in return I get to see where life's adventures take me, with you by my side.'

He relaxed then, his more usual broad smile spreading again across his face. 'I do love you so, Violet Mackenzie-Grant.'

'As I do you, Callum Gillespie.'

We were both silent for a mile or so as the train steamed onwards into the outskirts of the city. And then I said, 'So what was it you were saying about marriage?'

He laughed. 'Of course I want to marry you, Vi. And I'll buy you a ring to prove it, just as soon as I've saved up enough. But I do want to be able to provide for you, at least a little. So would you be prepared to wait until I can afford to give you a roof over your head?'

I nodded, thinking of the roof of the bothy the night before, the Samhain stars shining through the holes in it. The simple shack had been more than enough, and I'd felt a deeper contentment lying there with him beside me than I'd ever known before. But I understood that he felt the need to establish himself, that for his sense of self-esteem he needed to be able to give me that. Just as I too needed to prove I could stand on my own two feet. The least I could do was respect it in him. It only made me love him more.

'We'll save every penny,' he said. 'Then by the time you finish your studies we can marry.'

And so it was that I alighted at Waverley Station betrothed to my true love and happier than I had ever known it possible to be.

Arriving at the Herbarium the next morning, I was sure our colleagues must see all that had passed between us, Callum's eyes meeting mine and filling with golden light as soon as I walked through the door. But as usual the other botanists scarcely acknowledged me, as I hung my coat on the back of the door and took my place at the workbench where Callum was already unpacking specimens from a newly arrived tea chest. It was stamped with exotic-looking characters and the words *Produce of Darjeeling.* He pulled out a newspaper-wrapped parcel and carefully opened it, revealing a species of rhododendron that we hadn't seen before. His hand brushed mine as he passed it across to me, and I held it up to the light to study it more closely. Then I reached for my paintbox and my sketch pad and was soon absorbed in my work, only raising my head now and again to smile across at him as he leafed through a heavy book, methodically identifying each plant or setting aside those that appeared to be previously unknown.

Just before lunchtime, the door opened and there was a slight stir amongst the others in the workroom that made me look up. To my surprise, the Regius Keeper himself stood there. He exchanged a few quiet words with the principal curator, Dr Kay, and then beckoned to Callum. I opened my eyes wide and gave him a smile of encouragement as he grabbed his jacket and hurried to follow the two men out of the room. The door closed behind them and, after a flurry of muttering amongst the others, quietness fell once more as we got on with our work.

It was a raw, grey day, the east wind blustering amongst the trees in the gardens, so I made my way to a sheltered spot behind one of the potting sheds to eat my lunch. I knew Callum would come looking for me there, once he had finished whatever business the Regius Keeper had with him. Sure enough, a few minutes later he appeared.

His face shone with excitement, but it seemed to be mixed with something else too, some sort of doubt. He grabbed both my hands in his. He opened his mouth to speak, but nothing came out at first and I realised he was struggling to contain his emotions.

'Well,' I said, drawing him down to sit on the bench beside me. 'It must be good news, so put me out of my misery.'

'Oh Vi,' he said. 'It's the best news, I think. I've been asked to accompany Colonel Fairburn on his next expedition to Nepal! One of their number has dropped out, so they're in need of another pair of hands, someone who can collect specimens and prepare them properly. And they've chosen me!'

I flung my arms around him, knowing how much it meant. The experience would make him an expert in the field, furthering his career and giving him the recognition he so deserved. At the same time, I swallowed a gulp of sadness at the thought of the two of us being parted by such a distance.

'When do you leave?'

'Very soon! We sail from Southampton in a week's time. I know it'll be hard for us being apart, but Vi, this is just the break I need.

I'll make enough money from this one expedition to be able to afford a place for us. It means we can marry as soon as I come home. Who knows, it may open up all sorts of other doors too. It's a chance to change our lives.'

I listened as he told me the plans. He'd be away for much of the coming year. The aim was to spend this winter in the southern part of Nepal, when the climate of the tropical forests and plains would be more bearable, before the expedition began to climb into the mountains in spring so that they could spend as much time there as possible exploring that largely uncharted territory.

'I'll miss you so terribly, Vi.'

'I'll miss you too. But I'll be waiting for you back here. And I'll look forward to opening the specimen cases you send back and seeing your initials on some of the notes.'

'Maybe I'll discover a new species. And then I can name it after you. Wouldn't that be a good wedding present?' His doubts set aside now, his enthusiasm bubbled over, and I tried hard to make mine match it. I think I succeeded because he didn't seem to notice the way I forced the tone of my voice to sound bright and cheerful. I wondered about it later. Why was I not as joyful as he was at the news? Perhaps I was just envious of him having the opportunity to travel to the places I could only dream of visiting, leaving me stuck in the damp winter chill of the Herbarium. Yes, it was only that, I told myself firmly, squashing the anxiety niggling in the back of my mind at the dangers he would face.

He hugged me before we parted that afternoon. He returned to his workbench to attempt to concentrate on the task in hand – although I knew his mind must surely be filled with plans for the expedition ahead of him – and I walked away, hurrying through the rain to get to an evening lecture, not daring to glance back in case he saw the tears in my eyes as the last leaves tumbled from the branches of the trees above me.

TUESDAY, 1ST JANUARY, 1929

Callum must have posted the letter and present he sent almost as soon as he reached Nepal to make sure it reached me in time for Christmas. Hetty brought the small brown paper parcel to me in my room when I arrived at Ardtuath House, knowing what it must mean to me. Coming home again was a part of my camouflage, to make my father and brother believe I was toeing the line they'd drawn for me. Hetty was the only one I'd taken into my confidence and so she'd intercepted the package when the postie delivered it, keeping it hidden until my arrival.

Callum's neat handwriting – so familiar from the notes he wrote on the entries he used to make in the plant catalogues when we worked alongside one another – brought tears to my eyes, juxtaposed as it was with the crumpled and stained wrappings that spoke of its journey from Kathmandu to Aultbea. I'd received a handful of postcards from him in Edinburgh since he left just over a month ago, sent from the ports where the ship had docked on the way to India. I treasured every single one of them, even though the messages were brief and necessarily a little formal since he knew they would have to pass through the hands of my landlady at The Laurels.

'It's lovely having you home, Vi,' Hetty said as she watched me begin to tug at the string tied around the parcel.

I set it aside for a moment and turned to hug her tight, my sisterly enthusiasm dislodging one of the pins that held her hair back from her pretty face in a rather too severe French pleat. 'And it's lovely to see you,' I said. 'I want to hear all about the plans for the wedding just as soon as I've unpacked.'

She grimaced, fiddling with the large sapphire engagement ring that sparkled on her left hand. 'There's no danger of you NOT hearing all about them. Ma can talk of nothing else.' She gave a short laugh.

I held her at arm's length for a moment and looked at her searchingly. 'But you *are* happy, aren't you, Het?'

She shrugged. 'I'm contented, Vi. Rufus is a kind man. And it's a relief to know I'll have a home of my own and be well taken care of. Charles and Helen are going to be living here at Ardtuath soon, now Pa has decided to hand over the running of the estate to him. Heaven only knows, moving into the north wing with Pa and Ma would drive me completely potty. Rufus's proposal came at an opportune moment.'

She couldn't conceal the flatness in her voice though. 'Oh Hetty, are you completely sure you want to marry Rufus?' I said. 'He's so much older, and not having children of your own is a big sacrifice to make.'

She smiled, shaking her head. The stone in her ring flashed as she raised her hand to smooth back the lock of her hair I'd dislodged and pin it firmly in place. 'I shall try to be the best step-mother there ever was. I truly am fond of him, and of Arabella and Angus too. It gives me a sense of purpose, having a role to play in trying to make up in some little way for the mother they've lost, and supporting him. And it will be exciting to live in London, when we're not up at Shieldaig. The house there is in one of the best squares. You must come and stay with us and we'll visit Kew Gardens together.' She patted my hand reassuringly. 'You're looking well, Vi. Gardening obviously suits you, even if you may be pining for your Callum.' She glanced at the parcel lying on my bed. 'I'll see you downstairs shortly. There's a fire in the drawing room so it's almost frost-free for a change!'

I tugged at the string, but Callum had tied the knot so tightly I couldn't make it budge, so in the end I resorted to unearthing my nail scissors from my case and cutting it. I unwrapped the most beautiful brown cashmere shawl – as fine as a cobweb and soft as thistledown. I buried my face in it, trying to detect a little of his natural scent of fresh air and wood smoke, but instead it smelled faintly of unfamiliar spices. I drew it over my shoulders as I settled on the bed, feet tucked up beneath me, to read his letter.

Namaste Guesthouse

Durbar Square

Kathmandu, Nepal.

Dearest Vi,
Well, we've reached Kathmandu at last and I'm very glad to have seen the back of ships and trains for the foreseeable future. When I stand still, I still feel as if the ground is pitching and swaying beneath my feet and my stomach churns all over again. We'll be spending a while here as there are provisions to be found and arrangements to be made before we start for the mountains. I've met Colonel Fairburn at last and he is just as impressive as we'd heard. So far, our meetings have been brief and have related only to the practicalities of preparing for the next stage of the expedition, but I'm sure there will be opportunities to get to know him better in the weeks of trekking that lie ahead of us.
The city is a dirty, sprawling place, and I will spare you the description of my digs, not wanting to put you off your Christmas dinner. Suffice it to say, our Samhain bothy seems positively palatial by

comparison. This is to be our base for the next few weeks as the weather is against us even in the sub-tropics here on the plain. I'm champing at the bit to get going, as you can imagine, but it will be a while until we can start exploring the more clement valleys in the hills north of the city, let alone begin to climb into the mountains. The other chaps laugh at my impatience and tell me to make the most of being here. Even though conditions in the city are grim, they say this is pretty luxurious compared to what we'll be in for on the trek. I doubt the countryside will be as filthy though . . . personally, I long for fresh air and a mountain stream to wash in. And hillsides covered with lilies the colours of the sunrise and poppies the colour of sky, just like you said on the first day we worked together.

I ventured out to the market this morning and found this shawl. I hope you like it. The woman I bought it from told me it's called a ring pashmina, because it's fine enough to pass through the wedding ring I will be buying you on my return. The colour reminds me of those hazelnuts we put on the fire. I hope you still feel the same way you did then. I miss you, Vi, and long for the day when we'll be together again.

I'm going to finish up now because there's a man leaving the expedition party today to return home to England, so he will take this with him and post it to Scotland from there. I want to be sure it's waiting for you when you get to Aultbea for Christmas. The poor blighter's health has taken a battering in the tropics and his skin has turned quite yellow. But the doctors

here have given him some local medicine and say he
should make a full recovery once he returns to Great
Britain. The Colonel is paying for him to return by
aeroplane from Delhi. He's a decent chap.
   Sending you all my love, Vi.
   Callum

◆ ◆ ◆

It was in church on Christmas morning that I realised I've been carrying a secret within me ever since the night of Samhain. As usual, the first carol was 'Once in Royal David's City', but as I sang the words '*Where a mother laid her baby in a manger for his bed*', a thought struck me. I stopped singing and instinctively laid a hand on my belly, imagining I could already feel a slight thickening there. It explained my feelings of tiredness and a faint nausea, which I'd put down to missing Callum and the hard work of the last few weeks since his departure. The gesture made Hetty glance down towards my lap and then she quickly looked straight ahead again. But I saw the colour drain from her cheeks, and the way she studiously avoided catching my eye told me she, too, had realised at that moment. I took a deep breath and we both began singing the words of the second verse.

Once the service was over and we'd emerged from the kirk, she drew me to one side. Ma and Pa were busy shaking hands with the minister at the door. She didn't say a word, but she put her arms around me, hugging me tightly. Sudden tears sprang to my eyes as I leaned against her because it was as if she was hugging my baby too. In that moment, I knew she would continue to help me keep my secret.

'We'll talk later,' I whispered, and she nodded, then let go of me and we followed our parents back through the little graveyard to the waiting car. Charles and Helen had arrived by the time we got home, bringing little Alec with them. The dear wee soul was dressed up in a sailor suit and was allowed to come and show us his new spinning top in the drawing room, until Nanny whisked him away to the nursery to eat his lunch.

Hetty and I didn't have a moment to ourselves until the evening. Charles dominated the day, as usual, although he seemed in fairly good spirits for once, holding forth on his plans for the estate and his imminent move to the big house. I was thankful for him distracting Ma and Pa, so they didn't notice me pushing the sprouts around my plate and scarcely swallowing a sip of the fine claret with which Pa insisted on making a special toast to Hetty's last Christmas at Ardtuath. I saw my sister's frequent glances in my direction, though, but she was careful to provide a distraction too, engaging Helen in conversation about the furniture she'd like to keep in the main part of the house when Ma and Pa moved into the north wing.

Helen is a dear soul, a far nicer and gentler wife than our brother deserves, and she looked across the table at me and said, 'Violet, I know you love Edinburgh and will probably go on to become a famous flower arranger like Mrs Constance Spry, whose shop I've just been reading about in *The Lady* magazine, but I want you to know there will of course always be room for you here with us at Ardtuath. Little Alec would love having at least one of his aunts around. And you could always redesign the gardens here. I know Mrs Hanbury would love to be able to talk about plants with you at Inverewe as well, just as you used to do. So you will bear us in mind, won't you?'

I knew she meant well. But the thought of Charles's face when he heard Alec would have a baby cousin within the coming year – the illegitimate child of his wayward younger sister and a mere gardener – almost made me choke on the piece of pudding

I was attempting to swallow. I felt as if the walls were closing in around me and a sudden flush of heat overcame me. *Do NOT faint!* I told myself firmly, knowing it would only draw attention and make them fuss, asking questions that might arouse suspicion about my predicament. Hetty quietly topped up my water glass and pushed it a little closer before filling hers and Helen's too.

I was thankful to get up from the table and flee to the bathroom, where I splashed my face with cold water before rejoining Ma, Hetty and Helen in the drawing room. The menfolk were obviously still smoking their cigars in the dining room and for once I didn't resent the women being banished. One single whiff of that pungent smoke would surely have made my stomach heave. Wee Alec was there and I sank to my knees beside him on the floor, making up a game with his box of model cars.

At last, Charles proclaimed it time to leave. Nanny gathered everything up and Helen took Alec by the hand, bringing his dear little face up to each of us for a kiss goodbye. Once we'd waved them off down the drive, I made my excuses and retired to my room. A few minutes later, I wasn't surprised to hear a quiet tapping on my door and opened it to find Hetty standing there.

Without a word, I pulled her inside and closed the door behind her. She sat on the edge of my bed and drew me down to sit alongside her. We looked at one another in silence and then she said, 'I have just two things to say, Violet.'

I braced myself, expecting a lecture.

'The first is, I'm so very happy for you. I know how much you love Callum. There are people who will condemn what you've done, but I am not one of them. Don't let this be anything but joyful for you and your child.'

My hug, squeezing the air out of her lungs, prevented her from telling me the second of the things she wanted to for a few moments.

When she could breathe again, she went on, 'The other thing I wish to say is that I will do whatever you want to help you and support you. If it means calling off my own engagement, then so be it. Perhaps we can rent a little cottage in the country somewhere, far away from Ardtuath and from our brother, who will surely explode when he hears the news, and I will live with you and help support you financially until your baby is born and Callum comes home.'

I was stunned she'd managed to give it so much thought, even as she'd carried on so calmly throughout all the other demands of the day. I'd scarcely been able to absorb the realisation of my condition, let alone think about practicalities and imagine what it might mean for the rest of my family.

Once I could find the words, I said, 'Absolutely not, Hetty. I won't let you sacrifice your chance to make some sort of a life for yourself on my account. You must marry Rufus. And, besides, his children need you. How lucky they will be to have you there.'

She shook her head, then reached out her hand a little tentatively and placed it gently on my stomach, just below the waistband of my frock. 'This child will be my niece or nephew . . . a blood relation. If I have to choose then I'll stay with you until it arrives safely in the world. You can't do this on your own, Vi, and with Callum so far away I don't see any other option.'

'I can't let you do that.' I placed my own hand over hers. 'What will your life be if you give everything up for me? This . . . situation . . . is only for a few months. You have so many years ahead of you.'

I thought about the years to come. I'd be all right once I had Callum by my side again, but there were going to be some very hard months ahead when I – and my baby – would be shunned and berated and looked down upon.

Hetty was quiet for a few moments, thinking. 'Callum's parents live in Perthshire, don't they? Do you think they might take you in?'

I gave a hollow laugh, recalling Mr Gillespie's demeanour on my one and only visit. 'It would probably mean his father would lose his position and their home on the estate. That is most definitely NOT an option.'

'Could you try to stay on in Edinburgh for a few more months, whilst your condition is not obvious, I mean? Then perhaps I can ask Rufus if we can find you somewhere nearer us . . .' She tailed off, a frown creasing her forehead, and I think we were both imagining her fiancé's reaction when she told him his new sister-in-law was to bring disgrace upon his family as well as her own.

'Oh Het, you are such an angel. But I won't let this affect your future security. It's my predicament and I shall just have to find a way to manage it until Callum comes home and we can bring up our child together. I know it will be all right.' How, though, I wondered. I'd be told to leave the gardening school and my digs as soon as my condition began to show, so finishing the course I'd dreamed of for so long wasn't an option any more either.

Hetty wept on my shoulder then and I smoothed her hair and patted her back, my eyes dry. I looked around at my childhood bedroom, at the mirrored dressing table, and the walls papered with rosebud sprigs, and the pink candlewick counterpane softened with age. Would my own child ever know such comfort? Then I felt a surge of new determination. Hetty was right, I mustn't allow anything to take this joy away from me. I would protect my child. I would not let society stigmatise us and take away our happiness.

We sat like that for a while, Hetty with her sorrow and I with my new sense of fierce protectiveness for my baby. Then at last I patted her back and got to my feet, saying, 'Time for bed, Het. We're both in need of a good night's sleep after all the emotion of today. Things will look better in the morning. They always do.'

But I tossed and turned for hours, fretting about what I should do to make a life for my child. I must have exhausted myself with my worrying, though, because I woke in the darkness, before the first glimmer of morning light could creep through the crack in the curtains, and my sister was shaking me.

'I know what we can do, Vi,' she said. Her hair had escaped from its plait, forming a wild halo around her face. Judging by the shadows under her eyes, she hadn't slept much either. 'I have enough money saved up. I know you've had to spend every penny of your allowance to be able to live in Edinburgh, but I've had nothing to spend mine on. I can buy you a ticket and you can go and find Callum. Tell him about your baby. He will think of a way to make it all right. You can get married in India, or Nepal, or wherever it is he is now, and then come home again. Or you could stay out there until he can come back with you. So many women are colonial wives these days. Spending time living abroad is quite respectable now. And surely there must be some decent accommodation for you to stay in whilst he's off hunting for plants? You'll probably be able to have help around the house, so you won't be on your own. Then, when you come back to Scotland together, with your baby, time will have passed, and everything will be fine again.'

I rubbed the sleep from my eyes, trying to absorb what she was saying. My thoughts were as jumbled as my emotions. She was offering me salvation, but the plan was a wild one, filled with risks.

'No, Het, I can't possibly take your money. For one thing, I doubt I'll ever be able to pay it back – and that's just talking about the money, never mind the rest of the debt I'd owe you . . .' Even as I said it, though, I was thinking how much better it would be for all of us if I were out of sight and out of mind. It would save face, not just for me and my unborn child, but for Hetty and our parents, and Charles and Helen too. My protestations tailed off and we sat in silence for a minute as I imagined the possibility of a life on the other side of the world, far away from the judgement and disapproval of Scottish society, closer to Callum, raising our child in a place where the horizons stretch far wider than they do here. The surge of strength I'd felt the night before, born of protectiveness for my baby, had seeped away in the dark, sleepless hours, replaced by doubts and fears. But it returned now as the grey light of dawn suffused the room and my sister offered me a lifeline.

Hetty scanned my face, no doubt reading my thoughts. Then said, more quietly, 'You know this is by far the best plan, Vi. Didn't you tell me it's possible to get an aeroplane ticket? We could get you out there within the next few weeks, before Callum's expedition leaves for the mountains. We'll tell everyone you couldn't bear to be apart from him, that you wanted to be closer, and you're determined to see what opportunities there might be to do some botanising of your own over there. You've always been so headstrong; people will be a bit exasperated with your flightiness, but everyone will take it at face value.'

I knew she was right. The last words she said to me, as she saw me off at the station at Achnasheen three days later, were, 'I'm glad you have this love in your life, Vi. Remember, there is no shame in it.' I saw the wistfulness in her eyes then and hugged her tight.

'I wish, with all my heart, that you will know such love too,' I whispered. She squeezed my shoulder, extracting herself from my grasp, and turned away as the conductor blew his whistle and shouted, 'All aboard!'

I pressed my hand to the window, and she raised hers in reply as the train drew out, putting the first yards of an unimaginably long distance between us.

And now I'm back at The Laurels, and just as soon as the banks reopen after the Hogmanay holiday Hetty will transfer the funds for my ticket. I've already begun packing my things, preparing for the journey ahead and a new life in Asia. Kathmandu doesn't sound like the most suitable place to have my baby, but I'll see Callum there and we can decide where best to base ourselves. Northern India could be promising as there are hill stations where the British mem-sahibs go to seek respite from the heat in the summer. If Callum and I can marry in Nepal, then perhaps I can establish myself in Darjeeling in the spring and the colonial wives will accept me and offer support when the baby arrives at the end of July.

Writing this in my journal is a good way of putting off the things I must do next. I'm trying to pluck up the courage to write the letter I'll need to post to my parents and the one I'll ask Marjorie to deliver to Miss Morison when classes resume next week. I hate deceiving people, but there's no alternative. I'm doing it to protect everything and everyone I love. I'm doing it to make the best possible future for us all.

In my mind's eye, I can still see the smile in Callum's eyes that night in the bothy when I said, *Sometimes you just have to throw your heart into the river of life and dive in after it.*

I can picture the way his face will light up when I arrive in Kathmandu too and tell him the news of our child. And that gives me the courage to make this leap.

Daisy – March 2020

The trek from Phakding to Namche Bazaar is a challenging one. We set off early, the porters shouldering our packs and heading off first, while I settle up what I owe the teahouse owner for my food and accommodation. To my relief it's not very much and scarcely makes a dent in my wad of rupees.

Tashi Sherpa takes the lead and Sonam follows behind me, so I feel obliged to set off at a brisk pace, trying not to hold them up. Fairly soon, though, the path starts to climb, and my legs begin to feel as heavy as lead. We must be at over two and a half thousand metres now, although we have a climb of another eight hundred to do today. I do the sums in my head . . . that's more than two and a half thousand feet. Less than a Scottish Munro, I tell myself, and I've climbed a few of those in my time. But the air is thinner up here and my breathing is laboured, as if I've already climbed a mountain before we've begun.

As I begin to fall behind, the Sherpas slow their steps to match mine. The gentler pace helps me breathe a little more easily. 'Just put one foot in front of the other, again and again, slowly, slowly, along the path,' Tashi tells me, and his words become a mantra that I repeat over and over in my head. One foot in front of the other, again and again, slowly, slowly.

We walk through pine forests where more rhododendron flowers spill down the hillsides beneath us and silver strands of lichen, like greying hair, festoon the branches of the trees along the path. Tiny blue gentians, the colour and size of forget-me-nots, cling to the dusty earth and here and there the purple pom-poms of primulas emerge from the mat of dry grass that carpets the sides of the valley.

We cross flimsy-looking bridges spanning deep ravines, festooned with prayer flags that flutter in the wind. Every now and then we have to stand aside and wait for pack animals to cross, cumbersome loads of gas canisters and sacks of rice strapped to their backs.

After four hours, we reach a rocky riverbank and I sink down thankfully to rest. It's only eleven o'clock but the sun – whose strength has been camouflaged by the cooling wind – burns through the sleeves of my top. My shoulders feel tight against the pull of the straps of my backpack. I gulp from my water bottle and then take in my surroundings. A gusting wind tosses the branches of the scrubby trees growing beside the river. The water is an extraordinary shade of milky turquoise, carrying finely ground debris from glaciers high up in the peaks towering above us. And from the Khumbu glacier itself, I suppose, where those Sherpas lost their lives in 2014.

I'm lost in my thoughts, picturing the icefall tumbling in frozen perpetuity from the mountainside, when Sonam nudges me and points upwards, into the distance. It takes me a moment to register what he's saying.

'There it is. The Hillary Bridge. The highest and longest one we'll cross.'

Despite the water I've just drunk, my mouth feels dry as I focus on what looks like a fragile thread, suspended in thin air several hundred feet above us. If it weren't for the prayer flags tied along their length, the wires of the bridge would hardly be visible against the dazzling blue sky beyond.

A helicopter swoops overhead, swinging right to follow the line of the valley. 'Usually many more flights, taking supplies to Everest Base Camp,' says Tashi. 'But not now. Just a few. Bringing people out. Everyone leaving.'

I wish with all my heart I could hitch a lift and be transported effortlessly to our final destination of Phortse. But I know it's important for my body to adapt slowly, acclimatising and avoiding the threat of altitude sickness, which can be a silent killer. A ride in a helicopter to the higher altitudes we're aiming for could do more harm than good. So I get to my feet and take a deep breath, trying to fill my lungs with the thin air in preparation for climbing the long flight of steps leading up to the bridge.

As we approach it, I can't help imagining the wires suspending the bridge snapping, the whole thing twisting from its fixing points and sending us tumbling into the abyss. Even close up, it still looks flimsy, made from just a few cables and some planks of wood. But Tashi and Sonam seem completely confident in the structure. And our porters have probably already walked across it, I remind myself, far more heavily laden than we are. My legs and lungs burn with each upwards step, but I trudge onwards, trying not to think about anything other than putting one foot in front of the other, until, at last, we're standing at the start of the bridge.

The only sound is the rushing of the wind and the fluttering of the prayer flags streaming from the suspension wires. Then from behind us comes a soft clanking of bells and we have to stand aside to let a man drive his pack animals across. The bridge bounces and sways with their weight and Sonam grins, seeing the look of fear on my face.

'No worry, Mrs Daisy,' says Tashi, with a serene smile. 'Bridge is good. And we send Sonam first to make sure!'

His son laughs, shouldering his pack and stepping out confidently on to the planks suspended over the void.

'See,' says Tashi. 'No worry, like I say.'

I go next, trying to emulate Sonam's assured strides, but I can't help clutching here and there at the wires to steady myself as the bridge lurches and sways beneath me. For several moments, there is only the wind and the streaming prayer flags and a sense of vast, suspended nothingness. I glance to one side and see the turquoise river far, far below. *One foot in front of the other*, I remind myself. And then my legs are pushing me up the final section and I'm back on solid ground again, with Sonam congratulating me. 'Well done. Not so bad after all, was it?'

I turn to look back the way I've come and watch as Tashi strolls across in my wake, as nonchalantly as if it were a walk in a park, never once losing his balance or grabbing at the wires the way I did.

I know the steepest part of the climb to reach Namche Bazaar is still ahead of us, but the bridge crossing has filled me with adrenaline that helps my tired legs carry me onwards and upwards, one step at a time. I've learned to emulate Tashi and Sonam when we stop for brief rests along the way. Instead of sinking down on to the ground, they remain standing, leaning their packs on the stone ledges that have been built up alongside the path at regular intervals. They're just the right height to take the weight off your shoulders, I've discovered, and it's possible to perch there without your leg muscles stiffening and seizing up, making getting going again all the harder. We only stop for a few moments, just long enough to swallow a few bites of the protein bars I've stashed in my pockets and gulp down some more water, before setting off again.

After trudging up what feels like a thousand switchbacks, we reach a place on the trail where a wooden platform's been constructed. A woman sits beside it, in the middle of nowhere, beneath an umbrella, which casts a little shade over the bottles of water and packets of biscuits she's selling. Or at least she would be selling them if there was anybody here to buy them.

Tashi points to the platform. 'First Everest viewpoint,' he says. I set down my pack and walk across to take a look. On the other side of the ridge, through some pines, the great mountain stands proud against the blue of the sky, with a wisp of white cloud caught on its summit. I snap some pictures. Since I'm not going as far as Base Camp, this could be one of the few opportunities I'll have to see the mountain on a clear day. I know it's notorious for disappearing behind a veil of cloud whenever the weather begins to close in.

I buy a bottle of water and a packet of cookies from the woman, sharing them with Tashi and Sonam, who seem to love anything sweet. Then we shoulder our packs again and carry on up the next stretch of seemingly endless switchbacks. Over and over, I repeat Tashi's words in my head: *just put one foot in front of the other, again and again, slowly, slowly, along the path.*

It's mid-afternoon by the time the first buildings appear, and I stumble the last few hundred yards into the town, utterly exhausted. I almost weep with gratitude when Tashi turns in at the doorway of one of the lodges. And then I almost weep again, with frustration and tiredness, as I discover there are four more flights of stairs to climb to reach the rooms. My head aches as though it's being squeezed in a vice and my legs feel shaky with overuse as I force them to carry me upwards again.

At long, long last, I push open the door, let my pack drop from my shoulders, and fall, thankfully, on to one of the single beds.

After breakfast the next morning, we walk to the Everest View Hotel, a few miles away and a gain of another four hundred metres in height. We'll return to the lodge afterwards and spend a second night in Namche Bazaar to acclimatise to the altitude. Not that my Sherpa friends need it – they are as bright and nimble as ever, while I push myself upwards along the path. My head still hurts, and I've resigned myself to the fact that my legs are going to ache with exhaustion for the foreseeable future so I might as well just get on with it. One foot in front of the other.

'Slowly, slowly,' Tashi reminds me. 'Better to keep moving at steadier pace than push yourself too much and have to stop.'

The climb is worth it. In the clear morning light, the peaks of the Everest range are spectacular, their snow-covered summits breathtakingly beautiful against the cloudless sky. But by the time we get up to the top, the weather is changing again, and a curtain of cloud comes down, obscuring the mountains. And the hotel is closed, abandoned now that its clients can no longer hike in or pay through the nose for a helicopter to bring them here. Tashi had warned me it might be, although I'd secretly fantasised about ordering a cup of coffee and a cake to eat on the terrace looking out across the world's highest peaks. Instead, I make do with a gulp of water as I perch on a ledge, trying to shelter from the biting wind.

It's still only lunchtime when we walk back down to Namche Bazaar, so I retreat to one of the few coffee shops that's still open. To my relief, my headache seems to have lifted a little – like clouds from a mountaintop, I think with a smile as I sip my coffee and devour a large chocolate brownie. But outside the window, chilly clouds have enveloped the town and there's no view to be seen.

I pull Violet's journal from my bag and rest back on a sofa in one corner of the café to spend the afternoon reading.

Violet's Journal

SUNDAY, 27TH JANUARY, 1929

My feet have scarcely touched the ground since I last had a chance to write up my journal. And I can say that with some literal truth too! I'm sitting at a table in the foyer of the Grand Victoria Hotel, Delhi, beneath a large ceiling fan, in the hope of finding a little respite from the heat. The fan turns only sluggishly, barely stirring the soupy air, but it is at least not as hot as my bedroom upstairs, which is like an oven. The hotel has seen better days and the 'Grand' in its name is definitely stretching things. But after a whole week of flights and airport hotels I'm just grateful to have got this far. The Imperial Airways route hopped from France to Italy, Greece and Egypt and by the time we flew onwards to Baghdad, Karachi, Jodhpur – such exotic names to conjure with! – and finally Delhi, I had completely lost all sense of what day it was, never mind which country we were in. Despite the arduous journey and a good deal of nausea, as the planes lurched and swooped so very wildly at times, the novelty of flying didn't wear off one bit. I sat with my nose glued to the window as we passed over snowy mountain ranges, followed winding rivers, and crossed vast tracts of dusty desert as well as the bluest seas I've ever seen. I wanted to appear a seasoned and confident traveller to my fellow passengers, but I'm sure my rapt concentration on the landscapes unfurling beneath us as we bounced from one stop to the next must have given away my inexperience.

What a miracle it seems, to have been flung through the ether like that and arrived in the heat of India within a week of leaving the Scottish winter. I've written to Hetty to let her know I've got this far safely and tell her my extra bit of good news. A husband and wife boarded the plane at Karachi and were seated across the aisle from me, so naturally we got talking. They are missionaries, on their way to Kathmandu, and their church has managed to arrange a flight in a mail plane to transport them there from Delhi. They've kindly asked their local contact to find me a seat on their flight, which leaves tomorrow. It has cost me almost the last of the money Hetty gave me but saves me staying here longer to arrange trains and buses, so I'm sure it's worth it. And so, by the time Hetty receives my letter, I will have met up with Callum and am confident I shall be well on the way to establishing a base for myself in some suitable spot whilst he goes off exploring.

The gong has just been rung for dinner, so I must stop now. The food has been unexciting so far – more along the lines of boiled beef and potatoes than the exotic cuisine for which this country is renowned. Mulligatawny soup is about as spicy as it gets in the dining room at the Grand Victoria Hotel. It nourishes my baby, though, so I try to eat heartily even though I have the most dreadful heartburn when I lie down in my bed at night. It's probably partly nerves and too much excitement at the thought of seeing Callum so very soon. I must re-pack my case after supper, ready for tomorrow.

Kathmandu at last! I can hardly believe it.

Daisy – March 2020

Knowing what follows, I hesitate before turning the page to the next section of Violet's journal. Her joy and excitement at having reached Delhi mirror mine before getting on the plane to embark on this trip, little knowing how the world would change. And while my setbacks have hit me hard, they are nothing compared with what she faced on her arrival in the Nepalese capital.

The waiter comes over to remove my empty coffee cup and I order another latte. The café is warmer than the teahouse, where the stove won't be lit until this evening, so I'm in no hurry to leave. I raise my eyes to the window, but the clouds still obscure the view of the high mountains that encircle the town, and then I glance back down at the journal on the table in front of me.

I've marked this page with a pressed flower, a faded blue poppy stuck to a piece of ivory card that was tucked among the papers in the bottom of the cedarwood chest in the library at Ardtuath. The thought of home makes me swallow hard as I wonder how Mum and my stepfather, Davy, are doing and how they are all coping with the pandemic. I check my phone again, hoping for a message from my family, but there's been no signal all day and the screen stays stubbornly blank.

The waiter sets my coffee down with a smile and I thank him, then pick up the journal again. Just before I begin to read, an image flashes into my mind of the gilded gate in the corner of the Garden of Dreams and the devastation that lay on the other side of it. Dreams in ruins.

There could be no more fitting metaphor, I realise, for the next chapter of Violet's journey.

PART TWO

Violet's Journal

SATURDAY, 2ND FEBRUARY, 1929

Perhaps if I write down all that has happened, it will seem more real. Because I'm struggling terribly to absorb it. I feel my throat constrict again as I choke back my tears and I struggle for breath. A part of me wishes for an end to my life. But I know I must force myself to go on, to keep myself and my baby alive. And so I breathe in and I breathe out and somehow – impossibly – my heart keeps beating.

As soon as we'd disembarked on the dusty makeshift airstrip at Kathmandu, I took leave of my new friends and bade them good luck with their mission, then hurried to find a rickshaw and gave the driver the address of the Namaste Guesthouse. Durbar Square was easy enough to find, with its temples and market stalls, but once the driver had deposited me and my case beside the vast stone lions guarding the entrance to the square it took me some time to pick my way through the crowds. People jostled and shoved on every side. Beggars tugged at my sleeve, and I knew they didn't believe me when I shook my head and said I had no money. But it was true. My last few rupees had gone on the rickshaw. I'd gambled everything on getting here, on finding Callum.

After several wrong turns, I managed to ask a man selling incense if he knew where the guesthouse was, and he pointed to a distant corner of the square where the buildings crowded together to form a shabby terrace. Dragging my case behind me, I pushed my way through the throng. At last I saw the guesthouse sign, nailed to a wooden doorpost. I pushed aside the length of cloth that stood in for a proper door and stepped over the threshold.

It took a few moments for my eyes to adjust to the darkness after the glare in the square outside. It was stiflingly hot, despite the gloom, and a sickly stench made my stomach heave. I swallowed hard.

'Hello?' I called out, tentatively at first and then a little louder. 'Is anybody here?'

A shrivelled woman appeared from the other side of a door and peered at me suspiciously.

'Do you speak English?' I asked.

She nodded, not returning my smile. 'Little bit. You nurse?'

'No, I'm not a nurse. I've come to see my fiancé. I believe he's staying here. He's with the British expedition. Mr Gillespie.'

Without a word, she jerked her head towards the stairs, then disappeared back from whence she'd come, and I heard the clatter of pots and pans, the sound of a kettle boiling.

I left my case where it was and climbed the rickety staircase to the first floor. The stench was stronger up there and I held my handkerchief to my face, waving away the flies that buzzed angrily about my head.

'Callum?' I called.

I knocked at the first door I came to but there was no reply. At the second one, a man shouted, 'Who's there?'

'My name is Miss Mackenzie-Grant,' I replied. 'I'm looking for Callum Gillespie.'

The door opened a fraction, and I caught a glimpse of a dishevelled-looking character. 'Last door on the right,' he said, eyeing me with curiosity. 'Have you brought medicine?'

I turned away, panic rising in my chest now, and heard his door slam shut again as I hurried to the end of the corridor.

Callum didn't answer when I called his name. I pushed open the door to his room and gasped at the sight and the smell that awaited me. He lay in a tangle of dirty, bloodstained sheets, his face bathed in sweat. When I sank down on the floor next to him, his eyes were closed, and I could hear his lungs labour with every breath he struggled to take. I laid my hand against his brow and at the touch he opened his eyes, his gaze glassy and unfocused with the fever that raged within him. My foot nudged a tin pail beside the bed, and as its contents slopped over the rim I quickly realised it was the main source of the stench in the room.

He opened his mouth as if to try to speak, but no words came out. Hurriedly, I reached for a glass of water that sat on the bedside table and held it to his lips, supporting his head as he tried to drink.

'Don't talk,' I said. 'I'll fetch the doctor.'

He reached for my hand and stopped me getting to my feet. 'Vi,' he whispered. 'Come to say goodbye. I'm sorry . . .' His eyes closed again, and I wasn't sure he knew I was really there.

'Callum, listen to me,' I said. I tried to keep my voice level and firm, so he wouldn't hear the terror that threatened to over-whelm me. 'You have to get well. I'm here now. I'll take care of you. Everything will be all right. Try to drink a little more water, there you go.'

But he coughed as I held the glass to his lips again and I recoiled in horror as flecks of blood spattered my hand. I panicked then, calling his name as he sank back against the sodden mattress, but he didn't open his eyes and seemed to sink into unconsciousness. I heard a footstep on the floorboards behind me and turned to see the old woman from downstairs standing there. She set a basin of hot water and a strip of grey towel on the table. Her expression was frightened, wary but not unkind.

'What's wrong with him?' I sobbed.

'Is typhoid fever. He very ill boy.'

'We must get a doctor,' I said, scrambling to my feet. 'Where are the other members of the expedition? Where is Colonel Fairburn?'

She shrugged. 'Colonel he went away. The others, they move when fever comes. Only one man stay besides.' She gestured to the closed door back down the hall. 'But he ill too. Still sick but getting better now. I try to help.' She gestured to the basin.

'I'll do it,' I said. I dipped the towel in the water and wrung it out, using it to wash the blood from Callum's chin. 'Can you go and tell the doctor to come as quickly as possible?'

She disappeared down the hallway and I sent up several prayers for her to hurry. Whilst she was gone, I did my best to make Callum more comfortable, washing some of the sweat from his face and neck, opening the window to try to let in a breath of air and setting that ghastly bucket outside in the corridor in the hope that later I could find a suitable place to empty and clean it. I straightened the sheets a little, ignoring the stains, and knelt back down beside the bed to take his hands in mine.

'Help's coming, Callum,' I said, trying to make myself believe it.

His eyelids flickered open then and his gaze was clearer. 'Vi. It really is you. I thought I must be dreaming.' He smiled faintly, then frowned. 'You shouldn't be here. It's dangerous. Don't catch the fever.'

'I had to come. You see, I've discovered I simply can't be without you. So we're going to be together from now on.' I thought if I said it firmly enough, with enough conviction, then it might just come true. His eyes closed again, but I kept talking, more urgently, trying to keep him with me. There was so much to say, so much to tell him.

'There are three of us now, Callum. I'm carrying your baby.' His eyes opened again, meeting mine, and I knew he'd understood.

'We'll make a home for ourselves somewhere out here,' I continued. 'We'll raise our children in a beautiful place, free from all that snobbery back home, and they will grow up strong and happy and so very loved. We will walk into the mountains together and discover wonderful new plants. You'll find them and I'll paint them, and we'll publish a book, which will make our fortune. Just imagine it, Callum. We'll find lilies the colours of the sunrise and poppies the colour of sky.'

His breathing seemed to ease a little, becoming less laboured, so I kept on talking, watching as his face relaxed, smoothing his hair back from his forehead, holding his hand. His clear, hazel eyes never left mine and I thought he was listening. I lost track of what I was saying, I lost track of how much time had passed.

All I know is, I was still talking when the doctor appeared in the doorway. He stooped down and gave me his arm, helping me to stand. He stood by the side of the bed for a moment. And then he gently closed Callum's eyes and drew the sheet up to cover his face before he led me from the room, my legs collapsing under me.

Monday, 4th February, 1929

Yesterday feels like a dream now. Memories drift back, of smoke and brown water and a solitary marigold flower . . . If I could, I would have lain on the funeral pyre alongside him and gone with Callum as his body was burned. But the baby I carry is all there is left of him. There is no choice but to live.

As the doctor led me from Callum's bedside, he explained how urgent it was to arrange the cremation as quickly as possible. 'You must also wash yourself very thoroughly in the hottest water possible, Miss. Typhoid spreads easily.'

In my numb state, it scarcely registered as the guesthouse owner led me to a downstairs room and brought a large bowl of scalding water and a sliver of soap with which I washed the droplets of blood and the last touch of Callum's hand in mine from my skin. She brought my case to the room and took my dirty clothes away to wash them. I put on a clean dress and, as I fastened the buttons, I noticed the slight swelling of my belly. It was still scarcely perceptible at three months, but I rested my hand there, protecting our child, wondering how tiny it must be. I'd just watched a grown man die and yet this fragile scrap of life clung on within me.

Once the doctor had tended to the man in the other room upstairs, declaring him out of danger, he joined the guesthouse owner and me in the kitchen. The cup of tea she'd made sat untouched before me and he pushed it gently towards me. 'You must try to drink, Miss. You have had a terrible shock.'

I forced myself to take a sip. 'How do I arrange the cremation?' I asked, the tea easing my throat, which had closed up tight with my grief, speaking for the first time since leaving Callum's side.

'I will do it. As I said, it will need to happen as quickly as possible.' He exchanged a few words with the guesthouse owner, then said, 'I'll arrange for them to come and take the body to Pashupatinath tonight. That way we avoid the daytime crowds on the ghats. Although your friend is not a Hindu, with typhoid cases the practicalities are the most important consideration. Certain arrangements can be made for non-believers . . .' He must have noticed my look of bewilderment because he paused and patted my hand. 'I know it will be strange for you, but here we cremate our dead in the open air, beside the river. I'm sorry if it seems brutal. But it will be for the best. You don't need to be there. I can oversee it.'

'No,' I said. 'I will go with him. He has no one else.'

'Very well,' said the doctor. 'Then I will accompany you.'

They came and put Callum's body on the back of a cart, using his filthy sheets as a shroud. 'Wait,' I said. I fetched the nut-brown shawl from my case and gently laid it over him. A wedding-ring pashmina, he'd called it. But now there would be no ring. Although it wrenched at my heart to let it go, it was all I had to wrap him in, and there was no choice but to give it back.

The streets were dark and deserted as we travelled to the river. I knew we were drawing near when I smelled the smoke. A few people still wandered along the ghats and here and there a pyre smouldered low with the remains of the day's cremations, tended by men with sticks who pushed the ashes into the sluggish brown waters of the Bagmati River.

Two men carried the bamboo stretcher on which Callum's body lay. The doctor and I followed silently, walking past the temple and the funeral pyres to the furthest end of the ghats. A skinny waif of a holy man with wild hair and his face painted in a vivid mask of white and orange appeared, saying something to the doctor, who waved him away. There would be no religious rites, no ceremony, for Callum.

I forced myself to watch as they laid him on the pile of wood and added chaff. But I have to confess, I looked away as they lit the pyre, unable to stand seeing the flames lick at the edges of the shawl that covered him. I couldn't bear to watch, but I knew I needed to stay by his side even when the smoke choked me, making me retch.

At last, the fire burned low, leaving only embers.

I remembered the hazelnuts we'd put on the fire at the bothy on the eve of Samhain – was it only three months ago? – and thought how they had filled me with the certainty of our love and our future together. That was the only time I cried.

I sat there until the final ashes were pushed into the river. Dawn was just beginning to break, and the first birdsong floated on the faint breeze that dispelled the last of the smoke. I stood and wiped the grimy tear-stains from my face. Then I turned and took the doctor's arm as he helped me walk away.

The first funeral party of the day, everyone carrying garlands of golden marigolds, was beginning to assemble before the temple. A flower fell to the ground at my feet, and I stooped to pick it up. Then I took it to the water's edge and laid it in the stream, watching it slowly drift away. A solitary tribute to the man I'd loved.

When we returned to the guesthouse, the sun was rising, and the square was already filling with traders setting out their wares. To my surprise, we were met at the door of the Namaste Guesthouse not by the owner but by a well-dressed British couple. The woman stepped forward and clasped my hands in hers.

'My dear,' she said. 'What an ordeal you've been through. I'm so sorry we didn't know . . . I'm Roberta Fairburn. And this is my husband, the Colonel. He came to fetch me from Sikkim, so we've only just arrived back in Kathmandu and heard the news. You poor, poor thing.'

We sat around the table in the dining room and the guesthouse owner brought bread and jam and tea. The man who'd been in the upstairs room was there too, well enough now to eat a little. He introduced himself as Harold Andrews, another member of the expedition, and he explained to the Fairburns all that had transpired. The others had left the guesthouse when illness struck, moving to another one in a different part of the city. Mr Andrews had stayed to try to tend to Callum, he told me, but then had fallen ill himself. I was immensely grateful to hear at least one of Callum's comrades had stayed with him.

The Colonel sat quietly, letting Andrews talk and allowing his wife to ask me how I'd come to be in Kathmandu. I didn't mention the baby, of course. I just explained how Callum and I had met at the Edinburgh Botanics, that we'd worked together and become sweethearts, and that I'd wanted to be closer to him.

'What a brave young woman you are,' Mrs Fairburn said.

Then it was the Colonel's turn to speak. 'Don't worry, young lady, we'll make sure you get home safely. I'll sort out a ticket for you. If Roberta were not going to come with us into the mountains, she could have accompanied you back. But perhaps we can find a suitable chaperone.' He turned to his wife. 'What do you think, my dear? Perhaps one of the ladies in Sikkim will be returning soon?'

I was touched by their kindness and their offers of help, but the thought of travelling back to Britain in the company of a colonial wife, with my condition steadily becoming more apparent, filled me with panic. This whole endeavour would have been a complete fiasco, and I would still inflict shame and inconvenience upon my family. I thought of Hetty, making her wedding plans. I pictured the outrage and disgust on the faces of my father and brother, my mother's dismay, and knew I couldn't return. I was overwhelmed by everything that had happened, but I forced myself to try to take a steady breath, struggling to think clearly.

'Mrs Fairburn, if you are to be on the expedition, might it be possible for me to accompany you, do you think?' It was a desperate idea, but it would buy me some time, let me find my feet in this strange new country and work out a proper plan for a future for me and my baby. I saw the doubt flicker in her face and she turned to appeal to her husband.

'Colonel, I could be of use. I know how to prepare specimens for transporting them back to Britain. And I can make sketches and paintings of the plants you find. I can take Callum's place.'

He raised his eyebrows, but I could see he was considering my proposition seriously. 'Miss Mackenzie-Grant, I have no doubt you are an accomplished botanist, and we could certainly use your skills.

But do you have any idea how challenging the expedition will be? We will be trekking for weeks on end, at high altitudes. Sleeping in tents, sometimes in extreme conditions. It will be tough.'

'I believe I'm up to it, and if Mrs Fairburn can do it then surely I can too?' I said. *In spite of my condition*, I thought but didn't add. I was grasping at straws, trying to buy myself a bit more time to work out a plan. Accompanying the expedition would give me a few more months, at least, before my pregnancy became too evident and made it too challenging for me to continue. I'd cross that bridge when I came to it.

The Colonel smiled and the sternness of his features softened. 'But, my dear, my wife makes a habit of climbing hills. Even in India. She's been in Sikkim for months now and has acclimatised herself to the demands of this part of the world. You don't have that experience.'

'No, but I am young and in good health, and the hard manual labour at the gardening school has made me strong. I grew up climbing Scottish mountains.'

He turned to his wife again. 'What do you think, Roberta? Would you like Miss Mackenzie-Grant's company on our expedition? It would be nice for you to have a female companion, I imagine. And we certainly could use her expertise with the plants.'

So it has been agreed. After a bit more persuasion from my side, assurances of my readiness to undergo the privations of the trek ahead, and an offer from Mr Andrews to carry my drawing things in his pack to lighten my own, I am to join Colonel Fairburn's expedition.

I feel numb with a strange mixture of exhaustion, relief and trepidation . . . These emotions are so overwhelming that there's scarcely room for my grief. That will come later, I imagine. For now, I close my eyes to shut out the images of the past twenty-four hours that ambush me whenever I stop writing. When I do, I can see Callum's smile, encouraging me. Even though his body is nothing but ashes scattered in a river, I know he's still here with me. He will be with me forever.

I place my hand on my belly again. *I'm doing it for you*, I tell my baby. *And for your father. He would be proud of us.*

Daisy – March 2020

It's the final day of our trek to reach the Sherpa village of Phortse. I know it'll be another challenging one. We're climbing again, another thousand feet or so. But today's hike involves an uphill walk to Mongla – which is even higher than Phortse – and then a plunging descent into a deep river valley. I've learned by now that what goes up must come down, and vice versa. The final section of the path climbs steeply to where the village sits on an ancient terrace overlooking the valley. It would have been carved into the bedrock by a river, once upon a time. It's a reminder of the might of the forces at play, the ground rising as the Indian tectonic plate collides with the immovable object that is the Tibetan plateau. What was once the valley floor now hangs there, high and dry, halfway up the mountainside.

I can sense the village waiting for us, watching as we wind our way slowly towards it. For Tashi and Sonam, it's home. And in a way it feels like home to me too. At least, a temporary one. I've read about Phortse, imagined it, dreamed about it for so many years. And today, at last and against all the odds, I'll be there. No matter how hard the going, I remind myself, Violet went through far more on her own journey. After her arrival in Kathmandu – so full of hope – and the trauma of Callum's death, she had to walk in these mountains bearing her unborn baby as well as her burdens of grief and fear. My own preoccupations pale into insignificance alongside hers.

Just as we're preparing to leave the lodge, I check my phone one last time. There's a flicker of a signal and three messages flash up on the screen. One is a BBC newsflash: a lockdown has now officially been announced in the UK, to begin in a few days' time. There's a message from Mum: *Feeling so much better. Energy returning slowly. Wish I was there with you. Good luck with the final push to Phortse – send photos!* And the other is a one-liner from Jack, another one of his anagrams. He clearly has way too much time on his hands on his lonely voyage across thousands of miles of ocean. *SILENT = LISTEN.*

I smile as I shove my phone into my pocket and zip up my jacket. It's an early start and the air is crisp and clear as we begin to climb the steps leading out of Namche Bazaar and on to the path. My headache has gone this morning, and the sight of the snow-capped peaks soaring high above us on all sides lifts my spirits. Apart from the sound of my breath, which comes in gasps, it is silent up here. So I follow the instruction in Jack's message and listen, picking out the soft sounds the silence holds. There's the muffled tread of our boots on the path and the faint sigh of the wind. Every now and then I hear a harmonious clanking of yak bells in the distance, like a child playing on a xylophone. It reminds me of the joke, often repeated in the music school back home, paraphrasing the words of the late great comedian Eric Morecambe. *I wasn't playing all the wrong notes. I was playing all the right notes, just not necessarily in the right order.* Even though the sound of the bells is a little discordant here and there, it's still heart-stoppingly beautiful, and suddenly a surge of gratitude courses through my veins. All the doubts and setbacks to get this far have been worth it, just for this moment.

What was it Violet wrote? *Sometimes you just have to throw your heart into the river of life and dive in after it.* I feel I'm getting nearer to her, closing in on the half of her story that has gone untold. And that thought spurs me on as I repeat my trekking mantra, putting one foot in front of the other, again and again, slowly, slowly, along the path.

Phortse appears tantalisingly close on its perch on the far side of the valley as we leave Mongla after a lunch of soup and crackers. The teahouse owner – evidently another cousin, judging by the warm welcome he gives Tashi and Sonam and then extends to me – apologises that it's all they have. We are far from any town here and have left the main route leading to Everest Base Camp to take the path less travelled, leading up into the mountains. With the country rapidly shutting down, it's harder than ever to get supplies, the owner explains. The porters, who usually carry rice, bread, lentils and eggs up from Lukla and Namche Bazaar, have mostly returned to their homes. He also lists a number of friends – and cousins, of course – who have returned to Mongla and Phortse. 'Like the old days,' Tashi grins, turning to me. 'Usually, many people away from the villages at this time of year, for work as guides. But this year different.'

I insist on paying the teahouse owner for my bowl of soup. He tries hard to refuse, but it's only a few hundred rupees – no more than a couple of pounds – and I'm starting to understand how difficult the coming months are going to be for them all if this season's income from tourism is non-existent. As we embark on the final part of the trek, the sky overhead is heavy with ominous-looking dark clouds and a few icy droplets fall from above, stinging my cheeks. I can't quite tell whether they're sleet, snow or hail. I pull the hood of my jacket over my head and draw the zip up to my chin as we begin the long descent into the final valley before we climb back up to Phortse.

There's a metal bridge across the river on the valley floor and I simultaneously offer up thanks that it's firmly anchored to the solid rock, and wish someone had put up another flimsy-looking suspension bridge far higher to allow us to cross the void and to save us the effort of this final climb. It's begun to snow heavily now, and three yaks cluster alongside a vast *mani* stone, carved over and over with the Buddhist mantra *om mani padme hum*, trying to find shelter as the weather closes in. The wind swirls around us, shoving us off balance as it blusters against the steep walls of the valley, and even Tashi looks a little less serene as he glances upwards at the path leading to the village. 'Storm coming. We need go quickly now, Mrs Daisy.'

Quickly is not a pace I can manage very easily. My headache returns with a vengeance as I force my legs to carry me uphill once more, plodding along one switchback after another. The wind drives snow between the tattered tangle of rhododendron and birch trees that clothe the mountainside, offering little protection from the fierceness of the oncoming storm. The ends of the rhododendron branches are covered in tight buds, but there are no flowers out yet and I estimate they must be at least a couple of weeks behind the ones we've seen blossoming along the path at lower altitudes. We climb relentlessly, not pausing to catch our breath or look at the view. When I do glance back, squinting into the scouring wind, I realise there's no view left. Mongla and the path on the other side of the valley have been swallowed up. Even the bridge and the yaks have disappeared, obscured by the thick curtain of swirling snowflakes.

I think the climb will never end, as the altitude steals the breath from my lungs and the wind snatches at the hood of my jacket. I press a fist into the sharp stitch that grips my side, bending me double as it pulls tighter and tighter still. I think I'm going to have to give up. But there's no other option than to keep going, to keep putting one foot in front of the other, again and again, whatever my mind is telling me.

And then, all of a sudden, we're there, walking beneath the stooped trunk of an ancient birch tree guarding a brightly painted gateway. The tiled roof of the village gate shelters us for a few brief moments and I gasp in several deep breaths. Tashi reaches out his hand to turn the prayer wheels that line its walls, and I offer up my own silent prayer of thanks for having made it.

The climb isn't quite over yet though. The shelf of land on which the village perches is by no means as flat as it looked from across the valley. My calf muscles burn as we pick our way beside a long *mani* wall made of jumbled slabs of slate, each one carved with writing or images of the Buddha, left in memory of a departed soul. Tattered prayer flags flap wildly as the wind gathers force again, engulfing us in a swirling vortex of snow. I duck my head involuntarily as a flash of lightning and an ear-splitting crack of thunder simultaneously envelop us. Tashi and Sonam urge me on, turning into a smaller path that runs between a pair of rough stone walls. I stagger and stumble, completely exhausted now, blinded by the blizzard, and Sonam reaches to steady me, taking my pack from me and carrying it himself. I try to protest but the effort is too much and the wind snatches the half-gasped words from my lips.

The snowfall is so dense now that I don't see the wall of the lodge until it's right in front of us and Tashi pushes open the door.

I'm so numb with cold and tiredness and fear that I stand, stunned, my ears ringing in the sudden stillness. A cast-iron stove burns brightly in the centre of the room. A smiling woman, who is stoking the fire, gets to her feet. She picks up a silky white scarf from the counter and comes over to place it around my neck. Then she embraces me warmly.

'*Namaste*, Mrs Daisy Like-A-Flower,' she says, as if she's known me forever. 'Welcome to Phortse. I am your cousin Dipa.'

Violet's Journal

SATURDAY, 23RD MARCH, 1929

After four weeks in the field, I feel I'm getting into my stride at last. Once it had been agreed that I could accompany the expedition, Mrs Fairburn set about helping me procure everything I'd need. I'd confessed to her that I was almost entirely out of funds, but she told me not to give it another thought. 'Now you are a working member, the expedition will provide,' she declared. The Colonel has put me on the payroll and has given me the pay due to Callum, in order to tide me over. I confess, I wept with gratitude as I accepted it. It felt as though Callum was still watching over me, supporting and protecting his unborn child. As I push myself to climb the stony path ahead, I still see his smile and sense his arms around me, helping me along. Imagining him at my side gives me the courage to go on. And it feels good to be earning my own living for the first time in my life.

Mrs Fairburn has confessed to me that her husband has no great interest in plants. He's a soldier and a diplomat, but above all an adventurer who loves exploring the remoter corners of the world. 'The money to be made from finding new plants and sending them back to the botanic gardens in Edinburgh and Kew will provide us with a pension,' she said. 'That's why he relies on the knowledge and expertise of the likes of you and Mr Andrews.'

I listened with interest, mindful of the fact that once my employment is at an end, I shall need to find ways to fund myself now my father will most certainly have carried out his threat to stop my allowance. Between selling my botanical illustrations and the possibility of sending new specimens back home, I wonder whether I may be able to find ways to support myself and my child in this remote corner of the world.

The Fairburns have been so very kind, moving the whole expedition team out of Kathmandu and into a small hotel in Godawari, set in the hills south-east of the city, to escape the danger of typhoid. In the fertile green gardens surrounding the hotel, they allowed me time and space to mourn the loss of Callum and to begin to come to terms with the turn my life has taken. I was grateful to be left alone for much of the time, and to take my meals in my room, not just to grieve all I have lost but also because I was beset with morning sickness. Perhaps it was all the travelling, or the trauma catching up with me, but I could scarcely keep down a thing. At first, I thought I might have succumbed to the typhoid that had taken Callum, and a part of me wanted it to be so. I longed to be with him again and the thought of going on was too much to bear at times. It would surely be easier to die than to face what lies ahead of me without him by my side. But bear it I must, for the sake of our child. However, I developed no other symptoms, so I quickly realised it was no more than my body's natural response to pregnancy and the recent upheavals I had put it through. And so I forced myself to eat the rice that accompanied each dish, but I found I couldn't tolerate the richer foods, nor even the pots of strong black tea that were brought with every meal.

The kindly waiter who delivered the trays to my room soon noticed my lack of appetite and took it upon himself to bring me an infusion made from mint leaves instead, which soothed my stomach. I have found it to be the perfect antidote to the nausea that besets me. He also brought me some delicious jam, made by his wife from golden raspberries that grow in their own garden. I devour quantities of it, spread on toasted bread.

Despite my attempts to nourish myself and my baby, I must have lost a little weight in the weeks following my arrival in Kathmandu as the gardening smocks I've brought with me – being the most functional items of apparel for practical work as well as for concealing my expanding waistline – hang on my frame even looser than ever. Apart from a scarcely discernible swelling of my belly, which is easily concealed beneath my loose smock, my stomach still remains flat. Coupled with the bulky overcoat that I shall wear in the mountains where it's so much colder, my clothing will do a good job of concealing my condition for as long as possible and I don't believe there are any other visible signs of my pregnancy yet. During our time at the hotel, my listlessness as a result of the sickness could be entirely ascribed to my grief.

I wanted to do nothing other than sleep. Grateful to lose myself in exhausted oblivion; grateful not to have to think or plan. When not in my room, I passed my waking hours sketching and painting in the hotel gardens, immersing myself in the colours of the exotic plants that bloom there. A series of waterspouts, like dragons' mouths, fed a cistern from a hillside spring. Bougainvillea scrambled through the twisting branches of ancient fig trees, spilling waves of magenta and cerise through the dark leaves; sun-warmed jasmine breathed its sweet perfume into the air. There was also a curious shrub with the most heavenly scent, which bears flowers of pale blue, deepest purple and pure white all on the same branches. Mr Andrews – who would come and sit quietly alongside me sometimes to watch me at work – told me it is an import from South America and that its common name is the Yesterday, Today and Tomorrow bush because the successive flowers change colour so distinctively. It's a shame it wouldn't be hardy enough for the British climate.

Losing myself in my painting was a welcome distraction. Until now, I have had no inclination to write in my journal, nor to send a letter home to Hetty. She'll be very busy with her wedding preparations and I want to let her imagine me happily reunited with Callum for the time being. There'll be time enough to tell her all that has passed once her own nuptials have taken place. The Colonel has written to Callum's parents to tell them the sad news of the death of their son. He asked me if I'd like to add a note to his letter, but I said no. I told Colonel Fairburn I would write separately, later. But the truth is I don't wish to add to their anguish. Perhaps once the baby is born, I can let them know that they have a grandchild. I'm in two minds, though. I'm not at all sure how welcome that news would be to them.

So I was grateful for the time in Godawari whilst the final preparations were made for the expedition into the mountains. It helped me recover enough to face what lies ahead. Not just in terms of assuaging the nausea but allowing me to grieve and rest and restore a little more mental equanimity as well. Heaven knows, I shall need every ounce of my strength in the coming months.

The afternoon before we were due to leave, I was sitting, as usual, in the hotel garden with my sketchbook and my paints. Mrs Fairburn came to find me, to check that I was ready for the journey ahead of us. I reassured her that I was, having benefited greatly from three weeks of rest and recuperation since those terrible first days of my arrival in Kathmandu. She was full of optimism for the expedition ahead of us and described the preparations the Colonel has been making. 'My husband complains I do not travel light, but you should just see the amount he's accumulated to take with us. He's got more than a dozen chop boxes filled with food alone – enough tea, coffee, pemmican, butter and tinned milk to feed an army. Old habits die hard!' Perhaps she saw me blanch slightly at the thought of the tins of greasy meat paste, because she quickly added, 'But don't worry, I've made sure we have a few luxuries too, like chocolate and dates. I find I get such a craving for sweet things with all that hiking, don't you?' I forced myself to smile and nod, even as my stomach gave another silent heave.

In addition to the rations there are cases of medical supplies, plant-collecting equipment and our personal effects, as well as the canvas tents that will be our accommodation for the coming months. We formed quite the cavalcade as we set off the next morning, a string of porters urging their mules forwards, the cumbersome luggage strapped to the backs of both animals and men.

It felt good to make a start and I have discovered the relief there is to be had in walking. The simple act of putting one foot in front of the other focuses the mind, helping shut out the less welcome ruminations that run on a loop in my head. It gives me a purpose and seems to help quieten my nausea. Perhaps my baby enjoys the sensation of movement too, being gently rocked as I trudge along, up and down the hills.

We've skirted the city, passing through terraced rice fields, following paths uphill and down again, but slowly and surely gaining height with each day that passes. I've found I'm able to match the pace of the others with ease and feel my strength coming back. I'm thankful, now, for all those hours I spent at the gardening school pushing a plough or a wheelbarrow, and digging, mulching and turning the compost heaps. They've prepared me well for this.

As I walk, Callum is constantly in my mind. I talk to him – silently, of course – imagining him here with me, giving me the strength to keep going. Until this point, the climate has been largely subtropical. The hills to the north of the Kathmandu valley are a rich hunting ground and we've accumulated many interesting specimens. We forage in the mornings and then I usually return to camp to document our findings, preparing and annotating specimens to add to the collection that will eventually be sent home. I wonder who is working in the Herbarium back in Edinburgh these days and who will prise open the lids of the boxes and unpack my carefully pressed and wrapped folders. I hope they may spare a brief thought for the people who have walked so many miles and endured heat, rain and uncomfortable nights spent under canvas to seek out these new discoveries.

It's been worth a bit of discomfort, though, as well as the challenges of finding a little privacy here and there to undertake one's necessary bodily functions. The landscapes we've walked through have been so very beautiful – rolling green hills clad with verdant woodland in the main. But here and there we find valleys filled with the exuberance of colour one normally associates with the most highly cultivated gardens. This, surely, is how every plant would wish to live – unclipped, unpruned, growing free to realise its natural potential without being controlled and confined by man. Somehow, that thought reminds me of my father and my brother, and the life I've left behind. Perhaps, like the plants, I too shall thrive in the freedom of this environment.

Rhododendrons dominate, an unimaginable variety of subspecies bursting with clouds of red, pink and white blooms, growing to dimensions I have never seen back home. Cascades of wild roses tumble over rocky banks, scrambling into the branches of glossy-leaved camellias and towering magnolia trees. In one valley, the air was filled with the sweetest scent I've ever smelled. It turned out to be a variety of daphne, whose shy white flowers are the source of this heavenly perfume. We came upon a little hamlet where the inhabitants were engaged in making paper from it. They gather the fibres from the shrub's bark and soak it well until it forms a pulp. This is then spread thinly on wooden frames and allowed to dry in the sunshine until a sheet of paper forms. The final product – called *lokta* paper – is a little rough, with flecks of plant material still visible in the finished sheets, but I think this only adds to its charms. I bartered a box of dates and a bar of chocolate for a supply of sheets, which I've folded and stitched together to make a new notebook. It will be useful when I've filled the pages of this one.

Yesterday we reached a small village that the local people call Lukla, meaning the place of goats and sheep. It's obvious why – as we neared the village, we had to stop more and more frequently to allow the passage of bleating flocks. It's no more than a few shacks clinging to the steep mountainside, but we've been able to find accommodation in a teahouse. We were served plates of the local food – a tasty combination of lentils, vegetables and rice. It's simple fare, not overly spicy, and I must say it made a very welcome change from the slabs of Bovril pemmican we've been living on for the past month. I consumed about a gallon of mint tea as well and found it immediately eased the heartburn that has increasingly been plaguing me. I intend asking our guide, a cheerful Sherpa named Mingma, to bring a good supply of mint leaves with us on the next stage of the expedition.

It is such luxury to sleep under a real roof, albeit on a bedframe made of rough planks. The previous night our tents had frozen solid, jolting me awake as the canvas buckled and crackled with the weight of the ice. They had to be spread out on rocks in the morning sun before they thawed enough to be folded back into their packs. They never dry out properly in the humid forests at the lower levels and the canvas is spotted with black mildew, which smells unpleasantly musty. I'm glad we'll be staying here for a few days so they can be properly aired. I've noticed how much dryer the air seems up here now. I can feel it rasping in my throat as I breathe deeply with the exertion of the climb. However, other than that I have so far still felt no effects of altitude sickness. It's only now, though, as we are nearing ten thousand feet above sea level, that Mrs Fairburn warns we may begin to suffer a little more.

Blankets made of softest yak wool have been provided at the teahouse too. I slept the sleep of the dead last night, tucking one around me and folding another to fashion a comfortable pillow. I awoke to the strangest sensation. It was as if a butterfly were fluttering its wings deep in my belly. I put my hand there and felt the movement again. 'Hello,' I whispered, and my baby fluttered back its reply. 'So you're still there, are you, after everything I've put you through? I think you must be as sturdy as your parents.'

My underclothes are feeling a little tight in places now and I have to leave certain fasteners undone to allow myself space to breathe. Thank goodness my gardening smocks are still loose enough to conceal the bump of my stomach, and now we are reaching the cooler climes of the higher mountains, the folds of my overcoat will be a blessing as well.

From this point, Colonel Fairburn has decided to continue to follow the deep valley northwards. Then, when we reach the market town of Namche Bazaar, we will swing round to the west rather than making straight for the highest peaks that lie to the north-east of us. He's hoping we'll find richer pickings in the less well-mapped western valleys as we continue to search for more unusual spring flowers. The expedition will swing round towards the east later in the season to reach the glaciers marking the foot of the highest mountains of all, the home of Mount Everest and her sister peaks. Our guide, Mingma, who is a member of the Sherpa people, refers to the highest mountain in the world by the name of Chomolungma, the female deity they believe inhabits the summit. He would never climb it, he tells me. His people believe it would be disrespectful to stand on top of the head of the goddess. Those high valleys should be more accessible by the time our expedition's circuitous route leads us into them. It's intriguing to wonder what alpine plants – if any – might be found there. Tiny rosettes and cushions of leaves, perhaps, which have somehow adapted to life on the edges of survival and cling on in the most extreme of conditions.

Tomorrow we'll send off a tea chest full of specimens on the first leg of its long journey back to Britain. I've scribbled a letter for Hetty too, to tell her of the horror and devastation of losing Callum. At least I can reassure her now that I've managed to find a way forward once again. She must be counting down the final days to her wedding so, by the time my letter reaches her, she will be Mrs Rufus Ogilvy. I made sure to write the strange name and address on the envelope.

It put a lump in my throat. We are such worlds apart now.

Daisy – March 2020

The storm continues to rage around the lodge, rattling the corrugated iron roof and hurling thick sheets of snow against the windows, obscuring any last glimpses of the view from my upstairs bedroom as night falls. The accommodation is basic, but spotlessly clean, and I have a comfortable bed piled with pillows and duvets. There's a bathroom down the hall, but as I'm the only guest staying at the moment it's as good as an en-suite, even if the basins have no taps. Tashi has told me, with some pride, that they have a shower here at the lodge. But it turns out to be in a sort of cubicle outdoors and the water has to be fetched up from the river, then heated on the stove before being poured into a reservoir on the roof, so it's an experience I'll be foregoing for the time being.

As ever, the porters got here earlier and my bag's already in my room. I peel off my wet things and hastily put on some dry layers, shivering in the unheated room, and then make my way back downstairs in search of warmth.

I pull my chair a little closer to the iron stove in the centre of the room. My body aches all over after our hard day's trekking to reach Phortse. The glow of heat from the stove slowly permeates the layers of clothes I've put on, coaxing my frozen muscles to relax. It's such a relief to be here and I feel a sense of euphoria, mixed with a little disbelief.

The walls of the communal room of the lodge are decorated with prints of intricate Buddhist mandalas, held in place with sticky tape, alongside a series of framed photos of the surrounding mountains. In one corner, a picture of the Dalai Lama, cut from a magazine, is draped with a silky scarf – a *kata*, Tashi tells me – like the one Dipa presented me with earlier. There are wooden benches built around the walls, beneath the windows, covered with brightly upholstered cushions and soft blankets woven from yak's wool.

The kitchen door swings open, releasing a gust of laughter and a clattering of dishes, and Tashi appears with a cup of mint tea for me. He crouches beside the stove and adds some flat brown disks to it, stoking the flames. 'Yak dung,' he explains, holding one up. 'Best fuel we have because no trees up here. Just juniper twigs and this.'

I sip from my mug, savouring it as Violet would have done, cupping my hands around it to extract every last bit of warmth.

'Is this normal weather for this time of year?' I ask him. 'I wasn't expecting it. I thought Mum and I had done our research carefully and picked a good time of year for our trip – after the winter storms and before the early-summer monsoon.'

He shakes his head. 'Not usual at all. Weather all confused now. Very little snow in winter, and it comes now too late. Should be snow melt now so we prepare fields and plant crops for this year. But this weather gives us worry growing season will be too short.'

'What will you be planting?' I ask.

'Potatoes and buckwheat mostly. Phortse potatoes very good. Number one best in world. Known all over Nepal.'

Dipa appears from the kitchen, carrying a plate heaped high with my supper. It's a mixture of the famed potatoes with scrambled eggs and pak choi. I tuck in, ravenous after our scanty lunch of soup and crackers at the teahouse in Mongla all those hours – and miles – ago.

'Oh my goodness,' I mumble, through a mouthful. 'You're right about these spuds, Tashi. They're absolutely delicious.' I'm sure it's not just my hunger talking. The plateful of food is seasoned with garlic and herbs and the potatoes taste like the ones Davy used to grow in the lazy beds at Ardtuath, before the digging got to be too much for his back, with an old-fashioned depth of flavour.

'What is spuds?' Dipa asks, and I introduce them to the British term, which they repeat solemnly, committing it to memory.

'I will show you our spuds fields tomorrow if storm passes,' says Tashi.

'No, you won't,' Dipa interjects. 'You three have to stay inside for a week to make sure you didn't bring the virus to Phortse. Me too, now you are here. Everyone must do this now, to keep the village safe.'

'We should be okay in open air,' he replies, but she shakes her head firmly.

The advice seems a bit confusing to me. But I decide the best thing to do is follow Dipa's lead.

I notice a handwritten sign above the counter saying that Wi-Fi is available, so I pull my phone out and check the settings. 'Is there a password?' I ask Tashi.

'Sonam,' he calls, and his son emerges from the kitchen. 'Can you fix Wi-Fi for Mrs Daisy?'

Sonam takes my phone from me and taps rapidly, then shakes his head. 'Sorry, it's not working at the moment. This happens when the weather is bad.' He hands it back to me with a rueful grin and a shrug. 'Actually, it happens when the weather is good sometimes too. Yet another of the disadvantages of being in the back of beyond. But I'll set up your phone so you should connect automatically when we get a signal again.'

I thank him and his parents for all they've done. 'I didn't really believe I'd get here,' I say.

Tashi smiles. 'Mrs Daisy, you should have no worries. You know you travel with Sherpas, number one best mountain guides in the world.'

I laugh. 'Just as well – I very much doubt anyone else could have managed to get me to Phortse.'

Then Dipa adds, 'You have good determination though. Not surprising, just like your great-great-aunty Violet.'

She sees the look of surprise on my face. 'Tashi tells me why you want to come here. You have many cousins in Phortse. Sister-cousins and brother-cousins. Including me.'

I can't believe it! I'd come to search for some trace of Violet, hoping at the most to speak to someone who might dimly remember hearing about a heavily pregnant Western woman who visited the village almost one hundred years ago. I remember Dipa's words of welcome – 'I am your cousin.' I'd assumed she just used the term out of politeness, welcoming this stranger as one of the family, but now I turn to face her fully, my interest piqued as I realise perhaps she meant something more. 'Exactly how are we related?'

She frowns, trying to work it out. 'Brother of my sister's husband married to great-granddaughter of Violet. She called Pema. Means Lotus. Like-a-flower too. When phones working again, we will tell her you're here. And when quarantine over she will come. Her house over there, just down the hill.'

I sit in stunned silence. Violet's great-granddaughter is here! I peer out of the window, into the snowy darkness beyond. So near, and yet so far.

The next morning the storm has passed, leaving the sky as blue as the turquoise stones that dangle from Dipa's earlobes when she brings me my breakfast of pancakes with honey. The towering summit of Khumbila – the sacred mountain where the deity of the Khumbu valley is said to dwell, Tashi tells me – watches over Phortse, covered in a dazzling blanket of white. The village stretches down the hillside below the lodge, little houses dotted among the terraced fields, with threads of smoke emerging from their chimneys to mingle with the prayer flags that dance on the wind.

In the night, despite feeling exhausted to the very core of my bones, sleep had eluded me at first, my mind whirling with the knowledge that there were relations of Violet's still living in Phortse. Dipa hadn't told me much more, bustling back to the kitchen, and she didn't reappear. I waited a while, but my eyes began to droop in the warmth from the stove and at last I gave up and came up to my room. Despite feeling exhausted, I'd ended up lying awake for hours, listening to the howling of the storm, which sounded as if it was trying its hardest to blow down the lodge. I suppose I must have been drifting in and out of consciousness, but I distinctly remember thinking I could hear voices in the wind, crying and wailing, calling out in the darkness.

When I mention this now to Dipa, saying how weird it had been and that I must have been dreaming, she shakes her head. 'Not dream. They wind walkers. Souls of people who have too many regrets in life. After they die, they walk the winds, trying to find peace.'

'And do they eventually manage to find peace?' I ask.

She shakes her head, making her earrings swing. 'Of course not. Buddha say must find peace here on Earth in our lifetimes. Winds of regret take you nowhere.'

She tops up my teacup and heads back to the kitchen, leaving me to chew my pancakes thoughtfully, mulling over what she's just said in such a matter-of-fact way. There's been a lot of regret in my life: divorce; a feeling I've been a bad mum to my girls; giving up my career and settling for a job where I'm just going through the motions; living alone, cocooned in my flat, not really making an effort to go out and socialise . . . Outside, the strands of prayer flags dance and wave in the sunshine, making me think perhaps it's about time the wind changed in my life too. Otherwise, I'll end up walking the winds forever in a hopeless search for peace, having frittered away the opportunity to find it here on Earth.

It's incredibly frustrating not to be able to go outside to breathe in the mountain air and feel the sunlight on my face, but I know I have to resign myself to my week of incarceration. And in a way I welcome it. There's been so much to take in. Even just getting here has left me reeling, never mind the news that I have some living relations in this tiny, remote village perched on the highest edge of the world.

I bring the journals and letters downstairs and spread them out on one of the tables. And then, between frequent breaks for more cups of tea, I tell Tashi, Dipa and Sonam all that I know of Violet's journey and how my great-great-aunt came to be here in the first place.

Violet's Journal

Friday, 14th June, 1929

It feels strange to be writing in my journal again after so long. But only now can I look back and take stock of all that's happened in these past months.

In the weeks following our departure from Namche Bazaar, the expedition settled into a routine of trekking, making camp, hunting for plants, and then moving on again to explore the next valley. Our slow and steady gain in altitude, with weeks spent working from a campsite base, was a blessing. I didn't once feel the ill effects of breathing the thin air, the way some of the men did. Poor Mr Andrews, whose strength must have been sapped by his illness, was laid low for several days with a blinding headache when we reached the place called Thamo.

My morning sickness soon passed, too, and I felt a renewed sense of energy and purpose in accompanying the men on their forays in search of new species. It was noticeable, as we trekked deeper into the Khumbu valley, how the plant life around us changed. The pine and birch woods grew sparser, giving way to scrubby growths of juniper, which crouched closer to the ground. But other strange shrubs grew alongside the paths trodden by yak herders too, and I was kept busy capturing the forms of their leaves and flowers with my watercolours. I feel sure some of them will do well in the British climate as the growing conditions at these altitudes are so much cooler than the subtropics of Kathmandu. Indeed, some may even thrive in our milder temperatures and gentler weather. I have high hopes for one of the forms of pom-pom-like primulas we've found and can picture it growing by the pond at Inverewe, perhaps. I shall write to Mrs Hanbury, when I have the time and opportunity to send a letter. I haven't written to Hetty for weeks either, but told her in my last letter not to expect to hear from me for a while so she wouldn't worry.

We still walked through forests of rhododendrons, but only the earlier ones were in bloom above Namche. We had to rely on identifying them by their other characteristics and it was gratifying that my work in the Herbarium stood me in good stead. Once the men realised I had some useful knowledge, they began consulting me for help in identifying their finds. At first, some of them enthusiastically culled plants wholesale, pulling them from the stony ground and carrying them back to camp, roots and all, hoping instantly to have discovered some prized new find that would make their fortunes. I supposed they thought it would save them the effort of climbing repeatedly back and forth between hillside and camp. With the help of Colonel and Mrs Fairburn, who had considerably more experience in the field than most of the men, I managed to convince them to take more care, to mark their finds on a plan and bring back just a sprig at first, accompanied by descriptive notes, until we could ascertain which areas merited further investigation. I showed them how to mark the location on the ground of the plants worth collecting, so we could return later in the season to gather the seeds once they'd set.

I didn't mind scrambling up slopes and over screes to be shown their findings. Indeed, seeing plants growing in situ is of huge value in helping with their identification. But as the weeks passed and my baby grew within me, I began to find the exertion a bit more tiring and became a little more cautious about taking risks on the steeper rock faces. I think Mrs Fairburn must have noticed my slight reluctance because one morning she declared I should spend more time at the camp. 'Your drawing and painting skills are most valuable to the expedition, now the men are getting into their stride and know what to look for,' she said, then turned to her husband. 'Don't you agree, my dear? It would be best if Violet were to remain here a bit more.'

He looked up from the map he was perusing as he planned the next excursion. 'I suppose you are right, as you so often are, Roberta. Although if Miss Mackenzie-Grant wishes to accompany us, she has proven herself more than capable. But there are specimens to be prepared and labelled for sending back, so perhaps you two ladies could carry on with that whilst we're away.'

When I smiled my thanks to Mrs Fairburn, I caught her looking at me a little thoughtfully. Instinctively, I sat up slightly straighter in my camp chair and attempted to pull in the rounding of my stomach beneath my overcoat. She smiled back, giving no sign of suspecting anything, and I relaxed, relieved I was still managing to conceal my condition. The climbing has made me stronger and fitter, my muscles becoming more defined even as my baby pushes my belly outwards.

We based ourselves at Thamo for several weeks. It was less than a day's trek from Namche Bazaar but felt a world away. A brightly decorated monastery sits on high there above a few stone hovels, and the nuns who inhabit it were most welcoming. They have little enough to sustain themselves but insisted on bringing us gifts of food – little dumplings filled with savoury vegetables, and tasty pickles with which to break the monotony of our pemmican. Mrs Fairburn offered them a few tins in exchange for their gifts, but when they learned the contents were some form of meat they quickly handed them back. Mingma told us it is against their beliefs to consume another living thing unless it has died of natural causes. I was surprised to learn they eat meat at all, but the ancient form of Buddhism practised here seems rather a pragmatic one and I suppose when food is always so scarce and life so hard, it is only sensible to eat what is available. Some of the nuns are very young, mere children of ten or twelve years of age, and it is all too evident they don't get the nutrition they require. I could see one or two of them had the thickened ankles and bowed legs characteristic of rickets. We substituted some tins of condensed milk for the offering of pemmican, and these were gratefully accepted. I just wish we could do more to help them.

As the weeks passed, the weather improved, and I began to grow accustomed to the cycle of days in the mountains. The nights were bitterly cold, the sky clear and blacker than any I've seen in Scotland. But it was filled with breathtaking curtains of stars – far more even than Callum and I saw on the eve of Samhain. I looked up at them and wondered if he was there, somehow, somewhere, looking down on us. I wished I believed in reincarnation as the Buddhist nuns do, so that there might be some chance of him returning one day. But I knew I was alone, even in the company of the expedition, and that the time would come, soon enough, when I would have to fend for myself and my baby on my own.

Daybreak arrived as a cold, grey light at first and I would scramble out of my sleeping bag and into my clothes, emerging from my tent to seek out the first rays of warmth as the sun appeared from behind the wall of mountains enclosing the valley. Mingma and our porters would already have the fire going and a tin kettle steaming merrily atop it as, one by one, the expedition members came to sit in the sunlight, basking like lizards on a rock whilst the welcome warmth thawed out stiff limbs.

I began to notice that Mr Andrews would make a point of coming to sit beside me. He is a kind man, but I didn't wish to encourage his advances, nor to mislead him in any way. He probably imagined me to be rather shy and was being careful, too, not to encroach on my grief.

Whilst the mornings were clear and bright, more often than not a veil of cloud would accumulate over the mountaintops and roll down into the valley by mid-afternoon. Sometimes it became so clammy and cold that I was forced to retreat to my tent and wriggle into my sleeping bag for warmth, keeping all my clothes on whilst I attempted to finish writing up the day's notes. The men would usually arrive back from their excursions later in the day and we would all gather again beneath the awning of the cook tent to eat supper and discuss the latest findings.

One evening, alongside the assortment of plant materials the men had collected, they produced with some triumph a large slab of honeycomb. They'd found curtains of it hanging from the underside of a large cliff and one of the more intrepid amongst them had scrambled up to steal a chunk of it, braving the stings of the large and angry bees that quickly swarmed around him, making clear their displeasure. How we all longed for something sweet to break the monotony of our diet! But when I tasted the honey, I found it had a peculiar, bitter edge to it that did not agree with me and it rasped unpleasantly in my throat. My baby seemed to agree, giving my belly a good hard kick. I quietly passed the dish of it along, noticing that the Colonel and his wife did the same. But the men devoured it, spread on hard biscuits from our supplies.

That night, tucked up in my tent, I heard the most terrible commotion outside in the camp. I drew on my coat and stuck my head out through the flap of canvas. It was another crisp, cold night and the moon was almost full, illuminating the snow on the mountain peaks as well as the scene before me. For a moment, I wondered whether our camp had been invaded by werewolves, or some other sort of demons. Dark figures stumbled about, one of them seeming to throw back its head and howl at the moon. Then another of them staggered towards my tent. 'Violet,' it slurred. 'I love you. I desire you.'

'Mr Andrews!' I exclaimed, deeply shocked. He wore only his undershirt and long-johns and his feet were bare. I averted my eyes from his evident state of arousal. 'What on earth has got into you all? Have you been drinking?' I scrambled out of my tent to stand, feeling that he might attempt to get into it with me if I stayed inside and I would at least be able to make a run for it if I was out in the open. But there was no need – the men seemed too intoxicated to be at all coherent and could scarcely stand. Mr Andrews suddenly bent double before me and vomited copiously on to the ground.

I wondered where on earth they could have got hold of so much strong liquor. We had some bottles of whisky in one of the chop boxes, but the Colonel kept it padlocked and only he had the key, wishing to limit the amount consumed and make the supply last. He only broke out a bottle occasionally, dispensing a tot here and there for medicinal purposes, to toast a promising new discovery, or to keep spirits up after a particularly miserable day's weather. As more of the men began to vomit and retch, something stirred in a far recess of my mind. Back at Inverewe, Mrs Hanbury had insisted the beehives were placed as far away as possible from a certain grove of rhododendrons. 'Otherwise, they gorge themselves on the nectar and the honey tastes quite nasty,' she'd said. 'I've heard in some parts of the world it can even have an hallucinogenic effect if partaken of too liberally.'

Just then, the Colonel emerged from his tent. 'What in heaven's name is going on here?' he roared.

'I think it's the effect of the honey, sir,' I called. 'It's toxic.'

'Oh, for goodness' sake. What buffoons they are.' He stepped forward, used to taking command. 'Get back to your tents immediately!' But the men were beyond taking orders. By now they had all sunk to the ground near the fire and lay groaning and retching. 'Very well,' he barked. 'Stay there then and freeze.' He turned on his heel and disappeared back into his tent, from where I heard the muffled sounds of a conversation between him and his wife.

Realising that the men would, indeed, freeze to death if left there like that, I went from tent to tent, collecting up blankets and sleeping bags. Mingma appeared and helped me wrap them around the prone forms as best we could. 'Don't worry, Miss,' he said. 'I stay here and keep fire going. Make sure they keep warm. Make sure they don't bother you too.'

I handed the last blanket to him, to wrap around his shoulders. 'Is it the honey, do you think?'

He grinned broadly, his teeth gleaming in the firelight. 'Most certainly. It make men very excited. But not good if too much excited, I think.'

'Not good at all,' I said firmly. 'Thank you for keeping an eye on them, Mingma. Will they be all right?'

He nodded. 'It wear off after few hours.'

I didn't sleep much after that and neither did my baby, to judge by the somersaults it was turning. I suppose my agitation must have affected it. I placed my hands on my belly, reassuring it. 'I won't let any harm come to you,' I whispered. But I knew I wouldn't be able to conceal my pregnancy very much longer. It was becoming all too evident.

◆ ◆ ◆

As the weather improved, we climbed upwards to reach the higher elevations of the trail. Although it was still cold at night, by day the sun blazed down on us unremittingly. Sometimes we would find ourselves walking along a dusty track with clouds floating in the valley beneath us. It was a strange feeling, as if we were walking in the sky.

In places where the valley gathered shreds of clouds in the crook of its arm, we discovered new plants that seemed to survive largely by drinking the water in the air. Skeins of pale jade lichen hung from the trees there – scrubby birch and more rhododendrons – but the landscape was largely bare and dusty now, sparsely clad in low-lying cushion-like growth. The mountains were our constant companions, watching over us from all sides like vast, all-seeing Buddhas as we trekked further into the Khumbu. I could quite understand how the Sherpa people might believe them to be deities.

We climbed into the high valleys, following a milky river that gushed from the mountains as the spring sunshine liberated icy waters that had been stored up in glaciers over the winter. Even in the remotest places where there were no signs of permanent habitation, we still came across Buddhist shrines and carved *mani* stones. At the top of each pass we navigated, there were more heaps of carved rocks, bedecked with tattered prayer flags fluttering in the wind, and I paused at each one to give thanks that I'd made it a little bit further. The trekking was becoming a struggle for me though, and I gasped for breath in the thin air, the steep climbs becoming harder as the secret cargo I carried continued to grow within me. I moved at a pace as ponderous as that of the yaks that now carried the expedition's belongings, the atmosphere up here too thin for horses or mules.

By the middle of May, we reached a series of tranquil lakes at a place called Gokyo. There was much to explore in the surrounding area, so we made camp on a ridge of land between the water and a tumbling glacier. It was a beautiful, peaceful spot and whilst the rest of the party were away foraging, I could sit in the sunshine for hours at a time, sketching and painting, kept company by a tiny snowfinch who hopped from rock to rock in search of seeds and insects. Clouds drifted across the blue of the sky, their reflections floating past a pair of Brahminy ducks who had made the lake their home. The waters lapping at the shore and the sighing of the wind sang a lullaby to my baby as I worked, and I felt some sense of contentment at last. I had welcomed the momentum of the trek up to this point. The feeling of putting one foot in front of the other and moving forwards, away from the horror of my memories of Callum's death, had kept me going. But now I felt something shift within me. Perhaps it was instinct, my body telling me what my baby needed next, or perhaps it was simply exhaustion. I realised I needed to stop, to give myself and my child some rest in order to prepare ourselves for the birth to come in a couple of months' time. And I knew I certainly wouldn't be able to conceal my pregnancy any longer. It was time to confess.

One afternoon, before the others returned from their day's exploring, I asked Mrs Fairburn to walk with me down to the lake shore. We stood watching the ducks for a while, their rust-coloured feathers the only splash of contrast against the turquoise water. I was trying to pluck up the courage to tell Roberta what I had to say, when she began to speak first.

'They're very beautiful creatures, aren't they?' She nodded towards the ducks, which were reaching their bills towards one another as if in a kiss. 'They are believed by Buddhists to be sacred, you know. I've seen them depicted on images of the wheel of life. Legend has it that they're a pair of lovers who committed a sin in a previous life and returned in the form of these birds. They can be together in the daytime but have to separate at sundown and spend the nights calling to one another through the darkness.'

A single tear trickled down my cheek as she turned to me and took my hand. 'I know you are carrying a child, my dear. It's Callum's, isn't it?'

I nodded, unable to speak.

'I began to suspect some time ago. And, let me tell you, I have nothing but admiration for you, Violet. You have exhibited such determination and courage. But I don't think we will be able to conceal your condition from the men any longer. And I don't believe it is in your best interests, nor those of your child, for you to continue with the expedition. Are you about six months on?'

'Nearly six and a half,' I admitted.

'Then we need to make arrangements for you to get home in time for the birth. This environment could be dangerous for you, you know, now we are so high.'

'I realise that. But I feel fitter and stronger than I ever have done in my life. My body seems to be telling me this is a good place for me. I feel a freedom in these mountains that isn't available to me elsewhere.'

'You've done well, I agree. But I'm afraid my husband won't countenance letting you stay with us once he knows. You've been a very valuable addition to the expedition, but this changes everything. The others won't approve either, and it will unsettle the group. Don't worry, though,' she continued as I hung my head in shame – not for my baby, but for the way I'd deceived them all. 'I'll make sure we do right by you. You will receive the pay that's owed you and we'll organise a couple of porters to accompany you back to Lukla. From there you should be able to pick up a guide and travel the rest of the way to Kathmandu on horseback. Use your money to get a flight home. It will be safer for you to have your baby in Britain, whatever you decide to do thereafter.'

A sense of desperation rose within me at her words, constricting my throat so I couldn't speak. I knew she was right, but it felt completely wrong. There was no 'home' for me in Scotland any more. And I could not countenance the thought that I might be pressurised to give up my baby 'thereafter', nor the way Callum's child would be ostracised in that society. I pictured the long route back. I couldn't stay here at Gokyo, but perhaps I could find a place at Namche Bazaar or Lukla where there would be a doctor or a midwife who could assist me. The thought of returning to Kathmandu brought back memories of the stench of a filthy guesthouse room, a smoking funeral pyre and ashes drifting on a dirty river. I would far rather stay in the mountains.

Mrs Fairburn kindly took it upon herself to tell her husband that night, sparing me the ignominy of having to see the look on his face when he heard the news. As it was, he could scarcely look me in the eye when he emerged from his tent before the others were awake early the next morning, and found me sitting by the fire sipping the mint tea Mingma had made me. 'A word, please, Miss Mackenzie-Grant?' he said, already stalking off ahead of me towards the lake as I hurriedly set down my cup and got to my feet, following in his wake.

His wife had kept her promise to make sure I was paid what I was owed. The Colonel kept my dismissal short, handing me a brown envelope of money and telling me he'd ask Mingma to employ two local porters – being unable to spare any of ours – to take me back the way we'd come. 'It would be best if you don't say anything to the men,' he said. 'You can pack up your things and leave once we've set off for the day. I'll tell them the trekking was too much for you and we've had to send you home.'

Thus humiliated, I swallowed my pride and simply nodded, secreting the pay packet in the inner pocket of my coat.

After breakfast, at which I forced myself to choke down a bowl of porridge in preparation for the journey ahead, the others gathered up their collecting equipment and set off in search of alpine plants growing beside the glacier in the adjacent valley. Mrs Fairburn came to find me by my tent and gave me a quick hug goodbye. 'I wish you well, Violet,' she said. 'Here's a little extra for you. Keep it well hidden in case you need it.' She pressed a thick roll of rupees into my hand, waving aside my somewhat half-hearted objections. I knew I'd need all the help I could get.

'Thank you, Roberta,' I whispered. 'I'll never forget how kind you've been to me.'

I thought I saw tears spring to her eyes, but she turned away, a little abruptly, and walked off in the direction of the others without a backward glance.

I was sorry not to be able to say goodbye to Mr Andrews and thank him for his kindness, but he'd scarcely been able to look me in the eye since the night of the hallucinogenic honey incident. I suspect if he came to know about my own state of disgrace it would only disconcert him further, so it was probably better this way.

I was feeling considerably agitated, a few hours later, when there was still no sign of any porters. I certainly didn't want to be there when the Colonel returned, and began to think I'd have to set out on my own. But, at last, two rough-looking men leading a yak arrived in the camp, accompanied by Mingma. As they loaded my belongings and some supplies into the animal's panniers, the guide said, 'I sorry you have to leave, Miss Violet. Take care on journey home. The Colonel say to give you this.' He handed me a map. 'I wish I could take you. These porters not so good, I think, but they the only ones I can find. They go with you as far as Namche and then you find good Sherpa guide there.' He smiled at me kindly, adding, 'No worry, I give them mint leaves, tell them to make you tea for your baby.'

I glanced behind as I followed the porters back to the track, but Mingma was gone. The only other living things in the landscape were the two Brahminy ducks, bowing their heads in their daylight dance as they watched us silently from the mirror-calm surface of the lake.

◆ ◆ ◆

We took a different path to the one on which we'd come up to Gokyo. I was disconcerted at first and tried to ask the porters where we were going, but they seemed to have no English and just looked at me blankly. When I checked my map, I realised it must be a more direct route to Namche Bazaar, following the Dudh Koshi River south. I chided myself silently for not trusting the men. I didn't like the way the shorter of the two hit the yak with the stick he carried, though, nor the sullen look in the eyes of the taller one when his gaze slid over me.

Our progress was slow, and the valley was a narrow one, towered over by a peak marked on my map as Machhermo, in whose shadow we walked. The energy I'd felt previously seemed to have left me, so I was thankful when we arrived at a cluster of small stone buildings beside the river and the porters gestured to me to enter one of them. I'd assumed we'd just be stopping for a short rest, then pushing on, but they tethered the yak and unloaded my belongings from the baskets.

Within the stone shack, I was shown to a room with a lumpy mattress on the floor. 'Are we staying here tonight?' I asked the taller porter. He simply set down my bags, pointed to the makeshift bed, then turned away. 'What about supper?' I called after him, but there was no reply.

I took the time to wash my face and comb my hair, loosening the belt I'd taken to using to fix my skirt around my ever-expanding waist. I'd given up trying to fasten its buttons some weeks previously. The sun had disappeared behind the mountain and the valley was in deep shadow when I pushed aside the curtain that served as a front door and looked out of the shack. From the next-door building came the sound of laughter and a clattering of dishes, so I walked over to peer inside. There were several men – my two porters amongst them – sitting around a table playing some sort of dice game and making inroads into large mugs of drink. From the look of them and the level of noise they were making, I suspected it must be *chhaang*, the locally brewed beer, which I'd heard Mr Andrews and his colleagues on the expedition talk about sometimes, describing it as a filthy, strongly alcoholic brew made from fermented barley. A few others sat, more quietly, at smaller tables around the walls of the room, eating bowls of rice and lentils. The drinkers fell silent for a moment when I appeared, then the taller porter said something and threw the dice he was holding. They all burst out laughing again, returning to their game.

A woman appeared from the kitchen and gestured to me to take a seat in a corner of the room. She set a bowl of food before me and I shovelled it in, keeping my eyes downcast, not wishing to prolong my meal any longer than was absolutely necessary. When I'd finished, I slipped out of the makeshift inn and made my way back to my room. How I wished for a padlock to make fast the bedroom door. But there was none, so I piled my bags beside it to wedge it closed, wrapped myself, still fully clothed, in a blanket and tried to fall asleep. The sounds of carousing from the neighbouring shack continued, growing louder as more drink was consumed, and I lay awake for ages, my eyes wide open, staring into the darkness. At last, in the wee small hours, the noises diminished and then were silenced, to be replaced by the distant rasp of someone snoring and an occasional hacking cough. Thankfully, I let my eyelids close.

I don't know how long I was asleep for, if I'd fallen asleep at all, when suddenly my eyes flew open again at the sound of a stealthy footfall outside the shack. I sat bolt upright, terrified, groping around in the pitch darkness for something I could use as a weapon to defend myself. I had nothing.

There was a quiet tapping on the door. 'Who's there?' I called, cursing the giveaway tremor of fear in my voice.

'Please, Miss. I must talk with you,' came the soft reply in English.

I decided attack might be the best form of defence. 'Who are you? What do you want?' I hissed, kicking aside my bags and throwing open the door.

A man stood there, faintly illuminated in the moonlight, the outline of his hat visible against the doorway.

'My name Palden. I Sherpa, not like those others. I come to tell you there is big danger for you. Those men not good. They drink much *chhaang* and tell others they going to get good money for you from kidnap. Say you have baby coming. They say they can sell baby too, get good price.'

My skin prickled with a fear so visceral it made me almost double over with panic, instinctively folding my arms around my belly.

'Please, Miss, you must trust me. I help you, but we must go now. I take you to my village. My wife can look after you. You safe with us.'

I felt I could trust no one, but my only other option was to set off alone on an unknown mountain path in the darkness, with a pair of kidnappers hot on my heels. So I reached for my coat. The Sherpa picked up my bags and gestured to me to follow him quietly. We crept out into the moonlight, where the snoring continued from the adjacent shack to the accompaniment of the occasional clank of a yak bell as the animals shifted uneasily in the field alongside us. Palden picked up a pannier set against the wall of the inn and tipped out its contents of juniper branches. He stuffed my bags into it and heaved it on to his back, easily shouldering the load.

Then he handed me a stout walking stick to help steady my feet in the darkness and led me down a path leading towards the river.

Once we were a safe distance from the settlement and the noise of the rushing water was loud enough to cover our voices, I asked him, 'Where are we going? Won't those men just follow us?'

He shook his head. 'They not dare. They too much cowards and they know Sherpa people too strong. We go on different path now anyway. Up there.' He pointed across the valley to the opposite hillside.

We crossed a rickety bridge over the river, which foamed white in the moonlight, and plunged into a dense forest of rhododendrons. I had no idea how Palden was able to find his way. The path was a faint track, almost invisible in the darkness. But I plodded on steadily, keeping close behind him as he picked his way along it with ease. We climbed endlessly, up and up, zigzagging between the gnarled branches and their canopy of spreading leaves. I was grateful for their cover, which kept us hidden from anyone who might be watching from the far side of the valley, even though the climb left me gasping for breath.

We emerged on to a contour path just as the first faint light of dawn began to filter through the leaves, and Palden unstrapped the pannier from his shoulders, setting it down in the dust. 'We rest here a bit,' he said, and I sank gratefully on to a rock, my legs almost collapsing under me. He handed me a water bottle and I drank from it deeply, gasping between gulps, my chest still labouring with the effort of the climb. Suddenly, my belly cramped with a sharp pain, and I clasped my hands around it, fear gripping me. I breathed deeply and slowly, making myself relax for my baby's sake. As the muscles released again, my baby gave me a good kick by way of a reminder that I needed to take care of it, reassuring me it was still all right.

'You okay?' Palden said. In the early morning light, I was able to see his face properly for the first time. He had the same friendly features and warm smile as Mingma and I felt a little reassured that perhaps I hadn't leapt out of the frying pan and into the fire in entrusting my safety to him.

I smiled back. 'I'm fine, thank you. Just need to get my breath back a bit.'

'Don't worry no more, Miss. You safe now.' Then he grinned and said, 'You very good climber – almost as good as Sherpa. What your name?'

'Violet,' I replied. 'Like a flower.'

'Violet like a flower,' he repeated after me, nodding. 'We walk easy now. Be there in couple hours.'

'Where is *there*?' I asked, pulling the map out of my coat pocket.

He studied it over my shoulder and then pointed. 'My village is here. Called Phortse.'

As the sun rose high enough behind the mountains to peer at us, we continued on our way towards the Sherpa settlement. At a bend in the path, we paused again to drink some water as the sun climbed higher, bathing the landscape in gold. I took off my coat and Palden put it in his basket, despite my protestations that I could easily carry it. A few steps later, once we'd skirted another carved rock, I stopped in my tracks, astonished at the sight that met us. A hidden valley ran upwards to our left, carpeted with deep-blue flowers, looking for all the world as if a thousand pieces of the sky had tumbled down to form their petals.

'*Meconopsis*,' I said.

He shot me a quizzical look. 'What that mean?'

'The blue Himalayan poppy. On the expedition we spent hours searching for them. But we only found one or two – never anything like as many as this.'

'This Valley of Flowers,' he said. 'We bring yaks here in summer to graze. Collect flowers, mushrooms, leaves for making incense too. Phortse not far now.'

If I survive, I thought to myself, I shall come back here one day.

A few hundred yards further on, the path climbed to a point on the edge of another ridge where a small heap of memorial *mani* stones had been laid. And as we rounded it, the view opened up in front of us and there it was in the distance, bathed in sunlight: the village of Phortse. My first sighting of the place where I sit writing this. The place where – at last – I've been able to find a sanctuary and feel at home.

Palden and his wife, Dawa, have taken me in. I feel safe with them, and they've promised to look after me here for the coming weeks, letting me rest and recover from the trials of the past months until my baby is born. They feed me plates of lentils and rice and the most delicious potatoes I've tasted in a long time, even better than the ones we grew at the gardening school. I'm as round as an egg now and I've jettisoned my old, travel-worn clothes, preferring the traditional Sherpa costume Dawa has lent me, which all the women of the village wear. A silk blouse comes first, covered with a loose sort of pinafore dress, and finally a colourful, striped apron, the *pangden*, is tied around the area where my waist used to be. It's both comfortable and practical.

I spend my days working alongside Dawa and the others from the village, tending the crops of buckwheat and potatoes in the fields and picking mint leaves in the little garden she cultivates behind her house. Children run freely amongst the houses, playing and helping with chores. The sound of their laughter floats on the air, accompanied by the gentle clanking of yak bells and the sough-ing of the winds. From my mountainside perch, I stop often to ease my aching back and give thanks for the kindness of these people who have taken this stranger in when she had nowhere else to go.

My baby kicks and stretches, flexing its muscles, eager now to escape the protective cocoon of my belly. And I wonder at the possibility of a new future as I gaze out at the watchful peaks that hold us in their powerful embrace, and the valley filled with sky beneath us.

Daisy – March 2020

I close Violet's final journal and smile at Dipa, who's been sitting listening to the story of how my great-great-aunt came to end up in Phortse. Several days have passed since my arrival at the lodge, but the snow still lies thickly on the ground outside. It's warm indoors, though, sitting by the stove, and telling Violet's story to Dipa, Tashi and Sonam has helped pass the time as our quarantine ticks by, in the continued absence of any internet connection.

'There's just one more letter too,' I say, unfolding the flimsy sheet of paper. It must be one of the pieces of *lokta* paper Violet bartered for, made here in Nepal, because it's flecked and textured with little pieces of plant material. Violet's handwriting – so familiar from her journals – has blurred where the ink has soaked into the softness of the surface.

Phortse, Nepal

Early in the month of Bhadra

Dearest Hetty,
I write with joyful news! My baby is here, a little girl who arrived on what would have been the 28th of

July in Britain. Here, the Sherpas use another calendar entirely, and I have quite lost track of the days and months.

So you are an aunt again, this time to a niece named Themi. I've called her that because it's the Sherpa name for the little purple irises that push their way out of the dust at these high altitudes with such determination and survive against all the odds. She is utterly beautiful. She arrived quite quickly and without very much fuss. I'd been helping Dawa make tsampa, a flour ground from the buckwheat that is grown in the fields here, and stood up to ease a sudden pain in my back. She glanced up at me, then immediately got to her feet too.

'I'm fine,' I told her, and she grinned, taking my hand.

'You are fine, Violet, and so is your baby who is ready to come now, I think.'

I realised she was right. The pain in my back intensified, then faded a little before returning, redoubled, in the form of a strong contraction. I didn't feel the slightest bit anxious. She'd promised me, in her calm, matter-of-fact way, that she would help me when the time came and together we'd prepared everything in a small stone birthing hut set into the hillside a little way from the village. Over the previous weeks, we'd set kindling for a fire there and brought supplies of water and clean cloths, getting everything ready. Dawa had tied bundles of dried herbs around the walls, too, some to ward off evil spirits and others that are used, she'd told me, to help ease the pains of childbirth and prevent excessive

172

bleeding. As she led the way through the birch trees to the hut that morning, offering me reassurance and her arm to lean on when each contraction washed through my body, I felt a sense of strength and joy. And a few hours later, just as evening fell in the Khumbu valley, my baby drew her first breath, filling a pair of healthy lungs and giving a lusty cry.

I wish I could share her with you, Hetty, but I don't even have a camera to take a picture. I know how much you would love her and how much she would love you back. For the time being, I have no plans to go anywhere else. In spite of the extremes of altitude and isolation – or perhaps because of them – this place is safe, and the Sherpas have welcomed me into their community with such kindness and generosity of spirit. I don't know what the years ahead may hold for me and my daughter, but I think this will be a good place to embark upon the first of them together.

I'm sending you this parcel of my journals so that you may know the details of the journey that has brought me here. Perhaps you can share them with our parents when you feel the time is right, so that they may know the truth too. I'm enclosing some envelopes of seed as well. Please would you give them to Mrs Hanbury at Inverewe, with my kindest regards. I'll be interested to know which of them, if any, can be successfully germinated and cultivated.

I hope you are as happy as I am, that your own new family treats you well and gives you the love you deserve, as we do from afar.

Your sister, Violet, and your new niece, Themi.

◆ ◆ ◆

'The only other thing I have is this little shoe,' I tell Dipa, showing her the cracked, worn leather. 'I suppose it must have belonged to Themi at one point.'

Dipa smiles, picking it up and examining it carefully, before setting it back down beside Violet's letter.

'And now your stories are joined,' she said. 'After so many years separated, you bring them back together here at Phortse.'

'Against all the odds,' I say with a laugh. 'It's been quite a journey, and now I find myself stranded here for a bit, just as Violet did all those years ago.'

'Journey far, but travel within,' she replies enigmatically. Before I can ask her what she means, she continues, 'Phortse best place for you to be right now. This world no good. Virus too dangerous so you stay.'

Tashi comes in, carrying a little incense burner, which he sets on the counter. He lights it outside by the back door of the lodge every morning, to bless the coming day, he's told me, and even though it contains nothing but cold ashes now, it still scents the air in the room with its smoky-sweet perfume. 'You stay,' he echoes his wife. 'But no worry, Mrs Daisy. We will help you when it safe to return.'

'Tomorrow last day of quarantine,' says Dipa, counting on her fingers. 'Then you can meet your cousins. Sister-cousins, brother-cousins. Your Sherpa family.' She shoots me a shrewd look. 'Best of all,' she adds, 'you can meet Themi. Give her back her shoe.'

It takes a moment for what she's just said to sink in. I think I must have misheard her.

'Sorry, did you say Themi?' I ask.

She nods, beaming like a magician who's just pulled a rabbit from his hat. 'Daughter of Violet. Granny to Pema.' She taps her forefinger against the letter on the table between us. 'She old now. Ninety years. Very beautiful still, though, just like her mum was. Day after tomorrow, Pema will take you to visit her.'

Daisy – March 2020

That afternoon, a miracle occurs. A sudden pinging of phones and flashing of screens heralds the return of the Wi-Fi and all of us spend a few hours catching up with messages and news from the outside world. My joy at being able to communicate with my family again is tempered by a string of messages from Sorcha.

Are you there, Mum?

. . .

Where have you got to?

. . .

Can we talk?

. . .

Guess you're out of reception or data or battery or something. Just wanted to let you know things haven't worked out for Mara and me at Dad's. We're driving up to Granny's. Going to be locking down at Ardtuath with her and Davy. All good. Hope you're OK too and somewhere safe. Message us when you can xx

And then a brief and typically to-the-point one from Mara:

Dad's a plonker. We love you, Mum.

While I have to admit to feeling a certain amount of grim satisfaction at that last one, I'm concerned that they have been hurt again by their father's behaviour. I worry too whether they will be able to make the long drive north, presumably through a Britain that is rapidly shutting down, and I imagine roadblocks and police checks preventing people from travelling. I check the latest pandemic updates. The lockdown has taken effect as of today, so they should have made it just in time.

There's a message from my mum too, which I read next:

Delighted to have the girls here with us. Don't worry, will take good care of them. They were upset about their dad kicking them out, but it's time they realised who he really is. Will be good to be locked down together and there's plenty of space for them at the big house now it's empty. It's been way too quiet with the music school closed. They're filling the rooms with their voices and their laughter. Hope you're somewhere safe. Surely this lockdown can't last more than a couple of weeks? Hugs from me, and Davy sends love too xx

I try calling Mum's number and miraculously my call connects. Tears spring to my eyes at the sound of her voice. It feels extraordinary to be able to speak to her again at last, so effortlessly, at the touch of a button.

She reassures me she's feeling much better now, only occasionally pausing when a tight-sounding cough forces her to do so. She answers my torrent of questions: yes, everyone else is fine; the girls are okay, don't worry; they're holed up in rooms at the music school while they, too, keep themselves separate for a period of quarantine to be on the safe side; she and Elspeth have been delivering food to them, leaving it at the door; they talk to each other from a safe distance; Davy's been doing shopping runs in the Land Rover, not just for themselves but for anyone else in the community who can't manage to get out; only one or two others seem to have the virus and they're keeping themselves apart.

'But now tell me your news,' she says. 'I can't believe you've finally managed to get to Phortse! What's it like?'

'It's everything we imagined it would be and more, Mum. I wish you were here too. I think I've found Violet's family. We have so many Sherpa cousins! I'll have to try to work out how we're all connected and add it to the family tree. Best of all, her daughter's still alive. Yes, Themi! She must be ninety now. She has a granddaughter called Pema living in the village too. I'm meeting them tomorrow. I'll send you photos of everything. Don't worry, I'm fine. You keep yourselves safe.'

'That's so exciting! And you sound good, Daisy,' she says. 'Your voice sounds stronger than it has done in ages. Listen,' she continues, 'I'm going to let you go. Call the girls while the internet's working. I know they'd love to talk to you.'

After we hang up, I take a moment to breathe deeply and allow the feeling of relief at being able to speak to her – to reassure myself that they really are all right there – to sing through my veins. Then I call Sorcha's number.

'Mum? Are you there? Oh my God, I can't believe it! Hang on a minute, I'll call Mara. I'm putting you on speaker.' I hear her shout for her sister, the sound of footsteps, a shriek when she tells her, 'It's Mum – on the phone from Nepal!' And then I hear both my girls' voices and this time the tears don't just spring to my eyes but run down my cheeks as well.

'I'm so glad you're there safe and sound,' I say. 'Sorry it didn't work out in London. Want to tell me what happened?'

'Honestly, Mum, this is a much better place to be locked down,' Sorcha replies. 'Granny and Grandad are so cool, and we have fresh air and a whole country mansion to ourselves, filled with musical instruments. Couldn't be better.'

'Dad was a total pain,' Mara chips in. 'After about twenty-four hours of nagging us about not putting our things away because Sorcha dared to leave her laptop on the kitchen table and I was trying to charge my phone on his charger, he told us Claire needs space and we take up too much of it.'

'That's not exactly how he put it,' Sorcha interjects, ever the voice of reason.

'Yeah, I know, but it's basically what he was saying. Honestly, Mum, they made us feel so unwelcome. He was acting so different.'

'Well, it's a stressful time for everyone,' I say. 'Claire's shows will be cancelled and there'll be no work for him either. They'll be worried about your brother Max as well. It won't be good for a wee one being shut away from friends and fun now.'

'Yeah, yeah, we know, Max is his son. But we're his daughters. Honestly, we were talking about it in the car driving north – 'cause we just loaded up our things and headed for Granny's as soon as she said we could come – and we were saying how we saw a completely different side to him. We can totally understand now why you split up from him. He's such a control freak!'

Mara's indignation makes me smile. It sounds a lot healthier than being hurt, even though my twins must be smarting a bit. 'Well, I'm just glad you're at Ardtuath now. It's a good place to be locked down.'

'Anyway,' says Sorcha, 'tell us all about where you are. Have you tracked down Violet?'

'I have! Well, some of her family, anyway.' I fill them in.

'That's, like, so bizarre that we have cousins who are Sherpas, living in the Himalayas,' says Mara.

'Actually, they're called the Himalaya,' Sorcha corrects her.

'Whatever,' her sister replies. 'The Himalaya then. Anyhow, it's totally cool, Mum.'

'Send us photos when you can.'

'We love you . . .'

My girls' voices chime together as they talk over one another.

'I love you too. Take care . . .' And then I realise I'm talking into thin air as the connection has dropped and they've gone.

I notice a new message from Jack has arrived as well while I've been on the phone.

Made it to the Azores. Moored off Sao Miguel. Still not allowed to land, but food delivery (at a distance) and refuelling possible. Are you in the mountains now?

And then there's a photograph of whitewashed houses with red roofs set against a backdrop of lush greenery. He's captioned it with another of his anagrams:

THE EYES – THEY SEE.

I prepare a message to send him later too, Wi-Fi permitting. It's a picture of the pure blue sky outside the window of the teahouse, with Khumbila's snow-capped summit standing tall against it and not a cloud in sight. I add a caption too. *CORONAVIRUS: O, 'AV' NO CIRRUS.* It's the best I can come up with.

◆ ◆ ◆

I'd set the alarm on my phone, not wanting to waste time asleep when new-found freedom beckons with the opportunity to get outside and explore Phortse. But when I come downstairs to the dining room next morning, the sounds of chattering voices interspersed by great gusts of laughter are already coming from the kitchen. I tap on the door and push it open. Several smiling faces turn my way. A woman about my mum's age gets to her feet and hurries over to envelop me in a hug. 'Daisy *Didi*,' she says. 'I'm your cousin Pema. Violet's great-granddaughter.'

The word '*Didi*' seems to be added to the name of anyone close enough to count as a sister-cousin (and '*Dai*' is added for a brother-cousin), so I feel a flush of gratification and pride when Pema – my third cousin, if I've worked it out correctly – refers to me as Daisy *Didi*.

I take both her hands in mine. 'Pema,' I repeat. And then, in a very British manner, I say, 'It's lovely to meet you.' The words don't even begin to cover my emotions. How can it be that I feel so at home, so welcomed and accepted, in a place that couldn't be more foreign and a world that's been turned upside down?

Several others come forward to hug me too. I try to take in their names but am too overwhelmed by it all for now. Dipa herds us through into the dining room where there's far more space and we won't be under her feet as she prepares gallons of tea and piles of pancakes for everyone by way of breakfast. The stove hasn't been lit yet, but the room quickly heats up with smiles and excited chatter, as well as the steaming teacups and warmth of so many bodies, filling the teahouse with life after the quietness and emptiness of quarantine.

My long-lost, new-found family crowds round the table when I pull out the sketchy family tree and several new branches are soon added. There's much discussion and debate as to where each of them fits in and I have to resort to starting a new page to accommodate everyone. It's not so much a tree as a web now, and when it comes to adding Dipa's sister's husband's brother who is married to Pema, thereby connecting in a whole new strand of the family, Tashi brings out a roll of sticky tape so I can add another page out to one side.

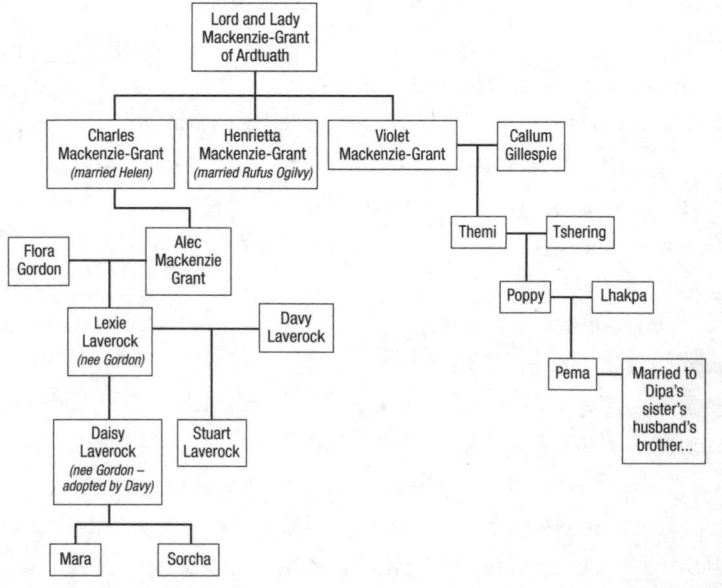

Filling in the spaces gives me the chance to ask questions about what family means to the Sherpa people. 'When the rest of the world talks about Sherpas, they think it means the guides who lead expeditions to the top of Mount Everest,' says Pema. 'But that's wrong. Sherpas are a distinct people. They were from Tibet originally, but they brought their yaks, their language, their faith and their traditions over the mountains from the east to settle here in

Nepal. And because they're so well adapted to living and working at high altitudes, they've gained a reputation for being the best guides to lead climbers wanting to reach the summits.'

'Number one best guides, like I told you,' Tashi interjects. 'This not something Sherpas very comfortable with though. Standing on heads of our mountain gods and goddesses disrespectful. Brings bad *karma*.'

Pema nods. 'Violet saw many changes here in her lifetime, and my grandmother, Themi, can tell you more.'

'And Themi is Scottish, like me?' I ask, pointing at the family tree. 'The daughter of Violet and Callum.'

'Yes, but she honorary Sherpa. Grew up at Phortse. And she marry Sherpa too,' says Tashi. 'She our sister-cousin, Themi *Didi*. Granny to us all.'

'It was rare in those days for the Sherpa people to marry anyone outside their own community,' Pema explains. 'But it's a bit more common now. We've become integrated, haven't we, Dipa? Dipa is a member of the Rai tribe,' she explains, 'so we're both outsiders in a way.' She smiles across at her sister-cousin, who is busily piling more pancakes on to my plate. Then she pushes a jar of honey towards me, urging me to eat. Thankfully, it doesn't seem to be the hallucinogenic variety.

'But you both make good choice, marry Sherpa men,' Tashi beams, reaching across the table to drizzle some more honey over the pile of pancakes on his own plate.

Luckily for me, everyone speaks at least a little English here. Pema's is particularly good, I suppose because Violet and Themi must have spoken it at home. When I ask her about it, she smiles. 'You're right, my great-granny, my grandmother and my mother made sure I learned English as well as Sherpa and Nepali when I was growing up. They wanted me to be able to choose where I lived. Somehow, though, we've all chosen to stay here. It has its challenges, as you've already seen, living at the limits of human endurance. But the world is a crazy place, and here, it seems to me, we are more concerned with the things that really matter. I guess having to work hard just to survive tends to focus the mind.'

'Is your mother still living here in the village?' I ask, pulling the family tree towards us and pointing at the name 'Poppy' that sits beneath Themi's name.

She shakes her head. 'No, she and my dad died many years ago,' she says softly. 'And once someone has gone, we don't say their names. Or if we do, we then say *Om mani padme hum*, as a blessing for their departed souls.'

I want to ask her more about her parents, but Dipa and Tashi begin to clear away the plates and teacups and Pema stands up, pulling on her quilted jacket. 'Are you ready, *Didi*?' she asks. 'Come and meet your cousin Themi.'

The others remain in the teahouse, catching up with the rest of the news from the outside world that Tashi and Soman have brought from Kathmandu, while I follow Pema up the path that runs to one side of the teahouse. The morning sunshine has melted most of the snow from the fields now and the people working yak dung into the soil to replenish it ready for this season's crops call out a greeting of *Tashi delek* as we pass. It's the Sherpa equivalent of *Namaste*, Pema tells me.

I'm quickly out of breath, and Pema slows her pace a little as we climb the path towards the monastery at the highest point of the village. A baby yak watches us with big eyes, its mother busily cropping the longer grass along the edge of the stone wall as we pass. We stop to watch a helicopter fly up the valley below us. 'They're running an emergency service only now,' Pema says. 'Just rescues and delivery of essential supplies. All the climbing expeditions have been cancelled.'

A series of stone steps continues upwards past a brightly painted prayer wheel towards the monastery, where giant prayer flags wave against the backdrop of the mountains, but instead of climbing them, Pema leads me on to a left-hand fork of the path, which follows the contour of the hill. We're above most of the other houses now. Up here there are just a few low-built stone cottages. Several look uninhabited, judging by their closed-up windows and doors. One, however, has a wisp of smoke issuing from a hole in its roof. Pema walks over to it and calls out, announcing our arrival.

And then she appears, drawing aside the traditional cloth curtain, with its appliquéd geometric design, that serves as a door covering: Violet's daughter, Themi. She's small and stooped, the years having bent and gnarled her slight figure like a rhododendron branch, and she wears the traditional Sherpa dress and apron. Her pure-white hair is twisted into a braid and a pair of coral and turquoise earrings dangle against her wind-reddened cheeks. My throat constricts so tightly I can't speak as she takes my hands in hers. Her smile crinkles her beautiful face into a thousand creases as she gazes at me with a pair of clear hazel eyes.

Without a word, she leads me inside and pats the brightly striped blanket on the bench, gesturing to me to sit down. She stands back, scrutinising me again for a long moment, and then says, in an accent that still carries a faint Scottish lilt, her voice soft with age, 'So you came to find us at last. You are very welcome, Daisy *Didi*.'

She and Pema build up the fire to make tea, giving me time to take in my surroundings. There's no stove in Themi's one-room home, just a low fireplace at one end, built from stones and mud. There's no chimney either, just a hole in the roof to let the smoke out, and I wonder how bitterly cold it must get in the depths of winter. The walls and ceiling of the simple stone dwelling are completely blackened with soot. In one corner is a low sleeping platform made of rough wooden planks, upon which sits a lumpy mattress covered in a pile of quilts and blankets. A small table stands beside the bench on which I sit, but there's no other furniture apart from a battered trunk and a large plastic drum, which, I imagine, must hold Themi's clothes. Everything else she owns is arranged on shelves lining the walls. I notice how, in the dim light entering through the age-frosted windows, every pot, pan and plate gleams, spotlessly clean against the soot-blackened stones.

Pema has begun stoking the fire with juniper twigs to rekindle it, but Themi waves her aside and sets about making tea the Sherpa way, her movements a fluid dance of familiarity. She pours water from a jerrycan into a pot and places it above the flames, then throws in a handful of tea leaves, some sugar and a good glug of milk. The whole lot is boiled up together and then she decants it into a tin kettle before pouring it through a strainer into cups. It's nothing like the tea I'm used to, but the strong, sweet concoction warms and energises. I feel the chill in my bones begin to ease, and the heavy tightness in my cold muscles lifts a little, as if someone has switched on my internal central heating.

I spread the newly extended family tree on the table before us and Themi asks about my mum and Davy, about my brother, Stuart, and his family, and about my girls. I pull out my phone and show her pictures of her long-lost relations in Scotland and she nods her approval at each one, her face crinkling in delight. 'We thought we must still have a Scottish family, didn't we, Pema? Although Violet didn't talk about them much. She always said her life was here in Nepal.'

I wonder, fleetingly, about saying Violet's name. Maybe it's okay if she wasn't born a Sherpa, or perhaps it's all right to say *Om mani padme hum* in our heads, because it seems to be acceptable to talk about her. There are so many questions I want to ask, I hardly know where to begin. So I start by pulling the tiny shoe from my pocket and placing it alongside the family tree. 'This was in the chest where I found Violet's journals and letters.'

Themi picks it up, a look of wonder spreading across her features. She gets to her feet and crosses the room to the fireplace. I hadn't noticed it before, but there's a little niche set into the stones forming the back wall of the house, camouflaged by the years of accumulated soot. She reaches into it. Then she returns to the table and sets the shoe's twin down beside it. The leather is cracked and blackened with age, but it's unmistakeably the other half of the pair.

'These shoes were mine,' she says. 'My mother told me my Aunt Hetty sent them out to us when I was born. I wore them when I learned to walk, but quickly outgrew them. So my mother put the single shoe in the wall. She said it was a Scottish tradition, to protect us from evil spirits and keep us safe. I never knew what happened to the other shoe. But now here it is. You have reunited us with it, just as you've reunited us with our Scottish family, Daisy *Didi*. Thank you.'

'I guess Violet must have sent it back to Hetty for safekeeping. There were envelopes of seeds in the box with all the papers, too. And some of her paintings of wildflowers.'

'Did you bring them with you as well?' asks Themi, her eyes bright with curiosity.

I shake my head. 'No, the seeds were ruined and the pictures are still in the library at Ardtuath. But we can send them to you if you like.'

She smiles. 'You will bring them next time you come, maybe?'

Her words take me by surprise. I'd always thought of this trip as a one-off, the holiday of a lifetime. It hadn't occurred to me that finding family here has set in place new connections, like strings of prayer flags stretching across the miles, linking us forever. 'Next time,' I say. And I grin, thinking how Mum and my girls would love to meet their Sherpa cousins.

'Now,' Themi says. 'Pema will make us some more tea and I will tell you what I know of my mother's life here in Phortse.'

I pull out a pen and a pad of paper to take notes so that I can transcribe them later and send them to Mum. And then, in that little one-roomed house, as the flames dance and leap in the fireplace and the mountain wind whispers outside against the stones, carrying upon it the voices of long-departed souls, she begins to tell me the rest of Violet's story.

When it's time to go, she holds up a hand and says, 'Wait.' She goes over to the large plastic drum in the corner and begins to unscrew the top. Her arthritic hands can't get a proper grip, though, so Pema helps her.

'These drums were once used by climbing expeditions to transport food and equipment up to Everest Base Camp,' Pema explains. 'Nowadays, though, they use weatherproof bags. So we've recycled the bins. You'll find one in just about every house in Phortse. They make good storage, stop the damp getting in.'

Themi reaches into the drum and brings out a plastic bag. 'Here,' she says. 'Take these away and read them.'

She and Pema smile as I look up at them in wonder. Because the bag contains a small pile of notebooks, made from *lokta* paper. And I realise I'm holding in my hands the next instalment of Violet's journals.

Violet's Journal

Thursday, 17th October, 1929

Today is the first day of the month of Kartik, in the season of Sharad or early autumn. This is a beautiful time of year, perhaps made all the more so by the fact that Hemanta and Shishir – the seasons of late autumn and winter – will soon be here. I think I'm looking forward to my first Himalayan winter with equal measures of fascination and trepidation. My main consideration will be keeping Themi warm and well fed.

My baby flourishes. She's a darling, loved by everyone in the village and passed from arm to arm by the Sherpa mothers who are helping me learn how to raise my child. Dawa and Palden continue to help and support me. Their kindness and generosity are quite astonishing, and I must confess I feel closer to them than I ever have to my own parents. How can it be that these two people, who've only known me for a few months, so readily welcome my presence in their lives? Perhaps it's simply the Sherpa way. Acceptance is an important foundation of their faith and that enables them to focus on the day-to-day challenges of having a warm shelter and food on the table each evening. Surviving in this place, on the very edge of human endurance, strips away any unnecessary pretensions and preoccupations.

It's the season of the harvest and, whilst the nights are bitterly cold, the days are awash with warm sunlight. I turn my face to it, knowing I'll store these golden moments away, just as we store away our caches of foodstuffs, to help sustain me in the months ahead. We work in the fields every day gathering in the crops, digging up the potatoes and preserving everything we can forage in preparation for winter, and all the while Themi snuffles and coos contentedly, tied to my back in a shawl of soft yak's wool.

When we're not working in the fields, Dawa and I carry arm-loads of washing down to the ice-cold river in the valley far below the village and then lug them back up again, damp and heavy, to be spread in the sun to dry. Fetching water is another daily chore, as is gathering juniper twigs and yak dung for fuel, and preparing and cooking meals. And so I hardly have a moment to think and I fall into my bed each night to sleep in the sweet oblivion of exhaustion. But I welcome that because, at the moment, focusing on the simple tasks that need doing each day helps me to walk through the pain and grief of losing Callum. It's the way we do things here in the mountains: slowly, slowly, one foot in front of the other.

It's hard and sometimes lonely too. But the reward for this hardship is a freedom to be myself, unlike any I've known before.

When the harvest is safely in, I will ask Palden to show me the way back to the valley filled with flowers. This will be the perfect time to start mapping the botany there and to collect seeds from the purple cranesbill and blue poppies that I saw growing there in such profusion back in the spring.

Daisy – April 2020

The next day I wake up early. Something's different, but it takes me a few moments to work out what it is. And then I realise. Instead of the mutterings of the wind walkers, carried on the constant buffeting of the wind against the walls of the house, there is silence. The air in my bedroom is milder too and so where usually I would pull the blankets around me and linger in bed, reluctant to brave the bitter cold, I jump up and pull on my clothes. Downstairs, the others are still asleep. I let myself out, quietly pulling the door closed behind me, and walk a little way up the hill.

At the top of the village, I perch on a wall beneath a string of faded prayer flags and look around. This view can't have changed much since Violet's day, and I feel closer than ever to her as I take in the sights and sounds of the village as it awakens. A raven calls from the branches of a birch tree, asking 'Why? Why?' and I remember one of Jack's anagrams: SILENT = LISTEN.

Most of the snow has melted now at this level and the fields are a rich brown, ready for planting. The sky overhead is still empty of clouds and aeroplane trails, and the wall of soaring white peaks dazzles against it. The first wisps of smoke drift from chimneys here and there, suddenly blooming into unruly billows as the kindling takes, before the fires begin to blaze with more heat and the smoke-swirls fade to a faint haze. The sun pulls itself above the ridge line and I hear the calling of birds and the faint clank of yak bells as the animals rouse themselves and begin to graze. I lift my face to the warmth of the new day, basking in the golden light.

A woman emerges from her house, tying on her apron, and then brushes her long black hair, twisting it into a braid and pinning it at the nape of her neck. She pulls the loosened strands from the brush, casting them away for the birds to use as nesting material, then shakes out a blanket and spreads it over a wall to air in the sun, before disappearing back behind the cloth curtain covering the doorway of her house. A man passes just below me on the path, carrying a bamboo basket of fodder on his back as he goes to feed his yaks, gently nudging aside the babies who crowd round him with curiosity as he approaches. Then the first sounds of Dipa busying herself with her pots and pans in the teahouse kitchen reach my ears, and I climb down from the wall and go to see if I can lend a hand with the breakfast.

The Wi-Fi is working well today and I'm able to send my email to Mum with what Themi has told me so far of Violet's life here. I push my luck, sending a few photos of the village as well, but am expecting no response as it must be the middle of the night in Scotland. So I almost jump out of my skin when my phone actually rings with an incoming call.

'Mum!' I say, excited to hear her voice again. 'What are you doing up at this time? Sorry if I woke you.' But the smile on my face quickly fades at her quavering words.

'Daisy, my darling, it's so good to hear you. But we're worried about Davy. He's caught the virus. He's been feeling bad for a few days, but then yesterday he was really struggling to breathe. We managed to get an ambulance to come, and they've got him in the hospital now. I'm not allowed to go and see him, though.' Her voice breaks with worry and exhaustion and she starts to cry.

'Mum . . . it's okay.' But it's not okay and my words sound hollow, even to my own ears.

There's a silence at the end of the line and then I hear her take a deep breath, trying hard to compose herself. 'It's so frightening, Daisy. This awful disease. We all feel so helpless. I can't get through to the hospital, the phone just keeps ringing and ringing. They must be overwhelmed, trying to cope.' I hear her hold the handset away as she chokes, coughing and crying again.

'I'm sure he'll be all right,' I say, although the words are empty platitudes, of course, because I have no idea at all whether or not he will. I try to sound more convincing than I feel, making my voice as strong as I can so it carries hope and reassurance to her over the thousands of miles that separate us. 'You know how tough he is. And he's in the best place to be well looked after. You still need to rest, yourself, you know. But he'll be back soon.'

She sniffs back her tears. 'I know, my love. Sorry, it's just getting to us all at the moment.'

'I'll try to come home, Mum,' I say, suddenly needing to be with her.

'No,' she says, her tone sharper. 'Stay where you are. You're safer there. I don't think you can travel anyway, but even if you can you'll be putting yourself at risk.'

I feel so useless, unable to be there when she needs me, and I swallow down the hard lump of emotion rising in my throat.

After a few moments' silence, Mum's voice comes through again, softer this time. 'Honestly, Daisy, please don't try to come home just now. Things will be better soon, surely. It helps me knowing you're safe and well. Just sit it out and wait until the Foreign Office says it's okay to travel again. Promise me?'

I sniff hard, then say, 'I promise. Oh Mum, I miss you so much. I wish I was there with you. Keep me posted, won't you?

And send my love to Davy if you manage to get through. He'll call you the minute he can, I know.'

She's quiet again.

'Are you still there?' I say.

'Yes, still here.' She sounds so tired, so weak. So unlike herself.

'Get some sleep, Mum,' I tell her. 'You need to look after yourself so you can take care of everyone else.'

'Okay, Daisy,' she replies. 'I love you.'

'I love you too, Mum.' Reluctantly, I ring off, not wanting to cut the tenuous thread that links us.

A few minutes later, a message pings on my phone from her. *Sorry, just tired. And everything always seems worse in the middle of the night. Going to get some sleep now. Take care xx.*

I send her one back, but the ticks beside it remain faint, showing she hasn't opened it. I hope it's because she's resting. I push my phone into my jacket pocket and follow Dipa and Sonam outside to help break the newly thawed ground in the field below the lodge so we can sow this season's crop of buckwheat.

Violet's Journal

News trickles through from the outside world only sporadically. Hetty writes of the financial struggles many are facing after the Wall Street Crash of last autumn. Her own situation has been affected, with Rufus having to sell the estate in Scotland. Although they do still have the London house and can always go north to stay at Ardtuath with Charles and Helen, so they've not been hit as hard as some. Apparently, the stock market crash has done nothing to improve Charles's humour!

Hetty asks whether I might come home now and bring Themi back to meet her family. Truthfully, though, I feel more at home here in Phortse, especially if there's little or no prospect of employment for me in Britain the way things are there at the moment. And whilst I miss my sister terribly, I know my parents and brother wouldn't welcome me back. A while ago, I plucked up the courage to write a letter to Callum's parents, telling them about their grand-daughter, but have received no reply. It's possible it never reached them, of course, but I suspect the truth is they want nothing to do with me. So I'm making a new family for myself amongst the

Sherpa people, who have shown me more acceptance and support than I ever knew in the society I've left behind.

Today has been a real red-letter day. Having spent the winter living with Palden and Dawa, keeping my baby warm, well fed, and cuddled from dawn to dusk, Themi and I have moved up the hill today to the top of the village. Palden explained they own a little cottage just below the monastery, where his grandmother used to live. She's long gone now, and the place has been standing empty for years. 'But if you want it, you can live there,' he announced last week. 'Weather getting better now. You and Themi need space for yourselves.'

Dawa, who was bouncing Themi on her knee, singing her a song, looked up and said sternly, 'But you come visit every day and I visit you. See Themi *Didi*.'

I could scarcely believe my luck. A home of our own! We went up to take a look at it that afternoon, and Palden prised away the boards that had covered the door and windows. It's a tiny 'but and ben', as we say in Scotland, although with just one room, and I fell in love with it at first sight, despite the soot-blackened walls, the rough slate roof with quite a lot of daylight showing through it, and the rook's nest that lurked in one corner of the single room. Dawa helped me clean it and gave me a mattress and some blankets. Once we'd lit a fire of juniper in the rough fireplace and she'd added a good handful of fragrant incense, the fustiness was dispelled and the place felt a good deal cosier. Best of all, the two small windows, with wooden shutters for me to close at night, offer a view over the village and across the valley to where the great hulk of Khumbila watches over us all protectively.

And so here I sit, writing this by the light of a butter lamp, with my baby sleeping in her crib, cocooned in the softest yak's wool. She snuffles contentedly now and then, her little hands opening and closing like the petals of flowers as she dreams. Our simple house may be described as basic, at best, but it reminds me of the bothy where I spent that night with Callum and the memory helps connect me to him. I talk to Themi about her daddy every day, keeping him with us.

Spring is coming. I'll be able to resume my plant-hunting once more and send the illustrations I've painted through the winter back to Hetty to see if she can find buyers for them. She's spoken to the Keeper of the Herbarium at Kew, who says they'll take any specimens I can send them. She's sent the prettiest pair of fine leather shoes for Themi. They were supposed to be a present for Christmas but only arrived a week ago. I've put them away for now, to await the time when my baby begins to crawl and then walk, as she starts to make her own way in the world one step at a time, just as her mother is doing.

Daisy – April 2020

The news of Davy isn't good the next day. Mum sends me a message to say he's been moved into intensive care, and I'm so upset that I can't sit still.

Jack's been in touch, sending messages of support. Elspeth's told him the news about Davy. I message him back, grateful to have a friend I can talk to, one who understands:

> *Can't bear to think of them going through this and not be there to help. I think I was definitely wrong to carry on with this trip. I should have turned back when I could.*

After a few minutes a message comes back:

> *You made the right decision, based on the information available to you at the time. From your mum and Davy's points of view, it was exactly the right thing to do. They would never have wanted you to cancel.*

Then a second one pings on to my screen, another one of Jack's anagrams, as an afterthought:

> *And anyway, WRONG = GROWN.*

I'm tempted to call him, suddenly overcome with the longing to hear his voice. But he doesn't pick up my reply of a series of emojis, so I know the connection between Nepal and wherever-he-is-now in the mid-Atlantic must have dropped.

I'm still full of anxious energy and want to put it to use labouring in the fields, but Dipa tells me there's nothing for us to do there today. So once I've finished breakfast I go in search of Pema. Her house is just below the lodge, a low, whitewashed cottage with a dark green tin roof, enclosed by a neat stone wall. Bedding has been spread out along the wall to air in the sunlight and a pile of yak dung discs is stacked between the posts holding up a little porch. I call out and Pema emerges from behind the door curtain. Her hug is very welcome, and I cling to her for several seconds. She draws back and looks at me searchingly. 'Is something the matter, Daisy *Didi*?'

I explain to her about Davy and she ushers me inside, sitting me down at her kitchen table and bringing me a cup of mint tea. 'I'm so sorry you have this news. It's hard for you, being so far away. But you are with your Sherpa family, and we will take care of you. Your mum will be happier knowing this, I think.'

Once we've finished our tea, she gets to her feet. 'Let's go and see my grandmother. I've made her an apple pie. She's always a good person to talk to when you have worries.'

As we climb towards Themi's house, Pema encourages me to talk about Davy. I find myself telling her how he's the only father I've ever known and the best one I could ever have asked for. I've loved going out in the boat with him since I was tiny. He taught me about the sea, about its moods and its power, and he showed me how – if you respect it – it will give you the best sense of freedom. I remember watching the spray fly like diamonds on the sunlit air as his boat ploughed through the waves, how he pointed out a pair of eagles soaring overhead and we saw dolphins dancing in the bow wave.

I share with her, too, the memories I have of a day when we climbed the hill above Ardtuath House and a thick mist unexpectedly closed in around us, scaring me. He picked me up and put me on his shoulders, taking long, loping steps through the heather and telling me I was a giant with my head in the clouds, to make me laugh. And then, as we reached the top, the mist swirled and lifted, and the sunlight played a magic trick. 'Look at that, Daisy,' he told me, pointing to where a giant's shadow was being cast over the hillside across from us, surrounded by a strange rainbow halo. 'It's called a Brocken spectre. An incredible sight, isn't it? It's just the light and the mist making an illusion.' He lifted me from his shoulders and set me on the ground so that I could cast a Brocken spectre of my own, alongside his. Our elongated, rainbow-encircled shadows looked to me like angels, and we waved our arms and danced, laughing as the strange, otherworldly figures copied us, the rings of light around their heads shifting and weaving across the hill.

Pema listens, smiling and asking me the occasional question as we continue slowly up the hill with frequent pauses for me to catch my breath. Walking and talking at altitude still isn't easy for me. When I describe the Brocken spectre, she nods. 'We sometimes see that here too, although it's quite a rare sight,' she says. 'Long ago, our forebears thought it was the shadow of the Yeti, because surely no human shadow could look like that.'

When we reach the fork in the path leading towards Themi's house, Pema says, 'Let's go up to the monastery first,' pointing to the steps leading higher still. I follow her a little reluctantly, resenting the additional climb, my lungs labouring in the thin air like a pair of bellows. But it's worth it when we get to the top. The brightly painted building has prayer wheels set into its walls and

Pema tells me to do as she does, setting them spinning. 'The prayers are for all,' she says. 'But today we send them out into the world especially for Davy. For your mum also.'

Up here, at the highest point in the village, the fields and houses stretch out beneath us to where the terraces suddenly drop away at the valley's edge. Huge white banners, inscribed with prayers, are hung on poles in front of the monastery, shifting languorously in the faint breeze, and the slopes above us are festooned with hundreds of strings of the smaller, more colourful prayer flags.

All those prayers, all those hopes, all those blessings, I think. *Please let them work for Davy. And for everyone else who's suffering in this terrible pandemic . . . the people who are ill and the families who are afraid. We're all in this together, no matter who or where we are.* I feel strangely comforted by that thought as Pema leads the way down from the monastery to Themi's little house. And it's a welcome distraction to sit on chairs pulled out into the sunshine, eating apple pie and drinking tea with my Sherpa cousins as Themi reminisces further about her mother, telling me stories of what she and her family endured when she was growing up.

One of Themi's favourite places was the Valley of Flowers, she tells us. She loved the days when Violet would take her there in search of more plants. They'd pack a picnic and then Violet would help Themi on with her little backpack before shouldering her own bigger one filled with her painting things and equipment for mapping and collecting specimens. Then she'd stride off up the path with Themi trotting in her wake.

'I learned to help identify some of the flowers,' Themi says. 'And I loved spotting my namesakes, the little irises that grow out of the rocks and dust above the path.'

They'd always stop at the water-driven prayer wheel marking the entrance to the valley to pay their respects to the deities that were all around them, in the mountains and the plants and the river. Then they'd follow the faint tracks made by musk deer and *tahr* – the mountain goats that inhabited the valley – winding their way upwards towards the rocky headwall.

'There were snow leopards too, living in that place,' Themi says. 'We would see their droppings, matted with the hair of their prey, and when I saw them I'd hurry along to walk a little closer to my mum, knowing I must look like a tasty morsel to those powerful creatures watching us, unseen, from the crags above.'

'They're still there,' Pema added. 'Only now they have baby yaks to feed on too. Herders take their animals into the valley in the summer and have built some huts up there. They've made stone walls to enclose their yaks safely at night, but even the prayer flags they put round them don't always keep the snow leopards at bay. I'll take you there one day soon if you'd like to see it.'

Themi tells me Violet spent several years methodically mapping the hidden valley, cataloguing the rich diversity of plants that thrived there. Her eyes grow misty with her memories as she talks, remembering her childhood. 'The best time was just after the early-summer monsoon, when the flowers blossomed. The ground would be carpeted with pink and purple and white blooms, and huge bumblebees drifted among them, drunk on the nectar. My favourites were the blue poppies, which looked like little bits of fallen sky, nodding on their tall stems, brushing our skirts as we passed by. I loved picking bunches of flowers to bring home and put on the table. But my mother would always tell me to be careful not to pick too many, to take just one bloom here and there so that the plants would be able to set seed and survive to grow again the following year. She herself got far more excited about the tiniest and shyest plants she found growing further up the valley walls – saxifrages and gentians and a much smaller variety of the blue poppy, which huddled close to the ground set in a rosette of spiky-looking leaves.

'She'd mark the precise locations of the most interesting plants on her map so we could come back in the autumn and gather some of the seed to send back to Britain. And then she'd spread a blanket on the ground and get out her sketchbook and her paints to capture them in pictures while I hunted for mushrooms and gathered bags of sweet-smelling leaves to dry for making incense.'

Themi cuts herself another sliver of apple pie and tops up our teacups before continuing. 'Those days in the Valley of Flowers were the best ones of all. But life wasn't always that idyllic. We had to work hard just to scrape by. Even as a young child, I would have to go out and collect yak dung to dry for the fire or to make into discs for cooking with. And every so often we'd have to put our packs on our backs and trek down to Namche Bazaar to sell the incense we'd made in the market there so we could buy supplies of salt and rice, which my mother would lug back home. As a result of carrying those heavy sacks, she suffered terribly from back pain, and although she never complained, there were days when she could hardly stand.'

Themi gazes across to where a pure-white rhododendron grows at one end of the house. 'She was like that tree,' she says, pointing a gnarled finger towards it. 'Her body became twisted and old, but she was still beautiful. And there was always an indomitable life force within her, which never stopped blooming until the day she died. No matter how hard life got, no matter what fate threw our way, she kept going, didn't she, Pema? She said life is like trekking: it's hard sometimes, but just keep putting one foot in front of the other, until you finally reach a place where you can see the sky beneath you.'

She looks exhausted, suddenly, and sadness casts a shadow across her face like a cloud passing in front of the sun. I think of the family tree and wonder what happened to Pema's parents – Themi's daughter, Poppy, and her son-in-law, Lhakpa. But just as I'm about to ask, Pema stands up and collects together our cups and plates, signalling it's time to leave.

'We'll see you tomorrow, Granny,' she says. 'Time for you to rest now.'

And so my question must wait for another day.

◆ ◆ ◆

Thankfully, the calmer weather stabilises communications with the outside world and I'm able to call Mum every day to get updates on how Davy is doing. The news is frustratingly unchanging: he's still in intensive care and they're keeping him sedated for much of the time as they try to help his body fight the virus. Mum tells me the nurses have been wonderful, letting her make video calls to their own phones so she can see Davy and speak to him on the rare occasions when he's awake. He can't talk, but she's seen him smile a little behind the mask that pumps oxygen into his lungs to keep him breathing.

'I just want to hold his hand,' she tells me, her voice cracking. 'It's horrible not being able to hug him and look after him. But at least he knows how much we love him and are longing to have him home again.'

My heart aches with helplessness, wanting to comfort her, wishing I could be with them. The pandemic is taking its toll – not just physically but in the devastating loneliness and isolation it's inflicting on humanity. How could we ever have imagined finding ourselves in this situation?

I think of Jack, too, sailing his boat across the miles of ocean. In the past, he and I would have been considered the risk-takers. But now it feels as if we're the lucky ones, safe from contamination, in places where we have a sense of purpose to keep ourselves distracted. It must be far worse for those who are locked down in their homes, cut off from their loved ones and living with the ever-present fear of the invisible threat that lurks beyond those closed doors.

I've made myself a little routine. Each morning before breakfast, I walk up to my viewpoint at the wall beside the prayer flags and give thanks, for the millionth time, that at least my girls are safe at Ardtuath and can comfort Mum while Davy's in the hospital.

I feel guilty, though, that my presence in the village is putting an added strain on its already scant resources and after a few more days I ask Tashi if it would be better for me to leave. I could trek back to Namche Bazaar on my own, then see if I could get accommodation there and sort out transport back to Kathmandu. But he tells me, 'No one go anywhere now. Government says to stay put. Not good in the world right now.' Then he reassures me. 'No worry, *Didi*. You stay here with us to be safe. And you help in fields, so you earn food like all of us.'

He waves his phone at me. 'Anyway, we just hear they sending helicopter to drop supplies every week. Keep us going. After the earthquake,' he tells me, 'Phortse completely cut off for months, all through winter. Whole country badly affected and no supplies getting through because roads and tracks have been destroyed. We living outside, sleeping in tents in snow. Your old cousin Themi too, she afraid to be in her house in case more earthquakes come. Then, once we have managed to build homes up again, we all work together to make place for helicopters to land. So can receive supplies that way if needed.' His phone flashes and he checks the incoming message. 'Ha! It coming now. You want to go see?'

I follow him past the school, along a path through the rhododendrons to where the hillside flattens out a little before falling away steeply to the valley floor below us. A flat stone circle has been constructed, just big enough to land a helicopter on. A few other villagers have gathered there too. After a few minutes, we hear the faint beat of the propellor blades and then the helicopter comes into view, flying up the valley beneath us. It soars higher, the noise reverberating from the mountainsides as it comes to hover above the helipad.

'We not allowed to help. Must stand back,' Tashi explains. 'Let pilot unload first so no risk of virus.'

A heap of sacks and boxes are offloaded, and the pilot gives us a cheery salute before climbing back into the cockpit and taking off again. Then we file down to the helipad and collect up the supplies.

'We bring to community centre,' says Tashi. 'Then everyone can get their share.'

Later in the day, I go with Tashi and Sonam to carry rice, bread and powdered milk up the hill to Themi's house. She emerges, grinning broadly at the sight of such a bounty, and insists on making us all tea. 'Sit, sit. I found something I wanted to show you, Daisy,' she says. From a tin box on one of the shelves, she brings out a sheet of thick paper, torn from a sketch pad, and passes it across to me. 'My mum painted that. I know she'd want you to have it.'

It's exquisite. A painting of a poppy, its petals the colour of sky and in its centre a circle of fine, sun-gold stamens. I can just make out the writing, in Violet's familiar script, in one corner. *Meconopsis grandis. (Betty's Dream)*.

Themi pours the tea and settles herself on the bench beside me, picking up her cup to take a sip.

'One day, an expedition came through the village. It was led by a well-known plant-hunter called George Sherriff and comprised a number of men plus his wife, Betty. They set up their camp just below the house here, and Violet was pleased to be able to talk to them and get news from the outside world. She showed them some of her paintings and said she could help him with his expedition, but George Sherriff was very dismissive of her. He didn't believe a woman could really know enough about plants to identify new species. He was an army man, used to giving orders, and he wanted to be the one to make the discoveries.

'Violet liked his wife, Betty, though. She was a kind woman. I remember her teaching me songs in English and she gave my mother some of the medicines and bandages they'd brought with them so we could use them for people in the village who needed them. Betty told Violet that, to be honest, she was getting a bit tired of trailing around after her husband and his men and then being left on her own while they went off exploring, but that George wouldn't rest until he'd found a new variety of the famous Himalayan blue poppy. He was jealous of another plant hunter, Frank Kingdon Ward, who'd already discovered a few, and wanted a poppy with his own name on it. And so the two women hatched a plan. Violet took Betty to the Valley of Flowers and showed her a place where this beautiful flower could be found.' Themi points at the painting in my hands.

'The women knew George Sherriff wouldn't take kindly to being told where the poppy grew, though, it had to be his own discovery. And so when he returned to the camp, Betty told him she'd had the most extraordinary dream the night before. In it, she'd walked up the hill and discovered a hidden valley full of flowers, where a poppy with petals the colour of sky grew. And she persuaded him it was such a vivid dream that he should go and have a look. He returned triumphant. And he declared he would take the seeds home and name the poppy *Betty Sherriff's Dream*, which he did. My mother had already painted this picture, but she added the new name beneath it, to remember how the two women had allowed him to have his wish of making the discovery. It was their secret.'

I pick up the painting to look at it more closely. 'I think I read about that story. It's a bit of a legend among gardeners who love growing Himalayan poppies. But it should have been named after Violet!' I say indignantly.

Themi smiles. 'Don't worry,' she says. 'Betty Sherriff made sure my mother received a payment for the discovery. And the medical supplies she gave us for the village were worth more to Mum than the fame would have been. She enjoyed knowing the secret too, I think. That was enough of a reward for her.'

'I'd love to see the valley,' I say.

Themi pats my hand. 'Pema will take you. Maybe I will come too. I haven't been up there for years, but it would be good to see it again. We'll give the flowers a bit more time to have a chance to blossom after all the snow that came so late, but we'll find a good time to go soon. I have one more thing to show you, too.' She gets up stiffly from the bench, and rummages in the tin box once more.

'Open your hand,' she says, and then she drops something into my outstretched palm.

Tears spring to my eyes as I realise what it is: the first gift Callum gave Violet, all those years ago.

Reverentially, I stroke the whittled palmetto leaf with my thumb before returning it to Themi for safekeeping. The small wooden talisman seems more precious than if it were made of solid gold. Because it embodies so much love. And it has endured where so much has been lost.

◆ ◆ ◆

After another week of warmer weather, the first tiny green spikes begin to push their way into the sunlight in the fields. One morning, we pack food and bottles of water and Pema comes to call at the lodge to take us to the Valley of Flowers. Dipa's coming too and she's added some cotton tote bags to her own pack for collecting leaves to make incense, as well as anything else she can forage to add to her cooking.

I'm very thankful for the distraction. The news from home is no better. Davy's still in intensive care and Mum has told me they've put him into an induced coma to try to allow his body to rest and fight the virus. Every waking minute – and I know there must be many through the long nights as much as during daylight hours for all of us – is an agony of hoping for the best and fearing the worst.

I've been trying to throw myself into helping Tashi and Dipa with chores around the lodge to keep myself busy. Even the effort of doing washing has become a welcome ordeal. It involves clambering down to the river carrying a large metal bowl heaped with clothes, sheets and pillowcases, then scrubbing them in the freezing cold water. We rinse the items and wring them out between us, before hauling the bowls filled with the heavy, damp washing back up to the village, a climb of half an hour even at Dipa's brisk pace. Pushing myself physically is a way of channelling my anxiety about Davy, though. *If I can make the climb in five minutes less than the day before*, I tell myself, *then he'll recover*. With every searing breath, I think of him in his hospital bed, his own lungs labouring, and I feel as if I'm breathing for him, desperately trying to will him to stay alive.

On the day of our trek to the Valley of Flowers, we walk up to Themi's house, where she's already waiting in the sunshine outside her door. She doesn't carry a pack, but neither does she use a stick to help her on the walk, and when I begin to breathe more heavily as we start to climb, she's the one who slows her pace to allow me to catch up.

It feels a little like a pilgrimage as we process in single file along the narrow path running above the village. Pema leads the way, then Dipa and Themi, and I bring up the rear: four women of different ages and backgrounds bound together by Violet's story.

While I can scarcely draw breath – let alone speak – Themi talks more about her reminiscences of coming this way with her mother all those decades before us. 'She would tell me about the plants, of course, teaching me to identify them so I could help her. But she would also talk about the plant hunters who'd come before us and the way they were greedy sometimes, taking everything they found. "It's our job to change that, Themi," she'd say. "Always remember, there's a big difference between being given something and taking it. We're the guardians of this place now. If anyone else comes looking for plants, choose carefully which ones you decide to give them." She was one of the first people to realise how important it is to conserve what we have.'

Pausing to catch my breath and press a hand into the stitch that's gnawing at my side, I picture the envelopes of seeds I'd unearthed from the wooden chest back at Ardtuath. How sad it was that the damp had got in and I never managed to get any of them to germinate.

We push on along the path, which, to my relief, mostly follows the contours of the mountainside once we've made the initial climb from the village. I stop beside a small heap of *mani* stones piled on top of a deeply carved rock and draped in a string of prayer flags so old and tattered they've become bleached of their colours. I turn and look back the way we've come. Phortse is spread out beneath us, dwarfed by the might of the snowy peaks surrounding it and the valley that plunges away to the thin ribbon of turquoise river a thousand feet below. The fields and houses look so tranquil from up here on this beautiful day, and yet it takes such determination and strength to be able to survive in this environment where Mother Nature can be as cruel as she is kind.

I notice Themi has taken a new string of prayer flags from her pocket and is winding them round the carved *mani* stones. 'This is my mother's memorial,' she says. 'We remember her here.'

I reach out and trace the outline of a stylised flower, incised into one of the slabs. I realise this is the point where the path twists up and over the next ridge – the final viewpoint from which the village can be seen. In Violet's case, of course, it must have been the spot she described in her journal after fleeing from her kidnappers. It was from here that she got her first glimpse of the place that would become home for the rest of her days, Themi heavy in her belly, as Palden guided them to safety.

At last, we reach a point where the main path carries on ahead of us, but we turn to the right and scramble upwards alongside a little stream that tumbles over white stones. There's nothing much to differentiate the spot from the many other meltwater streams we've picked our way across, but Pema turns to smile back at me, saying, 'Here's where we enter the Valley of Flowers.'

We're climbing more steeply uphill now but, rather than slowing down, Themi's pace has quickened.

If I hadn't already been gasping for air by the time we reach the lip of the valley, I'd have gasped again at the sight that awaits us. The mountains seem to lean apart a little, as if making room to cradle this beautiful spot in their arms. The valley is a sheltered bowl, nourished by the tumbling stream, stretching away from us to meet a rocky headwall at its far end. At the lower end, where we now stand, the water becomes dispersed, meandering among white river stones, creating a broad meadow where swathes of purple candelabra primulas grow. The waters braid themselves together again into a single channel, turning the water-driven prayer wheel before rushing over the valley's lip to cross the path and carry on their way to join the larger river far below.

As we pick our way across the river stones, the years seem to fall from Themi's shoulders, and I catch a glimpse of the much younger woman who came to this place as a child and would have brought her own daughter, Poppy, here too. When we stop beside a low wall, she perches there, lifting her face to the sun, and smiles, closing her eyes, lost in her memories, while Pema and Dipa wander on, foraging for mushrooms growing beneath the birch trees in the most sheltered spots. I sit down beside her, thankful to be able to rest and breathe a little more deeply, taking stock of our surroundings. There are several small stone huts in the valley, where yak herders have come to graze their animals on the fertile meadow that stretches up the valley sides to meet the steeper scree. The faint clanking of yak bells drifts down to us from above and I shade my eyes to try to make out the herd among the distant scrubland of juniper and grasses. A pair of eagles soar against the endless blue of the sky, spiralling on the air currents between the mountains. And we stand among a tapestry of flowers, just beginning to open their petals to the sun after the recent cold snap.

A sense of peace washes through me as my muscles release tension born of anxiety and stress. They're tight with a coldness as well, which has more to do with something internal, I think, than with the chill Himalayan air. I feel my heart tentatively begin to open too, where it's been frozen for so long by fear and loss and sadness: not just from my current preoccupations with the pandemic and what it's doing to my family, but from years of loneliness and emptiness.

Like Themi, I close my eyes for a while, absorbing the warmth, letting it soak through me, and what Mum said to me at the start of my journey comes back to me: *Try to find out a bit more about where Violet went. And while you're at it, try to find out what's happened to the fearless, audacious girl you once were, Daisy.*

Well, I've managed to find Violet's family – my family too, now – and in doing so I've gained a whole new perspective on the world. In following Violet's journey, putting one foot in front of the other just as she did, I've reached a place where I can see the sky beneath me. I've both lost and found more than I ever thought

212

possible. I've left behind the person I'd become, and while that's frightening, it's liberating too.

I open my eyes to find Themi scrutinising me closely. I smile and say, 'Thank you for bringing me to this beautiful place.'

She nods, her expression shrewd. As if she's been reading my thoughts, she says, 'You are beginning to find what you came looking for, I think?'

I laugh. 'Is it that obvious? Am I such a cliché? Another tourist coming to try and find myself in this foreign land? Looking for answers?'

She shakes her head. 'My mother often used to say that life is not about finding yourself – it's about creating the person you want to be. Life doesn't always give us answers. She taught me we have to accept there are some things we can't understand, and in the end our lives will be defined by what we do with that fact – how we accept it and pick ourselves up, facing reality and adapting to it, rather than denying or ignoring it. Violet made a life for herself here, even if she had to do it the hard way, and she gave me a future that I could never have had if she'd returned to Britain. She gave me freedom. And the hardships were worth it because they gave Violet her own freedom too.'

We're both silent for a moment, lost in thought. Then Themi continues, 'It's never easy, making changes, is it? It takes quite a bit of work because, as we Buddhists know, the natural human way is to cling blindly to the desires and beliefs that make us suffer. Wishing life was otherwise keeps us stuck. Accepting where we are and focusing on finding the goodness in every day can go a long way to getting us out of that downward spiral of suffering. Life can be very overwhelming, and that's especially true right now, while the virus is making things so hard for everyone, everywhere. But we can still choose to be like those eagles up there.' She nods towards the distant birds, just flecks in the sky now as they circle far, far above us. 'If we can let go of the thoughts that are keeping us trapped, stop fighting with them and struggling against them, we will soar upwards, where the currents take us.' She pats my hand. 'Come, let's walk again. I want to show you something.'

I follow her as she threads her way up a faint track, deeper into the valley. Every now and then she pauses to point something out to me: the tiny white stars of a saxifrage growing through a cushion of emerald moss; the hoofprint of a musk deer in a patch of damp sand where it's come to the river to drink; and, as we begin to climb higher towards the scree, the droppings of a snow leopard, matted with the hair of its prey.

Perched on top of a boulder, a large bird squawks a warning as we draw near. Its plumage is extraordinary, an iridescent peacock-blue. '*Danphe*,' Themi says. 'The Nepali pheasant.'

'It's beautiful,' I say.

'Beautiful, but slow. Tasty food for snow leopards and wolves. Easier to catch than deer and mountain goats.'

'There are wolves here too?' I ask, casting an anxious glance towards the rocky heights above us. Are those grey shapes just boulders, or predators silently watching us?

She nods, unperturbed. 'They follow yak herders coming through the mountains from the Tibetan plateau. Sometimes when they're hungry in the winter they come right to the edge of Phortse looking for food.'

She lifts the hem of her skirt in order to scramble more easily over a pile of rocks. 'This is where some of the blue poppies grow, the ones Violet showed Betty Sherriff. No flowers to see at the moment, it's still too early and that cold spell will have set them back even more this year. But look, here are the first leaves starting to sprout.' She shows me the tiny, hairy blades just beginning to unfurl where the sun warms the earth. 'They'll grow to be this high in about a month's time.' She gestures to her mid-thigh level.

We climb higher until we reach a point where the scree begins, giving us a viewpoint over the whole of the valley. Themi sits down on a lichen-crusted boulder, spreading her apron over her lap. I take a seat next to her. She nudges me. 'Look,' she says, her face crinkling into a smile as she points her gnarled forefinger towards the ground at our feet. 'That's what I really wanted to show you.'

I see the bud of a tiny blue flower huddled between the stones, hidden away, nestling in a low-growing coronet of spiky leaves, determined to lift its face to the sun. '*Meconopsis horridula*,' Themi says. 'It's a rare type of Himalayan poppy. Keeps to the high places and never grows big. I was up here with my mother when she first discovered it. But she said we must keep it a secret because she knew people would come and take it from here otherwise. Others have found it elsewhere since, but only we know it's here in the Valley of Flowers.'

I touch it gently with my forefinger, marvelling at how something so beautiful and fragile can survive in such a tough, inhospitable environment.

Then Themi says quietly, 'I named my daughter after it. Poppy. Of course, her father insisted she had to have a proper Sherpa name too, so we called her Nima because she was born on a Sunday and Nima means "sun". But to all of us, she was always Poppy. Violet absolutely adored her, as only a grandmother can.'

'What happened to her?' I ask softly. I've scoured Violet's journals for any mention of how she lost her granddaughter, but she stopped writing them in the late 1970s. I'm guessing whatever became of Poppy may lie behind that silence.

Themi gazes into the distance, her eyes not focused on the landscape stretching out below but on something else, something only she can see. 'The same thing that has happened to so many of our families. Mount Everest. You see, Daisy, that mountain is both a blessing and a curse for the Sherpa people. It changed our lives and our fortunes when people around the world realised it could be conquered. But it's the Sherpas who are the key to climbing it. They find the routes, fix the ropes, set the ladders across the ever-changing crevasses in the ice fields. They carry the oxygen and the supplies up to the camps higher up the mountain, allowing climbers to survive in the death zone. They're paid well for this work, of course, but they risk everything in order to try and improve life for their families.' She sighs, reaching out a finger to stroke the face of the tiny blue flower in the stones alongside us.

'My Poppy grew up in the village surrounded by her Sherpa family and friends,' she continues. 'Even though we were outsiders, everyone had accepted Violet into the community, and they just sort of adopted me as one of their children. I'd married a Sherpa – my husband, Tshering – so when Poppy came along, she was completely assimilated, despite being half Scottish. She was loved by everyone, but she had one particular friend, a little boy called Lhakpa. They were inseparable. As they grew up, they trained together with my husband to learn how to climb. Poppy was always an adventurer, like her granny Violet. She loved the thrill of being able to see the world from a different angle, hanging from an ice cliff or scaling a rock wall. Her dad always said that, technically, she was the best of all of them. She had an instinctive feel for the mountains.

'Eventually, Poppy and Lhakpa became husband and wife. When I'd married her dad, we had a very small and quiet ceremony as I was from the outside. But when Poppy and Lhakpa were married we had a big traditional Sherpa wedding, which went on for days. People came from all around, dressed in their finery, and we celebrated and danced. It was one of the happiest days of my life. Violet's too, she always said. I think she sometimes felt a little guilty that she'd denied me an easier life in Europe, although it was never something I wanted, but on that day, she felt all the hardship had been worth it to give her daughter and granddaughter so much relative freedom and a sense of belonging in a community of equals.

'A year after the wedding, Pema arrived. That was another great day in all our lives. Violet was old and frail by then, but she loved being a great-granny. She'd rock Pema to sleep in her arms, singing the songs she remembered from her Scottish childhood.'

I smile, remembering the songs I'd grown up with – those same songs, I bet.

'Like so many Sherpas, though, Lhakpa wanted a better life for his wife and child. He was already a strong climber and he'd accompanied his father and brothers on expeditions, along with my husband. They were a tight-knit team, and became known as some of the very best Sherpas. Lhakpa's dad was what they call an "icefall-doctor". That's a Sherpa who has specialised knowledge of finding the way through the Khumbu Icefall, the very danger-ous area just above Everest Base Camp where the glacier flowing down the mountain meets the valley. Even though it's moving in slow motion, it crumples and breaks, making it a complicated and hazardous start to every climb. Lhakpa learned how to be an icefall-doctor too, because that way he'd be paid more. And so he'd leave Phortse at the beginning of each climbing season to go and live in a tent at Base Camp, where, early every morning, while the other climbers were still asleep, he was part of the team who went up on to the icefall to work out that day's safest route through it, fixing ladders and ropes for the other climbers to use.'

Themi pauses as a sudden gust of chill wind whisks a strand of hair loose from her braid, into her eyes. She tucks it behind her ear, then continues.

'Lhakpa was on the Khumbu Icefall when a towering block of ice – a serac – fell from the western side, right where he was work-ing. It triggered an avalanche. The other Sherpas in Base Camp rushed on to the icefall to try to help their brothers. They recovered two bodies. But Lhakpa was still unaccounted for.

'It was devastating for the brothers and cousins who retrieved the two broken, frozen bodies. But in Sherpa culture it's even worse for the families of those whose bodies can't be recovered because in the Sherpa faith if the body cannot be given the correct care and respect then the soul might never be at rest. Bereavement and grief are a natural part of our lives, but it helps us survive the devastation of loss if we can observe the rites we believe will help the soul leave the earthly realm and find peace. So you can imagine how distraught we all were – especially Poppy – when word reached us that Lhakpa had been lost.

'She was determined to go to try to find his body. One of the helicopter pilots summoned for the rescue mission stopped off here at Phortse to pick up more Sherpas to help at Base Camp and Poppy joined them, along with her dad. Helicopter operations are normally forbidden around the Khumbu Icefall because the reverberations can trigger more avalanches in that area, where lumps of the ice on the moving glaciers can easily be destabilised. So, to get to the scene of the disaster, the rescuers had to climb out of the helicopter and hang from a long line to be deposited on to the ice.

'My husband told me that once he and Poppy had landed, they heard from one of the men who'd been on the icefall when the avalanche struck that Lhakpa had been fixing a ladder over a crevasse, immediately below the serac that had fallen from the side of the mountain. It was terribly dangerous, going back to that place where everything was still shifting and settling, but Poppy was determined to find Lhakpa. She and her dad searched for hours, even after everyone else had given up, and then they came across a deep crack in the ice that had opened up with the immense force of the blow when the ice fell. Poppy was convinced that was where Lhakpa would be. Tshering wanted to be the one to go down, but the crevasse was narrow, and Poppy insisted to her dad that it would be better if she went in to search. And since he was the stronger of the pair, it made sense that he should hold the rope for her. They quickly set up a fixing point in the ice and rigged the ropes for Poppy's abseil. They knew they had to work fast, because it was late morning by now, so the air was warmer, beginning to make things even more unstable.'

Themi can't speak for a few moments as she tries to hold back the tears that have started to flow. I take her hand in mine and hold it tightly.

When she can continue, she says, 'She found him deep in the ice. My husband felt her tugging on the rope to let him know that. He let out more slack so she could tie Lhakpa's body to the rope to bring him up to the surface. Then he felt Poppy start to climb, and he busied himself managing the ropes. But all at once the fixing point broke as the ice sheared. He tried desperately to take the strain but couldn't hold them. He hung on to that rope for dear life – there was no way he'd let go – but the surface was slippery now and he began to be pulled towards the opening.'

She stops again, struggling to say the next words.

'Poppy was experienced enough to have realised what was happening. She knew she would drag her father to his death in the crevasse and then there'd have been three missing bodies, putting others at risk if they tried to recover them.' She pauses again, brushing her tears away with the back of her hand.

'And so my husband felt his daughter cut the rope, falling to her death alongside her husband's body in that deep, icy grave. The other Sherpas who heard his cry of anguish say it's a sound that's seared on to their souls. They scrambled to stop him from trying to climb into the crevasse himself. It was far too dangerous by then, the ice was creaking and groaning as it shifted around them, and they dragged him from the icefall. They promised him they'd come back early the next morning to try to recover Poppy and Lhakpa, when the night air had restabilised the ice. But by the next day, the movement of the ice had closed up the crevasse and it was impossible to get the bodies out.'

It's my turn to cry now, big, ugly, gasping sobs that shake my body, and Themi wraps her arms around me, our tears mingling as she presses her cheek against mine.

'How do you come back from something like that?' I ask at last, when I can manage to speak again.

Her smile is filled with sadness as she replies. 'I think you know the answer to that already. You go on because you have no choice. Baby Pema had lost her mum and dad in one fell swoop and we had to look after her. She kept us all going, Violet, Tshering and me. Tshering was never the same again. He'd often wake in the night, crying out as he relived that terrible moment when he felt Poppy cut the rope. The only time he was at peace was when he was holding Pema. She could always make him smile. He never climbed in the mountains again and he died a few years later. It was peaceful in the end. His heart, which had endured so much pain and so much love, simply stopped beating one night.'

She raises her hand to shield her eyes from the sun as she watches the eagles circling above us. 'You remember how Violet used to say you just have to keep putting one foot in front of the other, slowly, slowly, until you reach a place where you can see the sky beneath you again? Well, that's what we did.'

She reaches down again to brush the bud of the tiny blue poppy growing in the shelter of the rocks, then gestures towards the barren expanse of the scree above us. 'Life is like that scree sometimes, isn't it? It seems bleak and dead. But if you look really carefully, you'll find little signs of life. Tiny, fragile plants, like this one, determined to push their way into the light. Determined to change the desolation into something else – a place where there is still hope and beauty. Pema was our constant reminder of that in the desolation after we lost Poppy and Lhakpa.'

She reaches over to take my hand in hers again and gives it a squeeze. 'Unless we're incredibly fortunate, sooner or later we all live through such times. Often, it's something personal and individual. But just at the moment I think the pandemic has created an avalanche of sadness for the whole world. So it's all the more important to look for these tiny signs of life and hope that keep us going.'

I nod, pulling a tissue from my pocket to blow my nose and wipe my eyes.

'I hate that so many Sherpas still choose to climb,' she continues. 'The mountain gods have been angered by the disrespect shown to them and no matter how much we pray and make offerings, sooner or later they show their anger by taking lives. But we still have such limited opportunities to make money and support our families that many continue to risk it. Women as well as the men, these days. And it's the old and the young who are left behind to manage as best we can. One good thing to have come out of this pandemic, for us at least, is that all the guides have come home now the climbing season's been cancelled. The village feels like it did in the old days, before there was the opportunity to stand on the heads of the gods and be paid for it. For the time being, everyone is home, and everyone is safe here. That makes us happy, even if we will struggle to make ends meet this year. The future is very uncertain for us all.'

Just then we hear Dipa and Pema's laughter, carried on the breeze as they make their way up the hill towards us, dispelling the sadness. They hold up bags bulging with the foodstuffs they've foraged, waving them in triumph. Even Pema is a little out of breath when they reach the rocks along the lower edge of the scree and sink down beside us, but that still doesn't stop the pair of them from chattering on about the dishes they'll be able to cook with the mushrooms and herbs they've gathered.

Then Pema must notice my red nose and tear-blotched cheeks because she puts out her hand and pats my knee. 'Granny has been telling you some sad stories, I think?' she says.

I nod, feeling my mouth tremble and my throat close again as I think of how she lost both her parents so tragically.

She smiles at me, her dark eyes shining with compassion. 'I know how hard it is for you right now, Daisy. We Sherpas understand pain and sorrow, so we're right here with you in this. Whatever comes. One of the things we all share, though, is Violet's resilience. She led the way for us, fixed the ropes and set the ladders, so we could follow. So we could keep on with the journey she began all those years ago. No matter what the world throws at us, we will adapt and survive by helping each other. It's the love in our hearts that makes us invincible, isn't it, Granny.'

Themi nods, pushing herself up to stand and brushing a few flecks of lichen from her apron. 'Your great-granny taught you well, didn't she, Pema. And now I think it's time we took those supplies back to the village so you can show Daisy how to prepare the mushrooms for drying.'

We walk back towards Phortse in single file and when we reach that first viewpoint over the village, we all stop for a few minutes beside the little pile of *mani* stones with their bright wrapping of new prayer flags. I realise this memorial isn't just for Violet, but for Poppy and Lhakpa as well. I press the palm of my hand flat against the incised characters on one of the slabs, sending my love to the three of them.

I listen carefully as the wind gusts around us, but I don't think I can hear their voices among those of the wind walkers. I get the sense that they're at peace, that they lived their lives without regret.

And now the love of their friends and family has laid them to rest, regardless of whether or not their bodies were given the last rites.

Poppy must have had so many things go through her mind when she felt the rope give and her father struggle to hold her as she swung in the void of that crevasse: her love for her tiny daughter and her parents making her want to fight to live, but outweighed by the knowledge that she'd lost Lhakpa and her attempt to recover his body could kill her father too. And so I think she must have made her impossible decision without regret, reaching for her knife and cutting the rope.

Because, as Themi said, Poppy and Lhakpa always were inseparable. Even in death.

PART THREE

Violet's Journal

THURSDAY, 5TH SEPTEMBER, 1935

Themi and I have spent the past week up at the Valley of Flowers, staying in one of the yak herders' huts there to save us the walk to and from the village each day. Themi is perfectly able to manage the distance, which is only a couple of miles, but it still takes us quite a time. Although she trots along at a good pace at my side on her sturdy little legs, she stops so frequently to wonder over a flower or a beetle that she's spotted that our progress can be slow. Like mother, like daughter, I suppose! She's completely outgrown the beautiful leather shoes Hetty sent, of course, and they've long since been exchanged for a pair of yak hide boots made for her by Palden. I remember, fondly, the days when she learned to walk by clinging to the hem of my striped apron to pull herself up. She was soon tottering around with the other children in the village, helping pick stones out of the fields and playing games in the dust. I've put one of the shoes in a niche in the wall behind the fireplace. It's a memory of the bothy in the Scottish hills, another way of remembering Callum and keeping him with us. Whilst I don't believe any evil spirits could harm my daughter in this place, I like to think of her daddy still watching over her.

I parcelled up the other shoe and sent it back to Hetty for safekeeping in the last package of paintings and seeds I sent her. She's doing a good job of finding purchasers for me in London and the money is transferred by wire to a bank in Kathmandu for me to pick up once a year. We're getting by and, like my daughter, I've learned to stand on my own two feet.

Now is the best time for gathering seeds, as we enter the autumnal spell of clear, dry weather. I think I must have combed every inch of this valley by now, and know where the shyest flowers hide their faces. There's a tiny blue poppy – *Meconopsis horridula* – that is a particular favourite of Themi's, growing up beside the scree, where it clings to the thin soil in the most inhospitable of crevices. She's turning into quite a knowledgeable botanist at the age of five!

There's talk in the village of another expedition coming through, perhaps bringing opportunities for the menfolk to get work as porters or guides. They come more frequently these days, making reconnaissance trips into the high mountains. Nepal still refuses to allow mountaineers access from the south to the Everest range though, and so far the Mother Goddess, Chomolungma, remains unconquered. But Tibet has started allowing expeditions into the region from the north and the demand for Sherpa guides, with their unsurpassed knowledge of the mountains and their tremendous physical endurance, has greatly increased.

As I write this in the last rays of sunlight, sitting on the bench outside the southern wall of my little stone house, I wonder again – as I do every now and then – whether the time is coming for me to return to Scotland. But from what I hear, Europe is still a turbulent place to be, with economies still struggling and political unrest fermenting like a bucket of *chhaang*. I feel no great urge to go back. It gives me far more satisfaction to sit here, looking out across the field of potatoes we planted back in the spring. The coverlet of dense green leaves holds the promise of a good harvest this year. In a couple of weeks' time, Themi and I shall dig them up and store them in bamboo baskets ready for the winter. And so the wheel of the seasons turns again and the snows will soon cover the valley, before giving way to the promise of another spring. I think perhaps I'll make plans to leave next year . . . or then again, perhaps I won't.

WEDNESDAY, 1ST JANUARY, 1941

A new year, at least in the calendar I once used to use. We have to be patient and wait for the Nepali new year, which only comes around when spring arrives in April. The fields lie frozen beneath their blanket of snow and the sun only occasionally shows its face through the gaps between the mountains, its light a precious rarity at this time of year. My feet feel as heavy as my heart as I force myself to go through the motions of my daily chores, feeding the fire with disks of dried yak dung, boiling water for our tea.

The telegram I received from Helen sits on the table before me, the words it contains as unwelcome and unbelievable today as they were when it arrived three days ago. Numbly, I ponder the journey those words must have made, across oceans and mountains, carried by electric wires and passed from hand to hand to reach me. If it weren't for the Red Cross, I'd still not know. I'd still think Hetty was alive. I'd still imagine there might be the possibility of being reunited with her one day. Killed in the Blitz, the telegram says. The house in London reduced to rubble. So many lives lost. And my sister – my lifeline – amongst them.

I've long since missed my chance to go back to Scotland. The war has slammed that door shut for now. When the news came that Britain had joined the fight, I felt concern for my family, of course, but I confess I felt such relief, too, that Themi and I were in this safe place. Stupidly, I thought the war couldn't touch us here. But it has. It casts its pall over the whole world.

And so I must find my own ways to grieve for Hetty. Palden says he'll speak to the monks and help me to arrange a *puja* for her. I will place a stone on the *mani* wall and wrap it in prayer flags. And I shall try to take consolation in the hugs Themi gives me. She climbs into my lap, wipes the tears from my face and begs me, 'Don't cry, Mummy. The flowers will come back again.'

The flowers will, but Hetty won't. And how will I manage to find buyers for my seeds and paintings? How will we manage to survive?

I've felt lonely before. But only now do I realise what it means to be truly alone.

Daisy – April 2020

The call wakes me in the middle of the night. I sit up in bed, reaching groggily for my phone. Through a crack in the curtains, I see a crescent moon hanging in the midnight blue of the sky, its faint light making the snow on the summit of Khumbila gleam dimly. I press the phone to my ear, saying 'Hello? Hello, Mum, are you there?' into the silence. At first I think the call must have dropped, but then I hear a ragged breath and I realise my mother is struggling to speak at the other end, across the thousands of miles separating us.

She doesn't have to get the words out for me to know it's the worst of news. But then she manages, 'Oh, Daisy, he's gone.'

All I can say is 'No'. As if denying it will make it untrue, will make everything okay again, will stop the virus from having killed Davy. And then I'm crying too, my sobs mingling with hers in the darkness.

She tells me she wasn't allowed into the hospital to be with him when he died. One of the nurses had called her, holding her phone close to Davy so my mum could tell him she loved him – we all loved him – and that we just wanted him home. If he could only keep breathing, hold on, get through this, we were all waiting for him. She said he was surrounded by our love. We were holding him, we were with him.

She tells me that even though he was still unconscious, she saw his eyelids flutter at the sound of her voice. She thought she glimpsed a faint smile. And then he took his final breath, and the nurse was on the phone saying, 'He's gone, Lexie. He's peaceful now. But he knew you were there.'

I let Mum talk, sensing her need to tell me. Then I say, 'I'm going to come home. When will the funeral be? I need to be there, whatever the restrictions are.'

'Oh Daisy,' she sighed, sounding utterly defeated. 'I don't think there'll be a funeral. They're not allowed now. The bodies have to be disposed of carefully in case the virus can still be spread.'

I lean my forehead against the cold window, wishing I could be with her to hold her and comfort her – and have her comfort me in return. If we don't have Davy's funeral, will he be at rest? And will we? How will we ever be able to come to terms with losing him in this terrible way? I'm desperate to find the words to give her some peace of mind, to help her be strong in this moment of complete despair. And then Violet's words come to me. 'Just keep putting one foot in front of the other, Mum. Slowly, slowly. We will get through this.' And I remember what Pema said and so I say those words too. 'It's the love in our hearts that makes us invincible.'

I hear her draw a deep breath. 'Thank you, Daisy. I know you're right. Davy filled our lives with so much love. That doesn't make it easier to lose him, but we know we were so lucky to have him, don't we?'

'We do, Mum. And we're so lucky to have each other. Who's there with you right now?' I can't bear to think of her suffering alone. No one should ever have to.

'Mara and Sorcha are here. They want to talk to you too. I'm putting you on speaker now, okay?'

I hear my daughters crying, calling for me through their sobs, and I try hard to make my voice reach out to them through the darkness, across the thousands of miles separating us. 'He loved you so much too, you know. He was so proud of you both, always calling you his beautiful girls. I know he will have loved having you there these past few weeks.'

'But Mum,' Mara says, 'what if it was us who gave him the virus? What if we brought it from London? What if it's our fault?'

'No,' I hear my mother say firmly, before I can reply. 'Don't ever think it was your fault.'

Gratitude chokes me, hearing her take charge and reassure my girls. Then I hear Sorcha's voice.

'We're worried about you, Mum, stranded there with nobody to support you. Are you going to be okay?'

I try to smile, so she will hear it in my words. 'I'm fine, don't worry. We have a great big sprawling family here. There are people I can talk to.'

But I realise how much I just really, really want to go home now, to be with them all there, giving and receiving comfort. 'The minute I can, I'll be on a plane back to Scotland, I promise. I'll contact the embassy in Kathmandu again first thing in the morning and see if there's any more news.'

'Okay. On the TV last night they said some countries are organising special evacuation flights to get people home,' Sorcha says. 'But Mum, the main thing is to stay safe. We miss you so much, and we want you back, but we couldn't bear it if you got the virus too . . .' Her voice trails off.

'What will happen . . . with Davy?' I ask.

'We don't know yet,' replies my mother. Her voice is grim, hardened with the effort of controlling her anguish. 'We're waiting to hear. Bodies are being kept in isolation for the time being until the authorities decide what can be done.'

I feel utterly wretched with helplessness. There's silence at the other end of the line and I can only imagine how helpless they must all feel too.

'I love you,' I say. Because they are the only words we seem to have left.

'We love you too,' they chorus.

'We'll speak again soon,' I promise, crossing my fingers that the Wi-Fi connection will allow it. Then the call cuts out, as if my words have immediately jinxed it.

I pull the blankets around me and sit, cocooned, watching the sliver of moon quietly set beyond the dark bulk of Khumbila. I remain there with my cheek pressed against the window until the first faint light of dawn spreads across the sky.

'Davy,' I whisper, hoping somehow, in some parallel universe, he can still hear me. 'You were the best dad ever.'

Tashi realises there's something wrong the minute he sets eyes on me when I finally come downstairs that morning. I tell him what's happened, and he envelops me in a hug. 'I so sorry, Mrs Daisy. Make us all very sad to hear your family suffering badly.'

Dipa and Sonam come through from the kitchen and sit down at the table beside me, offering kindness and sympathy too, while Tashi leaves the room. I go through several tissues before I can finally manage to drink some tea and choke down a bite or two of the toast they offer me.

Then Tashi reappears with Pema and Themi. 'Think you need your cousins now,' he says.

'When a person dies and you don't have the body, what do you do?' I ask them.

'When anyone passes, their physical body is no longer of the highest importance,' replies Themi. 'We would usually let the body lie in their home for three days so the monks can come and bless it, before it is washed and taken to a high place for cremation.

But whether there is a body or not, first of all, every person's spirit spends a period of transition in the *bardo*.' She sees the questioning look on my face and explains. 'There are six *bardos*, or states that occur at certain points in our lives when we lose our old realities and they're no longer available to us. They govern everything from life to death and beyond. The *bardo* of death is the place in between this world and next. In Tibetan it's called *ship chu shergu*, which means forty-nine days, because that's how long it takes. All souls go there to transition when they've finished with their earthly bodies. During that time, we hold a *puja* – a ceremony to mark their departure and commemorate them with respect – with monks saying prayers and lighting incense up at the monastery. The holiest souls, like the Dalai Lama, are reincarnated, to continue to bring their teachings to the world. But we believe most people who have led a good life this time around will simply go to rest. We all become part of the universe from which we originated, in some form or other.'

Tashi says, 'Mrs Daisy, would you like us to organise *puja* for your dad? It help you, I think, and we all can send prayers and blessings for him to make good transition.'

I realise I'd like that very much. It seems so important, suddenly, to do something to mark Davy's death and remember his life. 'Thank you,' I say, managing to smile, feeling comforted at being surrounded by them all so I don't have to go through this time alone. 'I'd really like that. And I think my mum would like it too, especially since she can't organise a funeral for him at the moment.'

'We make arrangements then,' he says.

◆ ◆ ◆

Five days later, on a morning shrouded in thick fog, a little procession makes its way up the hill to the monastery. I walk even more slowly than usual, thoughts of Davy in my mind every step of the way, carrying a yellow silk *kata* folded around a little envelope of cash, which Tashi has given me to hand over to the monks. He leads the way, followed by Dipa, Themi, Pema and me, with Sonam bringing up the rear. We walk in silence, each pausing to turn the prayer wheels set into the monastery walls when we reach the top. The tall white prayer banners hang limply in the still, damp-laden air, scarcely moving, and any sounds from the village below us are muffled by the mist.

We remove our boots and step inside. The monastery's walls and celling are richly painted, depicting scenes from Buddhist folklore, and a large gold Buddha sits serenely in the centre, one hand resting in his lap and the other raised as if in greeting as he contemplates us with a benign smile.

Three monks enter, their red-brown robes draped around them, and I bow and offer them the *kata*. They settle themselves, sitting cross-legged on cushions before a low table, and nod at Tashi. He ushers me forward to a small altar where a butter lamp burns next to three sticks of incense, telling me to light each one from the flame. As I do so, the monks begin to chant.

The perfume from the incense mingles with their deep, rapidly intoned words, filling the whole room, and I sit down beside the others and close my eyes, letting my mind drift as the sound and the scent engulf me. I feel as if I'm floating in a space between two worlds – one real, one imagined – and all of a sudden, in my mind's eye, I see Davy is there with me. And so are my mother and my daughters. All the people I love the most are here with us. The cold, heavy sense of grief I've been carrying in my heart for so long – since Davy's death, certainly, but probably for far longer than that too – is replaced by something else. Something lighter, filled with joy.

I open my eyes and the illusion vanishes. How can I be feeling such a sense of elation, I wonder, at this awful time? And then I realise. It's because I've been forced to accept there's nothing I can do about any of it. My old reality is no longer available to me. I've had to let go of struggling to regain control over my life, a struggle I've felt ever since my divorce took everything I thought I knew from me. I meet the eyes of the Buddha, smiling down at me, telling me to have faith, that this too shall pass. And I smile faintly back.

As the ceremony draws to a close, the monks' chanting slowly fades and we all sit in silence for a few moments. Then the others get to their feet, and I help Themi to stand, taking her arm as we walk to the threshold and put on our boots again.

We step out on to the terrace together and I gasp in amazement at the sight that awaits us. The mist has begun to lift, and a faint haze of sunlight burns through it from behind us, casting the shapes of our bodies into long shadows over the earth and on to the hillside across from us. And surrounding the head of each of those otherworldly shapes is a rainbow-coloured halo.

'Look,' smiles Pema. 'It's the Brocken spectre. As I told you, we only see them rarely here. It's Davy's way of saying goodbye to you.'

I stand, watching the spectral rainbow-encircled shadows we've cast shift and lengthen as the mist swirls around us, then disappear like melting snow when the sun grows strong enough to evaporate the water droplets in the air. Then I walk back down to the teahouse, arm in arm with my cousins, Pema and Themi, their comforting support making me feel stronger with every step.

That evening, once I've called my mum and the girls to tell them about the day, I reflect on how many people around the world must be experiencing the same feelings of fear and anguish and loss. I hope they'll be able to find their own ways to mourn. I hope they have family and friends nearby to comfort them. And I hope, one day soon, we will all be able to come together again, to cry and laugh and remind one another how our faith – in whatever shape it may take – kept us going through the darkest times.

Violet's Journal

The inevitable has happened at last. Word has just reached us that two men have stood on the summit of Mount Everest. One is a Sherpa, Tenzing Norgay, from the village of Thame, just one day's walk from here, close by the monastery at Thamo where I spent those months with Colonel Fairbairn's expedition. The other is a man called Edmund Hillary and he's travelled halfway round the world to conquer the mountain. So, on a day when a new Queen was about to be crowned in Britain, the Mother Goddess of the Himalaya surrendered her own crown.

There's much talk in Phortse about what this will mean. To stand on the head of the deity is an act of disrespect. Yet it's also focused the eyes of the world on this remote corner of the planet and opened up new opportunities for the Sherpa people. The Nepali government has finally opened the country to mountaineers and tourists and with the conquering of Everest the floodgates will surely open.

The day we heard the news, the entire village filed up to the monastery to pray and offer their respects to Chomolungma, hoping to appease the goddess and rebalance the *karma*. Themi and

I joined them for the ceremony and as I sat cross-legged on the floor, I sensed something new in the air: a tangible sense of hope, mingled with the smoke from the incense and the sound of the rapidly chanted prayers. In the fields and the teahouses, the men talk of the money they can earn from guiding, whilst the women's eyes fill with worry. And I ponder what it might mean for Themi and me, this opening up of our sanctuary to the world.

The safety and freedom I've known here have come at a price. After Hetty died, my source of income from the sale of my seeds and paintings dried up. To make ends meet, I've had to sell salt, which the men mine from deposits in the mountains. It involves lugging the heavy bags all the way to Lukla and going door to door. Themi is my secret weapon – one look at her rosy cheeks and glowing hazel eyes makes every householder smile and forget to barter down the price I'm asking. She never complains when we have to make the arduous week-long journey and is good company as she trudges the dusty path beside me, carrying our little bundle of supplies. I won't let her carry the salt. It's far too heavy. It twists my bones and makes every muscle in my body ache, but it's worth it when we return, feeling a great deal lighter in heart and mind, with a roll of rupees tucked safely into the pocket of my apron.

At night, as I huddle beneath the blankets for warmth and stare up at the soot-caked roof of our hut, I question again whether staying on is the right decision. The thought of my childhood home with its comfortable furnishings, electric lights and water on tap brings simultaneous pangs of longing and guilt. I've deprived my daughter of so much. But then I listen to Themi's soft breaths as she sleeps and I think of what I've given her: the freedom to discover who she really is, unfettered by social constraint; the strength to live on her own terms, rather than those imposed by others; the innate confidence that comes from being part of this community where non-judgemental acceptance and unconditional affection are taken as givens.

I ease my aching back as I turn over, cocooning myself more tightly in the layers of woollen covers as I watch the crescent moon sail above Khumbila's summit in its sea of stars. And I decide we should stay a little longer, at least one more summer, just until this year's harvest is in . . .

Daisy – May 2020

I'm not going to lie – despite the fleeting moments of hope and elation, I'm struggling. I know I'm not alone in that. The world is in mourning now, not just for the ones the pandemic has taken from us but for the life we thought we knew, the freedom we used to take for granted. I count my blessings every day, reminding myself how lucky I am. Instead of being locked down in my lonely London flat, I'm having the adventure of a lifetime. In this isolated place, which is probably a lot safer than most other places on the planet right now, I can enjoy the freedom of walking in the hills, working in the fields and visiting the Valley of Flowers to watch as spring turns to early summer there, bringing the rains, and the blue poppies begin to bloom. I'm surrounded by new-found friends and family, who couldn't be kinder and more generous. Violet's words bring me a new-found appreciation too, a sense of gratitude for where I am.

But the price of that freedom is being trapped here, thousands of miles from home and from the people I love the most when they are suffering. There's been no proper funeral for Davy. He was taken in a body bag to the crematorium, straight from the makeshift mortuary set up at the hospital. Under lockdown rules, no one else could be there. And so Mum has told me she feels stuck in a kind of limbo, unable to mark his death properly and unable to grieve properly until his ashes can be returned to Ardtuath instead of sitting on a shelf at the funeral director's offices.

I told her about the *puja* for Davy and sent some photos of the flickering butter lamps, the smoke from the incense and the monks in their burgundy robes. She listened carefully as I described the ceremony and the traditions surrounding it.

'I love that idea,' she said. 'Perhaps we can all use the forty-nine days of the *bardo* to allow ourselves time simply to focus on his life and give thanks that he spent so much of it with us.' She sounded a bit less strained, the strangling grief lessening its grip on her voice just a little, and I was glad the thought that there had been a ceremony for Davy – albeit on the other side of the world and conducted in such an unfamiliar way – was comforting to her.

Grief takes time. Forty-nine days may not be enough, but it's a start. It has given lockdown a new meaning. And it's given us all permission simply to sit with our thoughts, our memories, our feelings, without pushing them aside or judging them.

Unlike Violet, though, as the days tick by and the time passes, my desire to get home becomes stronger. Being apart is tough, no matter how hard I try to see the positives. I need distractions to keep me busy, so I go in search of Dipa and ask her again if there's anything I can do to help.

She looks at me a little doubtfully. 'Today I go and get fresh yak dung, make into pancakes for drying. Maybe you don't want to help me do that?'

But any task that keeps me busy is welcome, so I pick up a tin pail and follow her out to the pasture.

'Must be fresh,' she tells me with a grin as I survey the piles dotted across the grass. As I roll up my sleeves and begin to scoop dollops of damp dung into my bucket, I discover it's surprisingly un-smelly and not all that unpleasant to handle. Once we each have a bucketful, we carry it back to the wall beside the lodge. Dipa takes a good handful from her bucket, shaping it into a ball. Then she slaps it down on to a flat stone in the top of the wall and begins to pat it into an even circle, nodding as I follow suit. We carry on until the top of the wall is dotted with dark brown discs of dung, which will sit there for a week to dry in the sunshine before being added to the stack beneath the porch.

'Other way to do it is like this,' she tells me. She makes another snowball of dung – a dungball – and throws it with some force against the wall of the teahouse, where it sticks with a satisfying-sounding splat. She gives it a few pats to even it out. 'When it fall off we know it ready,' she says. 'You try too.'

My first attempt fails miserably, slipping down the wall and falling apart in the dust. 'Throw harder,' urges Dipa.

And so I do. And I find there's a huge amount of satisfaction to be derived from throwing clods of yak poo against a wall. I can highly recommend it as a way of relieving stress and lifting the spirits when you're feeling down. By the time we go back indoors my right arm is aching, but my heart feels lighter. The fresh air and exertion have helped clear my mind and it's satisfying to think that not only have I helped do something useful, I've also added a new skill to my CV.

As I sit in the kitchen with Dipa afterwards, sipping mugs of tea (having given our hands a very thorough wash first, of course), she grins at me as she begins to prepare lunch. 'You feel bit better now, Mrs Daisy?' she asks.

I nod. 'Much. If you need help with any other jobs like that one, I'm your woman!'

'You learn a lot, I think. You have mind like sand. But becoming like water.'

'A mind like sand? What does that mean?'

She takes a sip of her tea, before reaching for a pile of herbs to chop. Her hands are never idle, I've noticed. 'Buddha say three kinds of people. First kind have mind like rock: thoughts are carved there, like on *mani* stones. Stay angry or sad or frightened a long

243

time. Second kind have mind like sand: anger, sadness written there but pass away quickly as sand shifts. Third kind most pure and undisturbed: mind like water. Thoughts never can be written there, just flow through. Mind like water best. Let thoughts pass through. Doesn't mean don't be thinking them, just not holding on to them.'

'Hmm, I don't think my mind is always like sand, let alone water. Some of my thoughts are set in stone. They can be hard to let go of.' I think about my divorce, the pain and feelings of betrayal and abandonment it carved into my heart, alongside the fear I'd lose my girls.

'That's okay, we all working on it. It just like yak dung pancakes . . . Practice make perfect!' Dipa hands me the knife she's been using, then wipes her hands on her apron. 'You finish herbs. I put spuds on to cook.'

That night, as I lie in my bed waiting for sleep to come, a memory of the beach at Slaggan comes to me. Davy and Mum used to take us there, carrying a picnic from Ardtuath across a few miles of moorland to reach the isolated bay hidden between two rocky headlands. I would write my name with a stick in the damp sand near the water's edge, drawing flowers and hearts around it, then watch as the first waves of the incoming tide drifted over my creation, smoothing out what I'd written there. I remember one day Davy came to watch as I worked and when I'd finished my drawings, he took the stick from me and drew a big heart of his own. Inside it he wrote our names: Lexie, Davy, Daisy and Stuart. And then we stood side by side, watching the sea erase it, bit by bit. There's no sadness attached to that memory, only a sense of happiness and deep peace. I smile in the darkness, imagining I can hear the gentle shooshing of the waves as they wash away our names.

I think I must have fallen asleep still with that smile on my face, because the next thing I know it's a new day and the sound of the sea has been replaced by the sound of Dipa humming to herself as she begins to make breakfast.

Violet's Journal

SATURDAY, 28TH JULY, 1956

Today is Themi's twenty-fifth birthday. She's so grown up, my beautiful girl.

We've had a party and now she's finishing clearing everything away whilst I sit and write this, reflecting on the life we've made here. There's no doubt, things have changed a lot since my arrival all those years ago.

These days, the money the men earn from guiding expeditions to Everest and the other high peaks has had the power to change lives. It means the people of Phortse can afford to buy the materials to put proper roofs on their houses, instead of making do with slates and stones clawed from the mountainsides around them, and to purchase cast-iron stoves to heat their homes and cook their food. We can pay porters to bring food to the village too now – eggs and fruit and vegetables to nourish our children and prevent the malnutrition that used to bend their bones, crippling them, and made them susceptible to diseases.

Sir Edmund Hillary has expressed his gratitude to the Sherpas who helped him to the top of Everest. He's provided funding so that a school can be built in the village here, and the community is going to club together to employ a teacher so our children can have a proper education.

Standing on the heads of the mountain deities, though, has brought bad *karma*, just as the women foresaw. Climbing those peaks is never something the Sherpas would have done, were it not for the opportunity to try to improve life for their children. And so, whilst the Sherpa men take the risks, leading the climbers and going on ahead to find routes, fix ropes and set ladders across the gaping crevasses in the glaciers tumbling down the mountainsides, the women remain at home and send prayers to the gods to try to make amends for the dishonour the men are bringing upon their communities.

Sometimes the prayers seem to work. The men return home with cash in their pockets, lighting incense and making offerings to the gods to apologise for their transgressions. But other times the gods cannot be appeased. Men have been killed as avalanches thunder down on them, or as those hungry crevasses swallow them whole. Sometimes they lose their lives in accidents whilst trying to help and protect the less experienced climbers who now come to Nepal thinking they can conquer the mountains, only to find that the mountains have little regard for the ambitions of puny humans.

I've been doing my bit as well. I quickly realised that, for the community of Phortse, the most valuable thing I had to offer was my language. And so I run English classes in the newly built school, teaching the children and their mothers during the day, and in the evenings giving the men the vocabulary they need to be able to communicate, to lead climbs and instruct westerners how to keep themselves safe as they attempt to survive in the high-altitude death zone. I'm paid in cash from the guides as well as in foodstuffs, and Themi and I get by quite well.

I still spend my spare time in the Valley of Flowers. For now, it remains safely hidden from the groups of trekkers, who mostly stick to the main route to Everest Base Camp and bypass this forgotten corner. But past history has taught us how progress comes at a cost – a price paid all too often by the natural world around us. And so it seems all the more important to continue cataloguing what we have here. It may not be much, but I think of it as my legacy, and Callum's as well. He's still my constant companion as I uncover and document the valley's riches. Some days I imagine I can hear the long-ago echoes of a whistled tune, carried on the wind as it swirls down from the mountain peaks.

From indoors, I hear my daughter laugh and it sounds as melodious as the chiming of yak bells on the hill. Tshering is there with her. He stayed behind when the others left and is wielding a tea towel as she passes him the dripping plates. It's been more and more noticeable that he spends every minute he can spare, paying her visits or going for walks with her to collect juniper twigs and bamboo when he's not away guiding. His face lights up at the sight of her, the way Callum's would light up when the two of us were together. Although Themi and I are still outsiders, it seems the rules could be bent a little to allow them to marry despite the fact she's not a Sherpa. It would mean foregoing the three-day celebrations of a traditional marriage ceremony, but Tshering's mother has already intimated to me that they wouldn't mind that. Everyone loves Themi. The villagers consider her one of their own.

They've finished the chores now and Themi has just popped her head through the window to say she and Tshering are going to walk up the hill a little way to watch the sunset. I smile and nod, and remember a lily her father once showed me, back in the Herbarium in Edinburgh all those lifetimes ago. I painted its portrait, tinting the petals coral pink and gold, the colours of the clouds crowning Khumbila this evening.

It feels as though Callum is bestowing his blessing on them as they walk hand in hand along the path above me, dreaming, perhaps, of a legacy of their own.

Daisy – May 2020

Themi shows me a faded photograph of her wedding to Tshering. 'One of the mountaineers took it and sent it to us,' she explains. 'Tshering had just returned from his first ascent of Everest and his pockets were full of money. And he'd bought me that armlet as my wedding present.' She points with a crooked forefinger.

Then she brings a locked tin box out from beneath her sleeping platform and shows me the bracelet, ornately wrought in silver set with coral and turquoise.

Themi lowers her eyes, blinking in an attempt to stop the tears from falling. Her voice is low, choked with emotion as she continues, 'Look how young we were. We had such hopes and dreams that day. The whole world seemed to be changing for us, filled with the promise of a better future for all the Sherpa people. If we'd known what lay ahead, would we ever have dared set out on that path?'

I reach over and pick up the silver armlet, easing it gently on to her wrist. Then I take her hand in mine, stroking the gnarled, unyielding stiffness of her fingers. 'Of course you would,' I say. 'All that love you've known, for Tshering and Poppy and Pema – it's what underpins life, isn't it?' I point through the window to the snow-capped mountains across the valley. 'I think love is like Khumbila over there. It may be weathered and scoured, it may experience terrible avalanches and devastating rockfalls. But it only does so because it dares to be there in the first place. Our lives would be like trudging across a flat, featureless plain if we didn't have the courage to climb the mountains.'

She brushes away her tears with the back of her free hand and then wraps it around mine. 'You're right, Daisy. And I think that's what life has been like for you for a while, hasn't it? But now you've found the courage to climb again. I hope you will remember that when you leave us. Take home with you this knowledge the mountains have given you. You still have so much love to give and you should never forget how much your family loves you. Not just your Scottish family. Your Sherpa family, too.'

A flood of conflicting emotions washes over me. I feel warmed by her words. But at the same time I'm gripped by a deep-seated, visceral longing to be back at Ardtuath with my mum and my girls. To walk together along the path up the hill behind the house. To hug them and be hugged back. To cry together for Davy. To comfort one another with our love that's as solid as a mountain.

◆　◆　◆

Up until now, I've felt I've probably made the right decision, staying put in Phortse. But then the tides of the pandemic shift again around the world. Here in Nepal, the restrictions are still in place. There are no domestic or international flights, and the official recommendation is still to remain where you are. But the news from Britain is a little more optimistic. By the end of May, there's talk of the first, cautious lifting of the lockdown, of schools reopening and a return to the workplace for those who can't work from home. Non-essential shops remain closed, though, and the advice is to avoid using public transport. Mum writes that, like most people, she and the girls are staying at home. I read and reread the official advice, trying to work out what it means for me. In theory now, I could get back to Scotland if I weren't in Nepal. But the situation here remains unchanged as the country keeps its borders closed, to hold the virus at bay and protect its people. I try to make my mind like water, going with the flow, so the pendulum swing of my thoughts won't hook me and drag my emotions back and forth. It's not something I've perfected yet, but I'm working on it.

Then, out of the blue, an email arrives from the British Embassy in Kathmandu. With the cautious relaxing of restrictions in the United Kingdom, it says, an evacuation flight is being arranged for citizens still in Nepal who wish to go home. If I want to take it, I should register immediately and be in Kathmandu in three days' time. My heart gives a lurch. I want to be on that plane and get back to see Mum and my girls. But even if I could get myself to Lukla – a two-day trek I could maybe just about do if I set off at once – there are still no internal flights from there to get me back to Kathmandu in time.

I show the email to Tashi and Dipa. 'I think you want go home now?' he asks. 'Time to leave your Sherpa family and go back to Scottish one?'

'I do,' I say. 'But is there any way I can make that flight?'

He beams. 'No worry, Mrs Daisy. I speak to cousin-brother in Lukla. He helicopter pilot. Number one, best in Nepal. We make plan for you. Time to get you home.'

True to his word, as ever, by late afternoon the plan has been hatched. A helicopter is due to bring more essential supplies to Phortse the day after tomorrow. Once the food and medicines have been offloaded, I will get the return flight to Lukla and from there Tashi's cousin-brother will fly me back to Kathmandu, since he has a supply run scheduled too.

'What's the cost of two helicopter flights going to be?' I ask.

'No cost, Mrs Daisy. You family. And these flights essential anyway, funded by government, so pilots already get paid.'

I breathe a huge sigh of relief. I've not spent any of my remaining rupees, but I'm very much aware that I owe Tashi and Dipa for all these weeks of food and lodging. That'll take all the cash I have on me and more. I'm counting on the fact that once I get back to Kathmandu, I should be able to use a cash machine and take out whatever is left in my bank account, then find a way to get it to them.

◆ ◆ ◆

The next day – my final one in Phortse – I spend with Pema and Themi, wanting to make the most of every moment I have with them. Who knows when we'll meet again?

The early-summer rain falls steadily as I climb the hill to Themi's little stone shack. The white rhododendron at the end of the house has lost all its flowers now and just a few bruised blooms lie scattered on the ground beneath it. But Themi has planted bright orange marigolds in a row of empty powdered milk cans beside her front door and they lift their faces to the clouds overhead, like defiant little suns. Her small vegetable patch is neatly tended, its edges overflowing with burgeoning herbs, pak choi, and the green spikes of garlic.

'Hello?' I call out. 'It's me, Daisy.' I push aside the curtain and step into the black-walled room, where Pema comes to greet me with a smile before returning to the fire, where the pan of tea is coming to the boil.

Themi is sitting at the table and pats the bench beside her, gesturing to me to come and sit down.

'So you are leaving tomorrow, we hear?' she says, taking my hand. 'It's time for you to go home.' I clasp her gnarled fingers between my palms. They feel fragile, like dry twigs, and I nod, suddenly unable to speak as the realisation dawns on me that I might never see her again. Over the course of this trip, I've lost so much, but I've found so much too.

Themi must be thinking something similar because she smiles at me, the deeply weathered lines of her face crinkling, and she says, 'Every meeting holds the seeds of parting. Which reminds me . . .'

She gets up and goes over to the plastic drum in the corner of the room. Her stiff hands struggle to lever open the top, so I hurry over to help her. She reaches into the depths of the container and brings out a pile of sketches. I recognise Violet's handwriting, annotating them. She sets them to one side and rummages in the drum once again. This time she brings out a small glass jar. She holds it up to the light and squints at its label. It's clearly not what she was looking for as she replaces it and rummages again. Over her shoulder, I see the bottom of the container is filled with many more jars, each one neatly labelled. At last, she finds the one she's been searching for and hands it to me.

'*Meconopsis horridula*,' I read. The jar is tightly sealed, but the minute seeds it holds whisper softly against the glass as I turn it in my hands.

'Violet's legacy,' Themi tells me, nodding towards the drum. 'She saved these samples of all the seeds she collected, told me to keep them safe. She saw how fragile the plants could be and she knew it was important to protect them for the future, as this region opened up to the world. Take those seeds and grow them when you get home, to remind you of all you've found here.'

I tuck the jar into my pocket. When I can speak, I say, 'I feel as if my heart is breaking all over again at the thought of leaving you so soon after I've found you.'

'Ah, Daisy, your heart isn't breaking in a bad way. This time it's breaking wide open, like a seed. And when that happens, there's the possibility of a transformation, the birth of something new.'

'It's just so hard to say goodbye,' I say, still clutching her hand between mine.

'Yes, it is.' Her words are calm and matter-of-fact. 'But it's what we're all doing in this life – coming and going, loving and losing, living and dying. In the end, we're all just walking each other home, aren't we? Finding our way along the paths of life, sometimes alone, sometimes in the company of others, until we find a way to let go. This is what our faith is for. Because this is where all paths eventually lead.'

She extracts her hand from mine and gently brushes away the single tear that's running down my cheek. 'Don't only be sad, Daisy *Didi*. Be happy too. Make space for all those feelings, and know you have the space in that beautiful, broken heart of yours to contain them all. Violet used to say to me when I was feeling sad that even in the hardest times the joy is always there, like the blue sky behind the clouds. When we know that, maybe we can let the clouds drift away, letting happiness shine through again.'

Pema sets mugs of tea on the table before us and then comes to settle herself on the other side of me. We sit together for a couple of hours, talking about our families, and I show them the latest pictures Mum has sent me of Mara and Sorcha at Ardtuath, holding up their muddy hands to the camera. They've been resurrecting Davy's vegetable garden, digging a new potato patch, inspired by my descriptions of the Phortse spuds and how good they taste.

'Violet would definitely approve of her great-great-great-nieces,' Themi says. 'When you go home, Daisy, please will you send us pictures of the flower paintings you told us about? The ones Violet sent back from here. I'd love to see them.'

'I will,' I promise. 'And I'm going to go to the Botanic Garden in Edinburgh as soon as it's okay to do so, to try to track down more information about her. All those specimens and drawings she sent back from the expedition and afterwards, once she was living here at Phortse – they must still be there somewhere.'

'The rain has stopped,' says Pema, peering through the window. 'Let's walk down to the *stupa* together. Will you come with us, Granny?'

Themi shakes her head. 'I think I'll stay here.' She turns to me apologetically. 'My arthritis is always bad in the rainy seasons and today I need to rest. But I will come to the teahouse tomorrow first thing to see you before you go, Daisy. So there's no need to say our goodbyes just yet.'

As Pema and I walk down the hill, following the line of the *mani* wall, we stop frequently to stop and chat with people who've come out to work in their fields as the sun breaks through the clouds. I've got to know them all now, over the weeks I've been here, and they've all heard I'll be leaving on the supply helicopter tomorrow.

At last we reach the *stupa* at the foot of the village, startling a pair of *danphe*, which squawk indignantly before flapping off into the juniper bushes. Four pairs of all-seeing Buddha eyes watch over us as we walk clockwise around the white-domed shrine. A breeze has got up, sweeping the rainclouds from the valley and tugging at the skeins of prayer flags, scattering more of their blessings on to the wind.

'I shall miss all this,' I say as Pema and I stand by the wall, gazing out across the Khumbu.

She smiles. 'It will still be here for you when you're ready to return. All those lines on your family tree connect you to this place now.'

Practical as ever, she spots a plant growing in the shade of a birch tree with spikes of tiny white flowers and pulls a bag from the pocket of her jacket. She kneels down and carefully pinches off a handful of its bright-green heart-shaped leaves.

'Is that a variety of *Tiarella*?' I ask.

She nods. 'I use it to make a hot compress, which is good for my granny's arthritis.'

I snap a photo of the plant on my phone and then we continue slowly along the lower edge of the village, spotting several more *danphe* and a pair of musk deer grazing peacefully where the hillside falls steeply away beneath us. I drink it all in – the breeze ruffling my hair, the smell of the damp earth, the mountains rising above us and the random xylophone notes of the yak bells in the distance.

Pema walks quietly at my side until we reach her low-built whitewashed cottage. 'I'll see you tomorrow morning, Daisy,' she says, then disappears through the door curtain with her bag of leaves.

I trudge the rest of the way back to the teahouse, standing outside the lodge for a while, shading my eyes from the sun's rays that warm the fields, letting my muddled feelings wash through me like the turquoise river flowing in the valley far below. All at once, something falls from the wall above, tapping me softly on my shoulder, nudging my wandering thoughts back to the here and now. I laugh, then stoop to pick up the dried disc of yak dung and add it to the pile beneath the porch: my one last small contribution to this extraordinary community that gave me refuge when I needed it most.

◆ ◆ ◆

It doesn't take long to shove my belongings back into my pack the next morning and lug it downstairs. There are a surprising number of people gathered in the dining room, filling their mugs from large thermoses of tea. Dipa has made pancakes for breakfast and sets platefuls on the tables around the edge of the room, alongside jars of honey. 'Everyone want to say goodbye,' she explains.

The room is filled with laughter and chatter. I know I need to make the most of this gathering. Not only does it touch me deeply that so many people have come to bid me farewell, but I also realise this will probably be the last party I'll be at for the foreseeable future. The village has been able to form a self-contained bubble of community in this locked-down world, its natural inaccessibility making it safe to socialise and mix. Once I step beyond the wall of mountains that protects us, it will be a very different story.

Tashi checks his phone. 'Helicopter coming,' he says. 'Time to get ready.' And then an extraordinary thing happens. One by one, the people of Phortse come up to me to say goodbye, pulling *katas* out of their pockets and draping them round my neck. Each person clasps my hands between theirs, saying '*Tashi delek, Didi.*' Good luck, sister. I'm wearing so many of the silk scarves by the time they've finished that I can't do up the zip of my jacket.

Sonam shoulders my pack and Tashi leads the way to the helicopter landing area, while I follow, arm in arm with Pema and Themi. Dipa and some of the others bring up the rear. We stand beside the patch of rhododendron bushes, and I say my final goodbyes, promising Pema that I'll keep in touch and send her photographs and news from Scotland. The distant sound of the approaching helicopter signals the moment when I must take my leave of Themi. This particular goodbye is the hardest one of all, because I don't know whether I'll see her again.

She hugs me tightly, then holds me at arm's length, her hazel eyes searching mine, as if she's memorising my face. 'Remember what I told you the first time we went to the Valley of Flowers? That Violet always used to say life is not about finding yourself – it's about creating the person you want to be. You've taken the first steps, Daisy. Now keep going.'

'I know,' I say, laughing so that I won't cry, as the noise of the helicopter's motor reverberates from the mountains surrounding us and it comes into view, flying up the valley beneath us. 'One foot in front of the other, slowly, slowly along the path.'

She smiles and pats my shoulder beneath its cushion of *katas*. 'You listen to the lessons of the mountains and learn from them. That's more than most people do.'

With a roar, the bright-red helicopter rises to hover above the helipad, and we all cover our ears and turn our faces from the flying dust as it settles gently on to the stones. The pilot motions at everyone to stay back as he unloads the supplies, putting them in a pile at the edge of the stone circle. Then he beckons to me to come forward and I shoulder my pack and walk towards him, ducking my head beneath the helicopter blades. He hands me a face mask and loads my pack into the cabin before helping me in and closing the door.

As I fasten my seat belt and put on the set of earphones he hands me, he runs through his checks. Then he raises a thumb and I nod, letting the surge of emotions flow through me. There's fear and excitement at this, my first ride in a helicopter, alongside huge sadness at leaving my new-found Himalayan family and friends, as well as the strongest yearning to get home. I name each feeling and let it go, trying to make my mind like water as Dipa told me to, as the blades begin to spin so fast they become invisible and we lift into the air.

I press my face to the window, the paper mask covering my nose and mouth, waving goodbye to the little crowd on the ground below. And then we're off, whisking away down the valley, and the hills close in behind us, hiding the village of Phortse from sight, enfolding it and keeping it safe. *All those days of trekking*, I think, *and now it's going to take just a couple of helicopter rides – each one lasting less than an hour – to get me back to my starting point.* It seems much too fast, too sudden a re-entry into the real world.

Something Dipa once said, back at the beginning of my stay in Phortse, rings in my head. *Journey far, but travel within*. It makes sense to me now. Covering the miles to get to my destination, either by walking slowly, slowly through this landscape or by flying above it, was never really the goal. It's the fact that I took myself out of my familiar, comfortable life and put myself in a place where none of the usual, carefully constructed props and points of reference were available to me that allowed me to be myself again. To rediscover the essence of me. It lay hidden away, just as Violet's journals lay hidden for all those years in the cedarwood chest in the library, blanketed beneath layers of sadness and loss.

As we soar between the valley's green walls, following the turquoise thread of the river beneath us, a sensation of deep peace settles over me. Finding Themi, getting to know her and piecing together the final parts of Violet's story has given me a sense of purpose that's been missing from my life for some time. I turn the red string bracelet around my wrist. It's faded a bit now and the ends are beginning to fray, but it's still there as a reminder that I've walked the way of the warrior. I've done things I never thought I could. I've stepped into the unknown, fought some inner battles, and emerged on the other side.

And I've begun to create something new. Or, rather, some*one* new: the person I want to be.

Daisy – June 2020

'Goodbye and good luck,' I say to the German couple as we collect our bags at Doha Airport and go our separate ways to catch our onward flights. The plane from Kathmandu was half empty, a special flight allowed out of Tribhuvan Airport, arranged by various embassies to transport the last stranded tourists in Nepal back to Europe. I've sanitised and re-sanitised my hands and had my temperature taken countless times in the past couple of days. And now I join the queue to have it taken again at the airport checkpoint before heading to the departure gate for the flight to Glasgow. The face mask I've been wearing for hours feels grubby and limp and I gratefully accept the new one being proffered by the medics.

I go into the ladies' room to freshen up. Once I've washed my hands, carefully following the directions on the signs plastered on the toilet walls, I remove my old mask and splash a little water on to my face, washing away the staleness of the past twenty-four hours of travelling. As I go to put on the new one, I catch sight of myself in the mirror and am transported back to that moment all those weeks ago – in another lifetime – when I looked in this same mirror and didn't recognise the woman I saw there. The woman I see now has changed. Her face is tanned by the wind and sunshine of the mountains. Her hair – as unruly as ever – frames her features in a thick tangle of curls but instead of scraping them back in a band, she lets them be. She looks strong, this woman, her muscles toned by weeks of trekking and walking in the thin air of the high peaks. She looks like someone I'd like to get to know better.

She looks like me.

I fix the new mask in place over my face and head back out into the airport, going home.

◆　◆　◆

By the time I reach Glasgow, the reality of what everyone's been living through has hit me hard. The connecting flight was even emptier than the one from Kathmandu and when I arrive at the airport it's like a ghost town. The few passengers in the baggage hall are careful to keep their distance, and everyone's eyes – the only features visible behind the ubiquitous paper masks – look wary. The virus has spread its tendrils of fear everywhere and being in a public space feels uncomfortably risky.

My footsteps echo as I walk out into the deserted arrivals hall, feeling uncertain what to do next. I'd planned on hiring a car, even though it'll cost a fortune, but the car rental desks are all firmly closed, metal shutters pulled down over the windows. I fish my phone out of my pocket to see if I can find anything online, but the battery is dead. I look around, wondering whether there's anywhere to charge it, but the cafés are all closed too and there are no other charging points here. Perhaps I should have taken the London flight instead, but returning to my lonely flat is the last thing I want to do. Now the rules have been relaxed enough, I simply want to be with my family. I want to hug Mum and my girls and be hugged back. I want to comfort them and be comforted in my turn, as we come together to mourn Davy.

The journey to Ardtuath isn't an easy one at the best of times though, even if public transport is running. I'll just have to wing it and see if I can get a bus into the city and catch a train from there.

The first thing I need is some money, so I start walking across the empty expanse of the hall towards a cash machine to check the balance in my account. I know there's almost nothing left in it though, and the pit of my stomach clenches with dread. Have I come all this way only to be stranded once again? But then a voice behind me says, 'Hello, Daisy. Need a lift?'

'Jack!' I exclaim, flinging myself at him, ecstatic to see his face – or at least his eyes, which twinkle with their oh-so-familiar smile above his mask. 'What are you doing here? I thought you'd still be at sea.'

'I made pretty good time from the Azores. Heard from my mum you'd managed to get out of Nepal and were due to be arriving today. I wondered how you were going to get back to Loch Ewe safely. Everything's still really weird here, even if the country is slowly opening up again. So I thought I'd take a little detour and come and pick you up. I'm moored on the Clyde. Your personal yacht awaits, to take you home.'

We get into one of the few taxis parked at the usually busy pick-up point and Jack gives the driver directions to the marina, a few miles down the Clyde.

In the car, he says flatly, 'I'm so very sorry about Davy. It's a terrible loss.'

I nod and reach for his hand. 'I know he meant a lot to you as well.' And even though there's so much to say, we sit in silence as the taxi speeds down empty roads, heading for the river.

The city streets may be deserted but the marina is crammed full of boats, with one or two people working on them here and there.

'With lockdown, everything's been parked up for the duration,' says Jack. 'But now people are allowed to be out in the open air, it's starting to get back to normal.'

'She's beautiful,' I say when we reach the berth where *Skylark* is moored. She stands out among the other boats with her elegant lines and teak deck.

'She is, isn't she? I found my dream girl at last,' he laughs. 'I never thought I'd be able to afford her, but quite a few people were selling when the pandemic began and a client of mine let me have her for a good price. She's no spring chicken, but she's still in great condition. I installed a bit of up-to-date technology to be able to sail her across the Atlantic on my own and she did a great job of getting me here. Come on, let me show you round. We've an hour or so to wait for the tide to turn, in any case.'

Once on board, I hesitate to remove my mask, as Jack has done. He's been isolated all these weeks, and risked coming ashore to pick me up, and who knows what germs I may have been exposed to on the flights from Kathmandu to Glasgow?

He notices my uncertainty. 'It's okay,' he says. 'I can risk catching the virus now we're so nearly home. There aren't many people I'd take that risk for, mind you, but you and I are in this together now. All we can do is take as many precautions as possible to protect others. The government's announced a new rule – we're allowed to make a bubble with another household, so I reckon this counts. When we get to Aultbea, we'll be self-quarantining in any case. I'll sound out Mum, ask her to let Lexie know we're safe and sound and on our way home, then they can decide whether they want to isolate with us until we're sure we're all clear or whether you and I should stay on the boat for a while to be on the safe side. That's another advantage of this old girl.' He pats *Skylark*'s wooden cockpit fondly. 'She can be turned into our very own floating isolation ward if need be.'

Below deck, everything is neatly stowed away apart from a set of charts spread out on the table. Once I've stashed my pack in one of the berths and plugged my phone in to charge, Jack brews up a cup of tea and shows me the route we'll take to get back to Loch Ewe.

'We'll aim to get as far as Arran tonight on the ebb, then make an early start in the morning to catch the flood tide and get round the Mull of Kintyre. Depending what this wind decides to do, we might be able to slip through the sound between Jura and Islay and make it to the Isle of Mull by tomorrow night. Then it's a long day's sail up past Skye to Loch Ewe. We should be home late on Friday.'

I pore over the chart and when I look up again Jack is sitting looking at me, his expression inscrutable. 'What?' I say, wondering whether I have a remnant of my airline meal on my face or something.

He smiles. 'You look good, Daisy.'

'I *am* good,' I reply. 'It was an incredible trip.'

To my surprise, because Jack McKinnes has never been one for displays of emotion, he reaches over and takes my hand in his. 'You've always looked good to me, Daisy Laverock,' he says. Then he clears his throat abruptly and gets to his feet. 'Well, I'd better start making ready for the off. And you'll probably be wanting a shower and a freshen-up after your travels. I've put a towel in the heads for you.'

I watch as his legs disappear up through the companionway and hear his footsteps moving across the deck above me. Then I shake my head, down the remainder of my mug of tea, and go to delve into my pack for some washing things.

◆ ◆ ◆

We cast off and manoeuvre out of the marina. Then Jack cuts the engine, and I help raise the mainsail as *Skylark* heads down the Clyde on the ebb tide in the early-evening sunshine.

I'm still feeling a sense of overwhelm as I try to absorb all that's happened in the past twenty-four hours. How can I have journeyed from a Sherpa village perched high in the Himalaya, via two helicopter rides and two international flights, to find myself sailing down the Scottish west coast at sunset? I've been running on adrenaline and now the sudden peace and quiet leaves me feeling a little dizzy and disorientated. I'm sure the jet lag on top of all that air travel doesn't help either.

As we head towards the rugged outline of Arran, I move forward to sit in the bow, trying to ground myself a little as I watch the water part effortlessly before us. When I close my eyes, I imagine I'm listening to the mountain wind blowing down the Khumbu valley and I think of Themi, Pema, Tashi and Dipa, wondering what they're doing. I glance at my watch and realise it's the middle of the night in Nepal, but I can still hear their voices and the sound of their laughter, which seems to warm me from within.

I think I must drift off for a while because the rattle of the anchor chain wakens me with a start. And when I open my eyes, I think I must still be dreaming because there in front of me is a skein of Buddhist prayer flags, fluttering on the breeze.

We've turned into Lamlash Bay, between Arran and Holy Isle, and Jack is preparing to moor up for the night. He points towards the prayer flags with a grin. 'Thought it might be best to ease you back in gently. There's a Buddhist community here on Holy Isle.'

We anchor off, keeping a safe distance from the island communities on either side of us. I make a feeble attempt to be useful, but I'm so tired I can hardly stand. It's flat calm but I still feel as if the deck is rolling beneath me and I stagger slightly, steadying myself against the mast as I make my way to the stern.

'Supper?' Jack asks. 'Or are you just ready for your bunk?'

'Sorry,' I say with a rueful smile. 'I'm not very good company, am I? I think I'll just head for bed. I'll be a bit more with it in the morning, I promise.'

I brush my teeth and crawl headfirst into my narrow berth. And the last thing I hear is the quiet slap of the wavelets against the hull and the calling of the seabirds, as the sea rocks me gently off to sleep.

◆ ◆ ◆

I wake early, to the rattle of the kettle on the hob and the click-click-whoosh of the gas being lit, and climb out of my bed into the cabin.

'You slept well,' Jack says, as he puts out some things on a tray for our breakfast.

The dawn is still and quiet up top, the only sounds the creaking of the anchor chain and the faint tap-tap of the rigging against the mast. We sit, nursing our mugs between our hands, watching the first rays of the sun spread across the eastern horizon. The prayer flags on Holy Isle wave in the breeze, and I picture the ones at Phortse waving in return from the other side of the globe. It's comforting to think how they link us across the miles, like the lines on a family tree.

Jack checks his watch. 'Right, the tide's slack now so we should be able to get round the foot of Arran to catch the flood. Let's get underway.'

We carry the breakfast things down below to wash them and stow them safely away. Then we raise the anchor and motor out from behind the shelter of Holy Isle, into open water. We hoist the sails, making good progress, and the tide and wind are with us as we round the Mull of Galloway, where *Skylark* spreads her wings and begins to fly.

I'm glad to be ending my journey like this, having a little more time to let myself catch up. It's another sort of *bardo*, I think, another period of transition from one stage of life to the next. Then a thought occurs to me. I count the days on my fingers. In two more it will have been forty-nine days since Davy's death. I'll get home just in time to be with my family for the final day, when his soul leaves us for good.

Instead of making me sad, though, the realisation makes my heart lift. I get the strong feeling Davy is still here with me today, seeing me safely home one last time. And I laugh through my tears, knowing how he'd approve of my mode of transport.

Jack nudges my arm. 'Here, take the helm for a while?'

I nod, stepping up to the wheel, being careful to keep us on course as he goes forward to undo the fastenings on the headsail, letting it unfurl, and as it balloons outwards it gives us another couple of knots of speed.

'You okay there?' he asks, coming back to stand beside me.

'All good,' I answer.

He checks our heading and puts his hand over mine on the wheel to adjust it slightly. 'Stay on this reach for a bit, then we'll begin our tack to get into the Sound of Islay.' I nod, noticing that he doesn't take his hand off mine straight away, but leaves it there, giving it a gentle squeeze. It feels good, the warmth of his fingers enclosing mine. Without saying a word, I incline my head to lean it against his shoulder and we sail on like that for a few minutes, closer than we've ever been before. So that's another thing this pandemic has brought us, I think: this new closeness.

And, of course, he's always been like a brother to me.

I'm glad Jack seems to share my sense that there's no need to say much yet. He's probably got out of the way of making conversation, anyway, after all those weeks alone on the ocean. I think we both feel that, instead of talking, all we need to focus on at the moment is sailing on across the wind-whipped waters, heading for home.

Many hours later, we slip into the narrow bay off Mull where we'll anchor up for the night.

It's a natural anchorage, usually popular with other yachties, Jack tells me, but this evening we have it to ourselves. Beyond the headland, the white sands of Iona glint silver against the sapphire sea. The stones of its ancient abbey, outlined against the setting sun, watch on silently as we take down the sails and slip into the inlet, gliding slowly through a narrow channel between pink-hued rocks.

The water is perfectly clear. I see a shoal of tiny fish dart under *Skylark*'s hull and decide to go for a swim, stripping down to my T-shirt and underwear. 'You coming in?' I ask Jack, but he shakes his head awkwardly and turns away, busying himself with retying a fender rope that doesn't look to me like it needs it.

'I'll get a few things sorted here.'

It's funny, we've swum together thousands of times before, but this time he seems oddly self-conscious.

I gasp as I immerse myself, gingerly, in the cold salt sea. Then I let go of the ladder and give myself to it. My body quickly adjusts to the chill, and I strike out towards a nearby rock. Suddenly, I realise I'm not alone. The dark head of a young seal bobs up out of the water ahead of me and the creature watches me with its luminous eyes, no doubt curious about this trespasser in its territory. Once it's decided I'm no threat, it seems in the mood to play. It dives, its body arcing sleekly as it disappears beneath the surface, then reappears behind me, following back and forth as I swim in the channel of light cast by the evening sun. It'll soon be the longest day of the year and the sun won't set here until past ten o'clock.

Eventually, the seal grows bored of the game and disappears back out into the deeper water. I'm shivering by the time I haul myself back on to the boat.

Once I've changed, I go up on deck again, clipping the tendrils of my damp hair into a twist at the nape of my neck. Jack's set out cutlery, wine glasses and a dish of grated Parmesan. I sip my wine and watch a pair of oystercatchers busily making a nest among the stones on the shore, calling to one another as they do so.

'Dinner is served.' Jack passes me a bowl of pasta and then brings his own, sitting down beside me on the locker that serves as a bench.

We eat in silence for a minute or two, savouring the good food and wine, and then I say, 'What do you think you'll do next, Jack, now you have your own boat? Will you go back to skippering charters in the Caribbean, once the world gets back on its feet again?'

He shakes his head, twisting a mouthful of spaghetti on to his fork. 'Been there, done that now. It was only ever a means to an end, really, until I'd saved enough to be able to buy a yacht of my own.'

'So will you stay put on Loch Ewe, do you think?'

'Most probably. I'll see. *Skylark* will need to earn her keep, so I'll probably do some charters out of one of the marinas near Oban. That's where most of the business is. But in between I think I'll be spending more time back home.'

'Funny, isn't it, how we both still call Aultbea home? Even though neither of us has lived there for years.'

'Home's where family is,' he replies with a shrug. 'Always has been, always will be. The pandemic's made me see that. And what about you, Daisy? How long do you think you'll stay before you head back south?'

I shrug. 'My job isn't exactly essential and I can't do it working from home. So it's all up in the air at the moment. I've been think-ing perhaps it's time for a change.' The thought of returning to my empty flat in London fills me with dread, so I quickly take another sip of wine and deflect the conversation back on to Jack. 'Won't you find it a bit too quiet at home, leaving behind your glitzy lifestyle?'

He shakes his head, his expression serious. He hesitates. The big brother figure I've known all my life looks a little unsure of himself for once.

'Daisy,' he starts, then stops again and takes a gulp from his wine glass, as if for courage. 'I've had a lot of time on my own to do some thinking over the past months. The pandemic, your mum getting ill, then losing Davy . . . it all made me realise how important it is to say things before it's too late. So I'm just going to put this out there. And you don't have to say a thing, if you don't want to. Because there's no pressure. And you might not feel the same way. And if you don't, then that's okay . . .'

Watching him struggle to get the words out, seeing how serious his expression is, I set down my fork and take his hands in mine. 'What is it? You know you can tell me anything, Jack. You've always been the big brother I never had.'

He shakes his head. 'Well, that's just the problem, Daisy. You see, I don't really want to be your big brother. Never have done. And I was too young and too stupid to tell you that when I had the chance and then you went off and got married and had your girls. When you got divorced, I thought now's my chance. But you were too sad and too lost, and I felt I had nothing to offer you. I needed to make something of myself, for myself. But everything is different now. You seem so much happier, like you've got your old self back again. Like you've regained everything that was taken from you and mended the things that were broken.'

He raises his eyes to mine and they're full of an honesty that's so raw, so unguarded, that I know how important it is for him to say these things. I nod, recognising the truth in his words.

Looking a little encouraged, he continues. 'If there's one thing this virus has taught us all, it's that life is uncertain. And tomorrow we'll be surrounded by our families and that'll be great, but if I don't say this now, I probably never will. So here goes nothing . . . I've loved you forever, Daisy. And I wonder if you could ever feel the same way about me.'

The silence that follows is absolute. There's not even the faintest sigh of wind to stir the surface of the water, not a peep from the oystercatchers on the shore, not a creak from *Skylark*'s rigging. It's as if everything is holding its breath, waiting to see what will happen next.

SILENT = LISTEN.

Is it as easy as this? A simple question of shifting my perspective? Of rearranging the letters to make a new meaning?

Jack sees me differently: not as a sister or just a friend. I find I'm looking at him with new eyes, too.

THE EYES: THEY SEE.

The world has changed – in so many ways – and perhaps I've been wrong about everything I ever thought I knew.

WRONG = GROWN.

Themi was right. When our hearts break wide open, there's the possibility of a transformation. The birth of a new future. One we've created for ourselves. One we really want.

I smile into Jack's handsome, familiar face, which is currently fixed in an expression of such a mixture of fear and hope it makes my broken-open heart do a somersault. I hadn't realised it could still do that at its age, after all these years, after everything that's happened to it.

Suddenly, I know what I really want. I want him.

But words alone don't seem enough. So, instead of saying anything, I lean over and kiss his lips. And I feel them curve upwards into a smile of their own beneath mine.

He puts his arms around me, and we sit gazing out across the cove, my head cradled on his shoulder, and it feels so right. As if this is exactly where I always should have been.

We're moored in a millpond of gold, the flamingo-pink of the sunset perfectly reflected, as if we're floating in the sky. Then the final words in Violet's journal come back to me and I rearrange them, just a little, to match my thoughts: *I wonder at the possibility of a new future as I gaze out at the sky beneath us.*

◆ ◆ ◆

The next day the wind and tides seem to understand our longing to be home, and they conspire in our favour as we navigate our way northwards up the coast. Anticipation rises within me as we round the headland, into Loch Ewe. We're tacking again now, and it's tricky sailing as the wind blusters and bounces from the hills enfolding the loch, so Jack's at the helm and I send a message to Mum and the girls, and to Elspeth too, to let them know we're nearly there. I can see my messages have been read, but I don't know whether they'll come to meet us or whether we'll need to keep a distance from everyone for a quarantine period, mindful of the virus and the need to keep them safe. But then, as we turn on our final tack towards the pier, Jack nudges me and grins. 'Looks like there's a bit of a reception committee gathering.' He reaches for a pair of binoculars and hands them to me.

I can make out Mara there, dancing with excitement, and then Sorcha and Mum, waving their arms. Elspeth's there too, waiting to hug her son. As we draw nearer, I hear them whooping and I call back, even though the wind snatches my words and flings them backwards. 'I love you all so much.'

I turn and scramble back to Jack's side, ready to help with the final approach. He leans down and says quietly, 'I love you so much too, Daisy Laverock.'

I turn my face to his and kiss him again. When I look back towards the pier, I see the whole lot of them are dancing now as they cheer us home. And I don't need the binoculars, now, to be able to tell they're laughing and crying all at the same time, just like us.

◆　◆　◆

My concerns about quarantine were answered yesterday when we moored *Skylark* alongside the pier: the six of us are isolating together in the big house for ten days but, as Mara declared, they decided they're prepared to risk catching the lurgy from us in return for a hug. Mum and Elspeth – whose age puts them at the greatest risk – reckon they're probably immune, in any case, since they've both already had the virus.

We wait until the sun is beginning to set, slipping inexorably towards the far horizon, and then we all walk together up the hill behind the big house to say our final farewell to Davy. It's late, but we don't want this day to end because then we know he'll be fully gone from us. We'll still hold him in our hearts and whenever we catch the scent of the ocean on a westerly wind, we'll remember him. But we have to let him go, as we all must do eventually. Because every meeting holds the seeds of parting, as Themi said. But how thankful we are that we knew him, that he was with us, that he loved us.

Before we set off from the house, I placed a *kata* round each of our necks, linking us with that other family on the other side of the world, and our pale silk scarves flutter in the breeze at the top of the hill, a little like prayer flags.

We take our time, still reluctant to say that last goodbye. The setting sun floods the clouds with washes of deep rose and lily-pink. Then Mum takes the lid off the cylinder of ashes and releases them on to the wind. She gives a little sob as she does so, and we gather close around her, holding her. She still looks tired and grey from her own illness and her grief, and I try to pour some of my strength into her to help her get through this moment. I know there'll be many more difficult moments for her – for us all – in the months and years ahead. The pandemic continues to make life uncertain at best, and it will take more time to grieve the loss of Davy. But I know, too, that we will walk that stony path side by side, helping and encouraging one another, giving each other comfort when it's needed most.

Mara and Sorcha lead the way back to the house, lighting the path with torches, and Jack and I help Mum and Elspeth pick their way among the stones and tussocks of heather.

Once back home, we turn on lights and gather in the sitting room. Jack pours a dram of Davy's favourite whisky for each of us, and we raise our glasses in a toast. 'To Davy.'

After we've taken a drink, Mara gives a wicked grin and says, 'And here's to Mum and Jack as well. May I just say it's about bloody time!'

They all laugh at the look of amazement on my face, rapidly followed by the heat of the blush that flushes through my whole body.

'Oh, come on Mum,' Mara says. 'It's been patently clear to all of us except you that he's had a thing for you, like, forever.'

Jack shakes his head, mock-ashamed. 'Was it really that obvious?' he asks.

'Of course it was, dear,' says Elspeth placidly. 'Ever since you were about three years old and you used to bring her shells on the beach to put on her sandcastles. And then you got so drunk at her

273

wedding and cried on my shoulder. You probably don't remember much about that night, do you? But I told you that you were a daft laddie not to have spoken up earlier and then I took you home and put you into your bed to sleep it off.'

'Oh well, we got there in the end,' I say, with a rueful smile, leaning into Jack's embrace. 'We both just had a bit of living we needed to do first.'

Davy's guitar leans against the piano in the corner, so I pick it up and tune it. I begin to play the chords of the 'Eriskay Love Lilt', softly at first, until Sorcha joins in on the piano and Mara starts to sing the words of his favourite song.

> *When I'm lonely, dear white heart,*
> *Black the night or wild the sea,*
> *By love's light my foot finds*
> *The old pathway to thee.*

Mum and Elspeth join in the chorus, Mum's voice still holding the traces of its former purity from her youth.

> *Vair me oro van o,*
> *Vair me oro van ee,*
> *Vair me oru o ho,*
> *Sad am I without thee.*

We all sing the final verse together, Jack's tenor adding a richness to the words, which seem to come from our hearts rather than our mouths.

> *Thou art the music of my heart*
> *Harp of joy, oh cruit mo chridh,*
> *Moon of guidance by night,*

Strength and light thou art to me.

Very gently, I set the guitar back in its place. Sorcha closes the lid of the piano and there's silence. The final, remembered echoes of the song evaporate into thin air as the *bardo* reaches its end. And Davy's soul goes with them, and then there's nothing left in the room but a sense of peace, mingled with our memories of the love he gave us.

Daisy – August 2020

I felt close to Violet in Nepal, but somehow that journey and my return make me feel even closer to her here. After all, this was a childhood home for both of us, and both of us had to leave it. Her only option was to make a new home, on the other side of the world. But my time away has shown me my real home was always back here, where I started. I think it's the same for Jack as well. We've both come home, not only to the place we grew up but to ourselves. To each other. So I've decided to remain at Ardtuath.

All of us have had a lot of adaptations to make. Sorcha is able to continue her degree studies online, but Mara's ambitions in performing arts have been completely curtailed by the pandemic. It's impacted on the music school too, since the restrictions have brought home to us very forcibly the fact that live performances of all kinds are the first things to be cancelled and the last things that'll be allowed to restart. I'd worried Mara might be devastated at having to put her dreams on hold indefinitely, but she's found new purpose in her passion for gardening, partly inspired by Violet's story. I suspect she shares quite a few character traits with her great-great-great-aunt, not least her determination, her independence and her strength of will. Together, we've put up a large polytunnel in the walled garden behind Ardtuath House and begun growing produce there, which Mara sells to local hotels and restaurants, as well as running a farm stall on the pier every Saturday morning for the community. Sorcha helps out when she has the time and has been a useful source of advice, too, when it comes to trying out different crops to plant.

The music school remains closed for now. But we have plans to set up online classes from the autumn, allowing teachers and their students to keep playing. When we're finally able to reopen, Jack and I will take over the running of the school, although I suspect Mum and Elspeth will continue to keep a close eye on us. So, even though we're still living through strange times and there are many things we cannot do, we count ourselves very fortunate to have been able to adapt, finding new ways to keep going.

I'm spending a day in Edinburgh, because there's something I need to do here. This afternoon, I have an appointment at the Botanic Garden where I've asked to see the papers of Violet Mackenzie-Grant, which are kept in their archive. I park beside the main gates and go in, carefully stepping on the disinfecting mats that have been placed there. Visitor numbers are limited to keep everyone safe, and even though we're outdoors, everyone is still wearing masks. The first autumn colours shade the trees with hints of red and brown and the flower beds are filled with yellow rudbeckia and purple asters in a final defiant show of colour before winter arrives. I'm early for my appointment, so before heading to the Library, I meander along the paths and make my way to the Nepalese Garden in the heart of the Botanics. A string of prayer flags waves above a gateway of stones, from which a bronzed bell hangs, transporting me back to the Himalayan pathways leading to Phortse.

I take a photo and send it to Pema. *Thinking of you all*, my accompanying message reads. I wonder how they are, what they're doing this evening. I picture them sitting round the stove in the teahouse, perhaps gathering round to look at the picture I've just sent if the Wi-Fi's working there tonight. In my mind's eye I see their smiles, etched into their faces alongside the hardship that's written there too, the beautiful combination of kindness and toughness that's such a Sherpa characteristic.

As I walk on, I stop here and there to peer more closely at the labels beneath the rhododendrons lining the paths. In some cases, the name of the plant hunter who discovered the specimen is acknowledged: Frank Kingdon Ward, George Forrest and George Sherriff feature. *But*, I mutter beneath my breath, *where are the women? Where is Violet?*

I take a detour to walk past the Caledonian Hall and stand for a while in front of the pretty Victorian cottage. Nowadays the building's used as a venue for weddings and other events and the Herbarium's been moved to the modern, purpose-built science block, which also houses the Library. I imagine Violet walking up to this same doorway with its carved gingerbread gable, plucking up her courage to enter the place where she would find Callum at his workbench. I think she'd like the fact that an alpine garden has been constructed across from it these days. The tumbling stream and low-growing, high-altitude plants would surely remind her of the Valley of Flowers in her home half a world away.

I rouse myself from my reverie and a glance at my watch tells me I need to hurry to my appointment at the Library. Once I've sanitised my hands thoroughly and been admitted, I sign in and follow the directions the receptionist gives me from behind his Perspex screen. As instructed, I leave my coat and bag in a locker before being allowed into the archives. The librarian shows me to a table where she's set out Violet's papers.

'I don't think these have seen the light of day for decades,' she says. 'You're the only one who's asked for them. Do you have a particular interest in this woman?'

My laugh is muffled by my mask. 'You could say that,' I say. 'She's a distant relation. I went to Nepal to track her down and discovered her descendants still living there.'

'Oh, well in that case I think one of my colleagues would like to see you, if you'd be okay with that? When we received your request for this collection, it piqued his interest. He works with the Flora of Nepal team.'

'I'd love to meet him,' I say.

'Great. I'll let him know you're here. But for now, I'll leave you to look through this lot.' She gestures to the two dog-eared boxes of papers on the desk. 'Just say if there's anything else you need.'

I pore over them for an hour or so. They're mostly lists of the specimens collected by Violet and sent back to Scotland, neatly catalogued in the flowing handwriting that I recognise from her journals. I imagine Hetty would have delivered them to the Botanics – to the Caledonian Hall where I stood just a little earlier – along with the seeds and plant samples. But there are no drawings, no thick paper folders containing the plants she so lovingly, meticulously gathered and prepared. I think of the labels I saw on the rhododendrons in the gardens and wonder again: where is her legacy?

Once I've finished looking through them, I replace the papers in their boxes and get to my feet. The librarian must have been watching from her desk by the door because she comes over, saying, 'My colleague is waiting in the staff canteen, if you still have time to see him?' Once I've retrieved my bag and coat, she points the way down the stairs.

The canteen is empty, apart from a very tall young man sitting at a table in the corner, a cardboard cup sitting in front of him alongside the book he's reading. His face mask dangles by its elastic from one ear.

I approach him a little uncertainly. 'Are you Dr Martin Walker?' I ask.

He unfolds himself, gangly as a stick insect, and extends a bony elbow in the new way it's now acceptable to greet one another. 'I am, and you must be Ms Laverock?'

'Please, call me Daisy.'

He grins. 'How apt. Are all the members of your family named after flowers?'

'Pretty much,' I say with a laugh. 'Especially the Nepalese branch.'

He raises his eyebrows in surprise. 'You have family in Nepal? I want to hear all about it,' he says. 'Take a seat and I'll get you a cup of something. Tea? Milk and sugar?'

We sit at the prescribed distance from one another, but I'm able to remove my mask to sip my tea and it feels almost normal for a change.

Martin tells me about the Flora of Nepal project, which has been running for some years now. 'There's always been a special link between the Edinburgh Botanics and Nepal, ever since Francis Buchanan-Hamilton's time. He was the Keeper here in the early 1800s and he'd spent time in the Himalaya before that. We know now, perhaps more than ever before, what a hotspot Nepal is in terms of its biodiversity. And with the way the world is at the moment, it's becoming more important than ever to map and conserve that wealth of resources before it's lost forever.

'There's still so much we don't know about the medicinal properties some plants may hold,' he continues, waving his arms, his passion for his work evident as he gets into his stride. 'Take the example of the Madagascar periwinkle. It was once used in traditional medicine and when scientists researched it further, they discovered it contained two compounds – vinblastine and vincristine – that reduce the number of white blood cells in the body. Those alkaloids have been developed to provide a key substance used in chemotherapy for the treatment of various cancers. It revolutionised the treatment of childhood leukaemia, in particular. Just imagine how many young lives have been saved by that little plant. Just imagine how many more such discoveries could be out there, waiting to be made.'

'So would you be interested in talking to people who can tell you more about the plants they use in their traditional medicines?' I ask.

'Certainly,' he replies.

I show him a photo I'd taken of the *Tiarella* that Pema had picked to make the compress for Themi's arthritis.

'This is exactly the kind of thing we want,' he says. 'Modern-day plant hunters are citizen scientists, taking photos on their phones rather than digging up specimens. Can you send this photo to me? And put me in touch with your cousin Pema? I'd like to know more about the other plants they use there too.'

We talk for ages, the tea growing cold in our cups, as Martin tells me more about the work he's been involved in and asks about my trip to Phortse.

'One thing I don't understand is where the rest of Violet's specimens have got to,' I say. 'Why are the species sent back by plant hunters like Frank Kingdon Ward recorded out there in the gardens, but there's nothing of hers?'

He nods. 'It's a terrible loss. As you know, the Herbarium was once housed in the Caledonian Hall. But, attractive though it is as a building, it was a bit of a white elephant, never built for scientific purposes. Back in the day, it would have been a damp and airless place to work. It had a terrible old heating system using paraffin oil, which generated so much water vapour it ran down the walls and black mildew grew everywhere. The specimens sent back by Violet were among a significant part of the collection that was lost due to that dampness. Seeds and plant material simply rotted. It's awful, isn't it, she went to all that trouble to collect them and send back to the Botanics here in Edinburgh, only for them to end up being destroyed. Thankfully, nowadays we have far better methods of preservation, and the move to the new building here helped too.

'One of the things I want to do, when I have the time,' he continues, 'is to go through Violet's papers in the archive and see what's there. It would be good to cross-reference the missing species with those on our main Flora of Nepal database. She may have made some important findings, even though it's such a tragedy that they will have been lost now.'

'I have some more photos on my phone,' I tell him, holding it out for him to see. 'I took them when Violet's daughter, Themi, showed me the Valley of Flowers and some of the plants she remembers her mother being especially interested in conserving. Perhaps they might give you an idea too, if you can link them to the notes you have from her.'

He reaches out an angular arm to take my phone from me, nearly spilling cold tea over the table in his excitement as he leans in to get a closer look. 'Is that *Meconopsis horridula*? And what's that primula growing by the stream? I don't recognise the exact form . . . Well, your photos are certainly a great start, Daisy. Would you be happy to send copies to me? It's just a shame we don't have a pictorial record of everything else she discovered.'

I nod slowly. Then I say, 'What if there were some drawings? Would they be of use? And what if there were some seeds? Do you think they might still be viable today?'

'That depends. They'd need to have been kept in the right conditions. Cool, dry and dark. And, above all, safe from the damp.'

And then, when I tell him about my discovery of the sketches and the neatly labelled jars of seeds in the waterproof plastic drum that sits in the corner of Themi's house, the tea finally does go everywhere as he sends his cup flying.

A smile spreads over his face as I describe what I remember seeing. And I smile too, as the realisation dawns that Violet's legacy may still hold the promise of new life. Thanks to her foresight, she may have saved some of the rarest species of Himalayan plants for generations to come.

Daisy – April 2023

The Hillary Bridge stretches away before us, festooned in its streamers of prayer flags. We ease our rucksacks from our shoulders while we wait for a lengthy train of yaks to plod their way across it towards us, setting it swaying, and Mara grins broadly. 'It's so awesome, Mum. I still can't believe you did this trek on your own.'

I laugh, stepping aside to allow the porters following the yaks to pass by with their broad bamboo baskets. 'Well, I did have the help of a number one best Sherpa, of course.'

Tashi nods, acknowledging the compliment, and smiles benevolently. 'Your mum, she do twice this distance for her trek, no worry. Strong as a yak,' he tells Mara.

'I'll take that as the highest praise,' I say, as we shoulder our packs once more and step out on to the bridge. 'Yaks are the most wonderful creatures.'

We're on our way to Phortse, where Sorcha will be waiting for us. She's been living at Tashi and Dipa's lodge for a month now, carrying out research for her undergraduate dissertation on the effects of climate change in the Khumbu valley.

Mara almost skips across the bridge. I follow a little more sedately, pausing in the centre to feel the wind sweep over my face and scatter my thoughts into the sky beneath us, mingling with the prayers from the fluttering flags. Far below, the milky-turquoise river winds its way through the mountains. And then I walk onwards, the bridge bouncing beneath my feet as I head for the other side.

'I wonder how Sorcha managed to cross that,' says Mara as she snaps some photos, looking back the way we've come. 'She's never had much of a head for heights.'

'She do okay,' replies Tashi. 'Sonam took her pack, led the way. I walk behind her. No worry.' Mara and I exchange a knowing glance. Sonam's name seems to feature rather often in Sorcha's messages, and he's apparently been in no great rush to return to Kathmandu while she's been in the village.

'You ready for Namche Bazaar tonight and tomorrow, Miss Mara?' Tashi asks. 'Many young people there, now climbing season open again. Irish pub, fancy coffee, nightclub?'

'I think I'll just be looking forward to my supper and a good night's sleep by the time we get there if the rest of the way's as steep as this,' she replies, hands on her hips as she puffs her way up the path.

'Just put one foot in front of the other, slowly, slowly. You get there, no worry.'

The familiar mantra buoys my spirits, helping me on my way. The trek seems easier this time. Perhaps it's psychological – the path is a familiar one and I know it's possible for me to make it. Or perhaps it's the fact that my heart is so much lighter this time around, even if my pack is heavier, full as it is with gifts for my friends.

It's taken three years to be able to travel freely again and return to the Khumbu. Three long years for the world to get the pandemic under some sort of control. Miracles have been worked, with vaccines being developed and programmes rolled out, with countries working together to try to halt the spread of the virus. But the pain and the loss and the fear have left their legacy too. Livelihoods have been lost, mental health has suffered, and the cruel illness continues to kill the vulnerable and the elderly. My mum's never regained her old strength after she had Covid and then it took Davy from us. Her exhaustion has meant she's not been able to make the trip with us. Three years ago, she might have managed it, despite her age. But now she's tired all the time, and her worn-out lungs make her susceptible to any further infections, so she can't risk international travel. It's hard to tell whether it's her physical or her mental strength that's been most affected. Either way, the virus has had a lasting effect on her. Jack's stayed behind at Aultbea to look after her, as well as Elspeth, and he's promised Mara he'll look after her garden, too, while she's away.

The music school has reopened now, so that'll be keeping them all busy. It's a consolation to know the rooms of the big house resound once again with the sounds of practice and performance.

When the second lockdown hit on Boxing Day of that same year, I think we all found it way tougher than the first one. Hope became the life jacket we put on each day to get ourselves through. We'd had to resign ourselves to the fact that the music school wouldn't be reopening any time soon. In fact, it remained closed for the rest of that academic year, but we rolled out a programme of online classes to help keep our teachers and pupils afloat. Performances by the Ardtuath Online Orchestra buoyed spirits the whole world over, judging by the messages we received.

The music-making helped. And so did the news from the botanic gardens in Edinburgh and Kathmandu. Martin Walker's colleagues in Nepal had received the collection of seeds from Themi and sent some of them back to him. Both teams had begun to cultivate them, hoping that between them they could coax Violet's discoveries back into life. When the first photos arrived from Kathmandu of tiny green shoots pushing their way determinedly into the light, we whooped and cheered. And then Martin sent pictures from the Glasshouses in Edinburgh of the same thing happening, and we rejoiced again, knowing Violet's legacy had survived, against all the odds, and her name would live on for all time.

Our other source of hope was Mara's garden. I loved working there alongside her. She set up a rota so that people from the local area could come and help in it, too, just a few at a time to keep everyone safe, paying them in produce as well as the satisfaction of working together as a community in the fresh air. It offered some much-needed socially distanced human connection for those who were isolated. In the polytunnels and our milder west coast climate, tempered by the Gulf Stream, we managed to grow crops all year round. In winter, fresh greens like kale, chard, herbs and cut-and-come-again salad leaves were all welcome additions to the staples of potatoes, turnips, carrots and leeks that she grew out in the open in Davy's old vegetable beds. Mara experimented with traditional techniques of companion-planting, enriching the soil with seaweed and resting areas so they'd remain productive. Everything not only thrived, it tasted great as well.

As Sorcha continued her university studies online, she grew increasingly interested in the impacts of climate change in fragile places like the high-altitude areas of the world, where conditions already meant species were being threatened. Over the supper table, she'd tell us about what she'd learned.

One evening, I described the snowstorm that had engulfed Phortse the day I arrived there and told them how worried the villagers had been about what it meant for the growing season and their crops that year. Sorcha nodded, considering the issue in her quiet way. But Mara, who'd been in the process of helping herself to some more of her home-grown potatoes, suddenly looked up and said, 'Greenhouses. They need greenhouses, Mum. It'll help protect their crops from these new extremes of weather and expand the range of things they can grow, just like we've done here.'

We set up a video call with Tashi and Dipa the next morning, where they echoed our enthusiasm for the project and said they'd consult the local committee. A couple of hours later, Tashi rang back to say everyone loved the idea and an area of common ground had already been identified as a possible community garden. Sorcha and Mara did some research to find the most suitable materials to use and the best way to build structures that could withstand the extremes of weather in the Khumbu valley, and we hatched a plan to raise the funds needed to bring greenhouses to Phortse.

◆ ◆ ◆

After our two-night acclimatisation to the altitude in Namche Bazaar, Mara, Tashi and I set out on our final day's trek to reach the village. Tashi insists we stop for tea at Kyangjuma, where – miraculously, given the remoteness and the altitude – there's a bakery selling the most delicious cinnamon buns I've ever tasted. It had been shut last time we walked this way, so I'd missed out. It's a popular spot, crowded now with guides, trekkers and climbers, but we find a seat at a table in the sunshine.

'Maybe I'll come back and do some climbing one of these days,' says Mara, taking a large bite of her pastry. She gathers up the last crumbs and licks them from her fingers, looking across towards the formidable, soaring peak of Ama Dablam. 'Actually, on second thoughts, I think I prefer walking through the mountains rather than having any great desire to stand on top of them.'

Tashi nods his approval. 'You show proper respect to the mountain gods. Your mum tell you about that? She very good teacher.' He begins to collect up our cups to take them back inside the café.

We reach the fork, with its half-hidden signpost, and take the left-hand path, leaving the main route behind and climbing towards Mongla beneath a canopy of rhododendron leaves. Even though the going is harder now, it's far more peaceful. The noise of helicopter blades chopping the air into pieces fades into the distance and the only people we encounter on this path are a few porters carrying supplies to the remoter villages. Up and up we trudge, our chests heaving as we gasp in mouthfuls of the thin air. And then, at last, we round a bend in the dusty track and see the prayer flags of Mongla ahead of us. Knowing we've made it to the highest point on our trek brings a surge of energy to our tired legs as we clamber up the final stretch to our lunchtime teahouse.

Once we've fortified ourselves with bowls of soup, we re-shoulder our packs and carry on, downhill now, the path leading us back towards the blue-green river tumbling its way along the valley floor.

Around one more shoulder of rock, the first glimpse of Phortse awaits. Mara stands with her hands on her hips, drinking in the distant view of the little village, its terraced fields clinging to the hillside dwarfed by the soaring walls of rock that surround it.

Then, without saying a word, she turns, reaching out her arms, and draws me into a tight hug. And I understand. It's her way of expressing it all: the joy and the relief of having made it; the significance of this place and the insignificance of mankind within it; and our sheer, incredible awe and admiration for the Sherpa people of Phortse, whose qualities of strength, resilience and generosity of spirit allow them to live here, at the very edge of what is possible.

Mara then regains her usual matter-of-factness.

'Don't tell me we have to walk all the way down there to the bottom of the valley and then climb all the way back up again to get to the village! Honestly, where's another death-defying bridge when you need one?'

Tashi smiles beatifically. 'No need for bridge. When you can see home, feet carry you more quickly because heart grows lighter.'

And he's right. Because about an hour later, as we pick our way between the branches of the gnarled trees guarding the approach to the village, our aching legs and labouring lungs are completely forgotten when we catch sight of Sorcha, Sonam, Dipa and a small crowd of others standing at the gateway, smiling and waving, welcoming us.

Our packs are taken from us by a couple of little boys who run on ahead, up the paths between the stone walls leading to the lodge, while we follow at a more leisurely pace. We walk alongside the *mani* wall, its ancient stones a testament to so many goodbyes already said, the ones who have gone before us still here in our hearts. As we approach the lodge, I'm gratified to see there's still a neat stack of yak dung pancakes in the porch.

And then a white-haired woman, as gnarled and as beautiful as a rhododendron branch – just as her mother, Violet, was before her – emerges on the arm of her granddaughter and we step into the warm embrace of our Sherpa family.

◆ ◆ ◆

Two days after our arrival, the whole village gathers to watch for the helicopter. There's a buzz of anticipation, accompanied by much laughter. This is a day of celebration for all. At last we hear the sound of the rotors, and it comes into view. It's quite a sight, as the materials for constructing two sizeable greenhouses dangle beneath it from a longline. I hold my breath as they're gingerly lowered and set down safely on the ground. Then I put an arm around Mara and Sorcha, standing one on each side of me, and squeeze them tight. They look as happy as I feel to see the greenhouses reach Phortse.

What had begun as an idea over the supper table at Ardtuath one evening quickly turned into a project involving the whole community back home. We started small, with Mara raising funds from the sale of her fruit and veg at a roadside stall, along with pots of jam and chutney made by my mum and Elspeth. Then we raised money from the online concerts performed by the music school's lockdown orchestra. Perhaps it was our refusal to allow a second lengthy lockdown to stop us that people found so inspiring, or perhaps it was the realisation that a remote Himalayan community was being hit so hard by the effects of climate change in addition to the pandemic and needed our help. Either way, the project began to grow arms and legs and people got involved the whole world over. Jack told his sailing friends on the other side of the Atlantic and they sent donations and helped spread the word. And so, as lockdown fenced us in and restricted our movements, we expanded our horizons in different ways, escaping by helping others. Instead of the pandemic constraining us, it gave us the time and space to find new meaning in our lives, reminding us of both our fragility and our resilience, of what it really is to be human. And it seemed others shared our determination because the messages of support and the donations poured in, even at that time when so many had lost so much and were struggling financially.

It's been another bitterly cold spring in the Khumbu – the greenhouses have arrived just in time. Now, once the helicopter pilot has set the materials down safely, he lands and ducks out from under the blades to hand over the rest of his precious cargo. We hurry forward to take the cellophane-wrapped trays of seedlings from him and get them into the shelter of the community hall, where they'll be nurtured until the greenhouses have been assembled and they can be planted out.

These plants are a gift from the botanic gardens in Kathmandu, a few food crops to begin planting out in the greenhouses. Later in the season, once the weather is warmer and the rains have come, some of Violet's plants will be reintroduced to the mountains as part of a wider conservation project. The botanists are especially interested in two of her findings. One is a variety of yew, which has been found to contain a substance that can be used to fight certain types of cancer. And the other is the high-altitude, prickly little blue poppy, *Meconopsis horridula*. It turns out it contains a medicinal compound that is effective in treating bruises and circulatory problems. The latest research has found it has the potential to be used in the treatment and prevention of heart attacks. If it can be grown here successfully on a wider scale, it just might provide a whole new income stream for these remote mountain communities. And then, perhaps, the inhabitants won't be so dependent on risking their lives and angering the mountain deities in order to be able to provide for their families.

Some of the Sherpa guides have come home, taking time out from their work on the mountains, to help with the construction of the greenhouses. They walk forward to shoulder the heavy materials and carry them up the hill to the site of the new garden, led by a gaggle of excited children dancing ahead, with the rest of us following on behind.

In a couple of months' time, when the early-summer rains arrive, a team from the Edinburgh Botanics are planning to join their Nepalese colleagues and travel out to explore the Valley of Flowers. And Sorcha will show them the findings from her research. She's already been offered a position as their newest employee when she's finished her degree course. Her job means she'll be spending her time between the botanic gardens in Edinburgh and Nepal, part of the team working to conserve and protect the biodiversity of this place for future generations.

And so it fills me with great joy – and not a little maternal pride – that both my girls are following in Violet's footsteps, nearly a century on.

Daisy – May 2023

It's my final day in Phortse. I walk with Pema up the mountain to the Valley of Flowers.

When we get there, we climb up the track to where the scree begins, looking for the first glimpses of *Meconopsis horridula*. It takes a while, but at last Pema finds a rosette of the prickly leaves, nestling against a sun-warmed rock, protecting a tight bud at their centre. The little plant seems so fragile, yet at the same time so resilient, a tiny shoot of life among the expanse of weathered grey rock. To me, it embodies the Sherpa spirit and offers inspiration in this changed and changing world. The pandemic has been a lesson – a reminder that we need to practise building our tenacity every day so that when the time comes for it to be tested, we are ready to meet the challenges with the same qualities by which the Sherpa people live their lives: a fierce compassion; a gentle, good-natured strength; and a kind-hearted determination.

The breeze carries the faint sound of yak bells up from the pastures beneath us, at once both harmonious and discordant, reminding me of that old joke again. It applies to my life as much as it applies to music. Before I stepped out of my comfort zone and on to the path of the unknown, perhaps I wasn't playing all the wrong notes – I was playing all the right notes, just not necessarily in the right order. Maybe that's what Jack and I were both doing. We were playing the right notes, only it was the wrong tune. A bit like his anagrams: we knew all the letters we needed, we were just using them to spell out the wrong words. But now I think we're starting to get it right.

As if I've conjured him with my thoughts, my phone buzzes as a message from Jack lights up the screen. He reassures me that all's well at home. He'll be at the airport to meet me in a couple of days' time. Though, he adds, in a car this time, not a boat.

His message ends with a line in capitals: I LOVE YOU, DAISY LAVEROCK. I contemplate it for a moment, wondering if it's another anagram. But then I realise the letters are in exactly the right order, just as they are.

Pema and I begin the walk back, stopping at the place on the path where Violet first glimpsed the village. It's also the place where she is still remembered, in the flutter of the prayer flags and the carved flowers on the *mani* stones that are her memorial. I add another string of flags to the skeins already wound around the stones. This one is for Davy, as well as for Callum and Violet.

As I thrust my hands back into the pockets of my jacket, my fingers close around a folded sheet of paper. It's the last letter Violet wrote. But this one was never meant to be sent. It was tucked into the back of her final journal, addressed to her daughter, Themi, and her granddaughter, Pema. The ink may be smudged and the *lokta* paper it's written on softened by age and by the hands that have held it and read it, but Violet's words still resonate clearly down the generations:

> *Darling Themi, darling Pema,*
> *When I'm gone, please keep my legacy safe. It's here*
> *in these jars and they should be protected until such*
> *time as they're needed. In my lifetime, I've witnessed*
> *great changes to the world we inhabit, and I fear for*

its future at the hands of those who can't see what's happening. The day will come when the contents of these jars may be needed. I'm confident that you'll keep them for me, and that you will know when the time is right to share them.

I still have faith in the future, because it's populated by the two of you, by the likes of our friends in Phortse, and by those who will come after you all. Surely they will have the wisdom to learn the lessons of history from our mistakes and make this world a better place? Surely they will keep alive the traditions that matter but be brave enough to make changes too? That spirit of adaptation has got us here. Surely it will endure in the face of challenges still to come?

We live in a place that's both brutal and fragile. But those very characteristics have made us resilient, like the plants that grow here.

There is something very beautiful about that resilience. I know it will see you through when I am gone. When all that remains are these words and my everlasting love.

Violet xx.

I run my fingers across the surface of the paper, feeling the embedded fragments of the plants from which it was made many, many years before. And, silently, I promise Violet we'll do our best not to let her down.

Far below us, where the sky fills the valley, sunlight glints on the newly constructed greenhouses. People are already at work, planting out peppers and tomatoes grown from seeds and nurtured on windowsills, which they're trying out as new summer crops:

another form of adaptation, while they still preserve what they can of their traditions in a changing world.

The world has changed so much since the first time I stood here, but there's still so much beauty in it. Each of us is here to protect it for only a short time. These stones are a reminder of that, of the duty we have to care for it and pass it on to future generations. They're a reminder, too, of the legacies of Violet, Callum and Davy, which have become interwoven in ways they never could have imagined.

And what will our legacy be? How will we heal ourselves and the world? We don't have all the answers yet. But we do have the will. Because, like the tiny blue poppy the colour of the sky, discovered by Violet all those years ago, humankind is a beautiful, fragile, surprisingly resilient thing. It holds all kinds of untapped potential. And surely that's worth protecting.

I reach out my fingertips to trace the flower carved into the *mani* stone one last time and as I do so I glimpse the *sungdi,* the length of red string encircling my wrist. It's almost completely faded now. But it's still there to remind me every day that we have to be brave enough to walk the path of the warrior, stepping out into the unknown.

What does the future hold?

There's only one way to find out.

My stride is strong and my footing sure as I take the first steps.

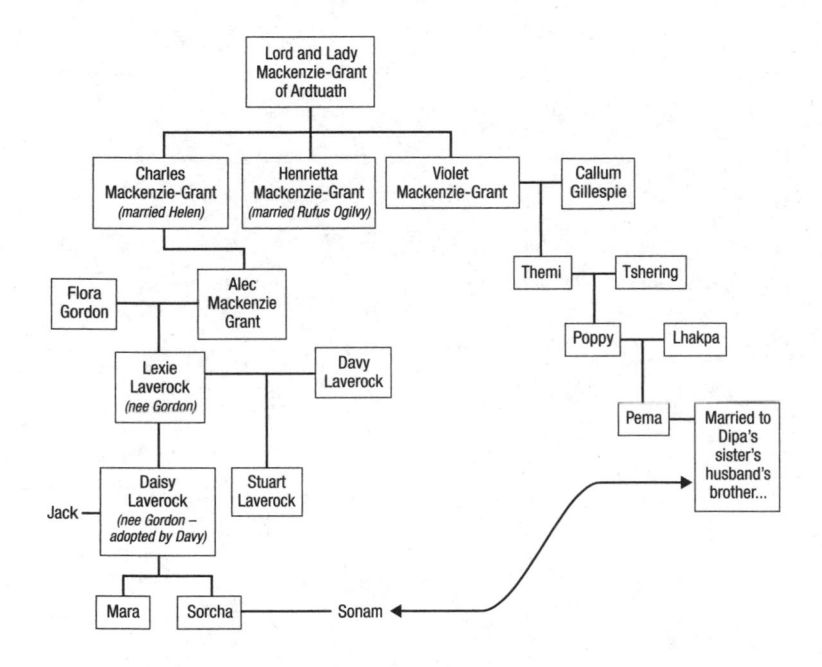

AUTHOR'S NOTES

All my books can be read as stand-alone novels, but some of the characters and their stories weave in and out between them. Readers of *The Skylark's Secret* will already have met Daisy as a young child and learned more about that side of the family tree, including how Lexie and Davy got together and why Lexie's surname is her mother's rather than her father's. Those characters have waited patiently in the background while I wrote two more books – and the world went through a pandemic – until it became their turn to step back into the spotlight and tell another part of their family's history.

In imagining Violet's life story, I've tried to retain as much historical accuracy as possible. Inverewe Gardens, the Edinburgh School of Gardening for Women and the Herbarium at the Royal Botanic Garden Edinburgh all existed in the 1920s, as described. I took a small liberty with the Imperial Airways route to Delhi, which was only officially established in December 1929, a few months after Violet needed to get herself there.

Other than known historical figures, identified in the sections below, all characters are fictitious, and any resemblances are purely coincidental.

WOMEN GARDENERS AND EXPLORERS

There were a number of women gardeners and explorers whose stories inspired that of Violet. One was Dawn MacLeod, who worked for many years alongside Mairi Sawyer (previously Mairi Hanbury, née Mackenzie), in the famous gardens at Inverewe. Her books *Down-To-Earth Women* and *The Gardener's Scotland* depict life on the north-west coast of Scotland and the cultivation of those gardens.

My thanks to Lindsey Gibb, storyteller extraordinaire, who introduced me to the redoubtable Ella Christie of Cowden, an intrepid explorer and creator of a beautiful Japanese garden. *Alicella: A Memoir of Alice King Stewart and Ella Christie*, by Averil Stewart, recounts Ella's global adventures through her letters home to her sister. Lindsey also pointed me to the book *Unsuitable for Ladies: An Anthology of Women Travellers*, selected by Jane Robinson, which is full of tales of courage and adventure.

Dr Deborah Reid – who is an extremely talented gardener in her own right – wrote her PhD thesis on *Unsung heroines of horticulture: Scottish gardening women, 1800 to 1930*, which describes the Edinburgh School of Gardening for Women, established by Annie Morison and Lina Barker, and provided much inspiration for Violet's time there.

And the first seeds of inspiration for Violet's journey were sown some years ago when I worked as a volunteer at the Explorers Garden at Pitlochry Festival Theatre. Julia Corden, a modern-day plantswoman and explorer, who was the manager there at the time, pointed me on the path that would eventually result in this novel when I asked the question: 'Where are all the female explorers?'

PLANT HUNTERS

This remains a sensitive topic to this day. The original plant hunters opened up new horizons and expanded the realm of botanical research, but in some cases they took rather too much, decimating the populations of some rarer species. Thankfully, nowadays there's greater awareness of the importance of conservation and protocols have been put in place worldwide, governing the removal of plants and seeds. Under no circumstances should plants or seeds be taken without adhering to these rules and the laws of individual countries. We can all have a role to play, though, as citizen scientists, collecting photos and data, helping to share knowledge and understanding in more considered ways.

Frank Kingdon Ward, George Forrest and George Sherriff, who are mentioned in the novel, were famed plant hunters, responsible for bringing back many of the plants we grow in our gardens and parks nowadays. Colonel Fairburn is my own creation though. There really was a Himalayan poppy named *Betty Sherriff's Dream* after she was said to have pinpointed its location while asleep in her tent on one of her husband's expeditions, which I relocated from Tibet to Nepal for the purposes of Betty's encounter with Violet. Thanks to Niall and Jane Graham-Campbell and The Meconopsis Group (https://themeconopsis-group.org) for the information about this.

Frank Kingdon Ward's collected writings *In the Land of the Blue Poppies* (edited by Michael Pollan and introduced by Tom Christopher) record his daring expeditions through Tibet, China and South East Asia in search of new plant varieties, including the legendary Tibetan blue poppy, *Meconopsis grandis*.

A Plantsman in Nepal by Roy Lancaster is a fascinating account of his plant-hunting expeditions in the early 1970s.

Ann Lindsay's entertaining and informative book *Seeds of Blood and Beauty* introduces the earlier Scottish plant hunters and details their exploits and discoveries around the world.

I'm also grateful to Mike Silburn and Charlotte Flower for book recommendations and loans.

Himalayan botany

The Royal Botanic Garden Edinburgh has had links with Nepal for over two hundred years, ever since Dr Francis Buchanan-Hamilton, a Scottish surgeon and naturalist who trained at the RBGE, made the first scientific collections of plants from the Kathmandu Valley in 1802, and became known as the 'Father of Nepalese Botany' when he held the position of official Keeper at the Botanics from 1815 to 1829. (During my research, I discovered a distant family link to the Buchanans of Callander. So, in Sherpa terms, that probably makes us cousins!)

Dr Bhaskar Adhikari of the RBGE was hugely generous with his time and most helpful in talking to me about the Flora of Nepal project. This UK/Nepal joint venture was established to explore and record the extraordinary biodiversity of the region. Via their website www.floraofnepal.org, a wealth of information about the botany, geography and climate of the country has been made available, and there's a companion volume to the website that gives a comprehensive overview: *Nepal: An introduction to the natural history, ecology and human environment in the Himalayas*.

Thanks also go to the Director of the National Botanic Gardens of Nepal, Mr Dipak Lamichhane, and to his assistant who kindly showed me round in the pouring rain, pointing out the species that have medicinal properties.

My reference to recent research into the potential use of *Meconopsis horridula* in protection against acute myocardial ischaemic damage was based upon an article published in the *Journal of Ethnopharmacology* (vol 258: 10 August 2020, 112893) by Feng Zhao, Ruifeng Bai, Junjun Li, Xiao Feng, Shungang Jiao, Shana Wuken, Fuxing Ge, Qian Zhang, Xiaochun Zhou, Pengfei Tu and Xingyun Chai.

SHERPA HISTORY AND CULTURE

I'm deeply grateful to Tshering Tashi Sherpa (Tashi Lama), Dipa Rai and their son, Sonam, for their generous hospitality at The Little Sherpa Lodge, and to all the people of Phortse for their warm welcome. It was an honour to spend time with Tshering Lhamu Sherpa, Tashi's ninety-eight-year-old grandmother, who shared her memories of what the village was like in the 1930s and remembered some of the expeditions coming through.

Without the support of James and Karen Lamb, I never would have been able to have the experience I did of trekking to Phortse and living there for ten days. I'm also very grateful to James and Karen for reading an early draft of this novel and weeding out some of my mistakes. Any that have slipped through the net are mine alone.

James Lamb and Tashi Lama set up The Little Sherpa Foundation in 2015 in the wake of the terrible avalanche on Everest's Khumbu Icefall that killed sixteen Sherpas in April 2014, leaving their families devastated and struggling to survive. I've pledged to donate 10 per cent of the royalties I receive from this book to support the charity, which helps build a future for the Sherpa people, adapting to modern challenges while still preserving the Sherpa culture. You can find out more about the foundation at www.littlesherpafoundation.com. One of the projects we're fund-raising for – which is not without its challenges! – is to help bring greenhouses to Phortse.

The BAFTA-winning filmmakers Richard Else and Meg Wicks were wonderful trekking companions, as well as filming the trip. Huge thanks to them for all their enthusiasm for this book and for helping me with my research. The film they made can be

viewed on this page of my website: www.fionavalpy.com/books/
the-sky-beneath-us/

The book *Sherpa: Stories of Life and Death from the Forgotten Guardians of Everest*, by Pradeep Bashyal and Ankit Babu Adhikari, is a good source of first-hand testimony of what it's like to be a Sherpa and earn a living in that dangerous environment, and Ed Douglas's book *Himalaya: A Human History* is another excellent source of information about life in one of the most extreme regions of the world.

Some of the Buddhist fables referred to in this novel are based on those in Robert Long III's book, *The Buddha's Journey Home: New Buddhist Fables*.

COVID-19 AND THE PANDEMIC

Over 10,000 tourists became stranded in Nepal when the pandemic struck and countries began to close their borders. Many were evacuated on special flights, organised by their embassies, a process that took some time to organise, especially for those who had become stranded in the remoter areas of the Himalaya. Some, though, chose to stay in places that were safer rather than trying to make the long and uncertain journey home. With customary warm-heartedness, the Nepali people made them welcome and shared their resources with them.

During the pandemic, I gained first-hand experience of what it's like to find yourself on a Covid ward, at Ninewells Hospital, Dundee. I extend my deep admiration and thanks to the staff there who risked their own health every day to care for their patients under harrowing conditions. It was a place of fear and suffering, but I also witnessed courage and grace, as well as hope and human resilience amid devastating grief.

I was reminded of what those dark days of the pandemic and life in lockdown were like for so many of us by *The Covid Chronicle*, a beautiful sewing project that records people's experiences from around the world. Thanks to one of my readers, Vicky Riches, a contributor to the project, who first told me about it. It's now on permanent display at Chelsea & Westminster Hospital and can be viewed online at: www.thecovidchronicle.org.

ACKNOWLEDGEMENTS

Heartfelt thanks go to:

The Lake Union team at Amazon Publishing, especially Sammia Hamer, Eoin Purcell, Nicole Wagner, Sana Chebaro, Mike Jones, Jenni Davis and Sadie Mayne.

Everyone at The Madeleine Milburn Literary Agency and especially Maddy Milburn, Saskia Arthur, Rachel Yeoh, Georgina Simmonds, Valentina Paulmichl, and Amanda Carungi.

My friend Lesley Singers for always being there, and to Ann Lindsay, Maggie Anderson, Gillian Galbraith and Debs Reid – the Laughing Literary Ladies who also happen to know an awful lot about gardening and have created beautiful gardens of their own.

And thanks and love to my family – James and Natalie, Alastair and Carey – for encouraging me to keep up the training schedule that would enable me to make the trip of a lifetime to Nepal, and for joining in the early-morning swims in the River Tay whenever possible.

ABOUT THE AUTHOR

Photo credit: Willow Findlay

Fiona is an acclaimed number one bestselling author whose books have sold over three million copies and been translated into more than thirty languages worldwide. She draws inspiration from the stories of strong women, especially during the years of the Second World War, and her meticulous historical research enriches her writing with an evocative sense of time and place.

For more information, to sign up for updates or to get in touch, please visit www.fionavalpy.com.

Follow the Author on Amazon

If you enjoyed this book, follow Fiona Valpy on Amazon to be notified when the author releases a new book!

To do this, please follow these instructions:

Desktop:

1) Search for the author's name on Amazon or in the Amazon App.
2) Click on the author's name to arrive on their Amazon page.
3) Click the 'Follow' button.

Mobile and Tablet:

1) Search for the author's name on Amazon or in the Amazon App.
2) Click on one of the author's books.
3) Click on the author's name to arrive on their Amazon page.
4) Click the 'Follow' button.

Kindle eReader and Kindle App:

If you enjoyed this book on a Kindle eReader or in the Kindle App, you will find the author 'Follow' button after the last page.